NO PAIN NO GAIN

Hanley broke off his narrative and looked at his audience. Harriet had a hand under the elastic of her knickers; Jennifer was openly masturbating, smilingly attending to herself; Simon's erection throbbed, but his hands were firmly on his thighs; Peter had slipped his briefs to his knees, but his cock still flopped tiredly to one side.

As for Hanley himself, the words had for him an overwhelmingly erotic ring to them. 'Whip', 'flog', 'cane', 'birch' – as Jennifer had said, mockingly but with truth, he could read a page of any book, magazine or periodical and immediately his eyes would come to a halt at a word which immediately travelled like an electric current from eyes to brain to cock.

He coughed gently. 'Er, would you like me to continue, or shall we interrupt the recital for a little practical application?'

NO PAIN NO GAIN

James Baron

This book is a work of fiction.
In real life, make sure you practise safe, sane and consensual sex.

First published in 2005 by
Nexus
Thames Wharf Studios
Rainville Road
London W6 9HA

Copyright © James Baron 2005

The right of James Baron to be identified as the Author of this Work has been asserted by him in accordance with the Copyright, Designs and Patents Act 1988.

www.nexus-books.co.uk

Typeset by TW Typesetting, Plymouth, Devon

ISBN 978 0 352 339669

Penguin Random House is committed to a sustainable future for our business, our readers and our planet. This book is made from Forest Stewardship Council® certified paper.

MIX
Paper | Supporting
responsible forestry
FSC® C018179

Printed and bound in Great Britain by Clays Ltd, Elcograf S.p.A.

Contents

You'll notice that we have introduced a set of symbols onto our book jackets, so that you can tell at a glance what fetishes each of our brand new novels contains. Here's the key – enjoy!

cp (traditional)

cp (modern)

spanking

restraint/bondage

rope bondage/hojojutsu

latex/rubber/leather/enclosure

fem dom

willing captivity

medical

period setting

uniforms

sex rituals

Introduction

Five people, three men and two women, meet regularly in the exclusive upstairs room of one of them – Gerald Hanley. Hanley is 52 years old, a bachelor and bi-sexual. He is a slim, good-looking man whose appearance of masculinity belies his true nature. He is, in effect, a sexual masochist who revels in humiliation and corporal punishment.

He is also a journalist, and a very good one. As an investigative reporter, he has, in his time, revealed sexual indiscretions involving TV personalities, actors and high-profile names in industry and commerce. He has kept his identity secret; he poses as an ardent member of the various SM clubs which exist around London where those so inclined go to receive punishment or administer it. Hanley is as keen to receive pain as the rest, but he is also, paradoxically, a pioneer against men – and women – who use their wealth and influence to persuade others less fortunate than themselves into the heady world of flagellation, domination and humiliation.

During his long-time association with others of his kind, over the years, he has gathered a small coterie around him who meet regularly to talk, have sex and indulge each other's fantasies to the best of their various abilities.

As far as Hanley's 'friends' are concerned, his only interests are matters concerning SM.

Hanley's book on the subject of sadomasochism – under an assumed name, of course – has become the 'bible' of his group. They, however, know nothing of his undercover activities as a reporter, even though they're aware, vaguely, that he is a journalist. Hanley has no intention of 'exposing them'; his will is merely to toy with them in the knowledge of what he could do to their careers if he so chose: much as the way he toys with the young men he meets who are reckless enough to place ads of a particular significance in the Sunday tabloid for which, ironically enough, Hanley himself writes.

So, let's meet his four compatriots. Ladies first, naturally.

Harriet Whippenden (yes, honestly, that's her real name – and who knows what mysterious psychological influences may have come to bear on her!) is 67. She is a tall and powerfully built woman, well corseted and long knickered (she buys her XOS directoires from the most established underwear manufacturer in the UK who thankfully continues to fashion this regrettably underestimated, sexually deviant item of women's undergarments – still favoured by those fortunate enough of both sexes to be 'in the know'). 'No more than four inches above the knee should the elastic be positioned' is her dictum and she is inclined to add presciently, 'Or even further down to skirt level for added voyeuristic interest!'

Harriet is fond of reciting, by heart, the well-remembered monologue from the John Osborne one-hour play *Under Plain Cover* in which Jenny, the young girl involved in a sadomasochistic relationship with her lover – who turns out to be her brother – extols the virtues of long, silk knickers.

2

After the Jenny character reviews various forms of women's knickers she arrives at the point which Harriet delights to quote:

'Finally we come to the flower of the form believed by most to be decadent. They have long legs, never more than four inches above the knee, which makes sitting down, getting out of cars, riding bicycles or going upstairs in buses a tremendous adventure. They always – repeat always – have elastic top and bottom. What the flying buttress was to Gothic so is elastic top and bottom to the Classic Perpendicular or Directoire style. And it is only in knickers that one is still able to find that strange repository of mystery – the gusset. Nowadays they are mostly worn by elderly or very square middle-aged ladies ... I suppose one might almost say that the end of the knickers came with the rise of nylon ... they were never quite the same afterwards. The heavy whisper of descending pink silk was soon to be heard no more. All was hard-faced, unembarrassed, unwelcoming nylon.

'Of course, in their most basic form, they can still be seen on schoolgirls trooping by the dozen into their gymnasiums in drab navy. But only very square little girls really still wear them long.'

Harriet's recital, while all the time she is smoothing the silken legs of her pink knickers and fingering the bunched elastic, always brings two of the group to extremes of erotic excitement, and we'll get to those shortly.

Harriet has been married, but only briefly. When she was forty, she encountered a young man twenty years her junior. His name was Jeremy, but she called him her 'prince'. Before long, after she had offered him a home – his parents were dead and he was a penniless student living in a hostel – she began to introduce him to her own particular tastes: dressing him as a schoolgirl; or as a schoolboy with short trousers and uncomfortable woolly underpants. He was thrashed; he thrashed her; they had extraordinary sex, usually with Harriet dominant. Jeremy, however, rebelled one day – perhaps, as Harriet thought afterwards, he had suddenly realised that life was more promising elsewhere – and left abruptly.

Now, Harriet was seeking another Jeremy. But, though Hanley had tried to make various introductions on her behalf, all had failed. In the meantime, at the end of every meeting, she demands a flogging and, naked, takes her punishment with a large photograph of Jeremy – underpants down, masturbating – pinned to the wall in front of her.

The other female member of the club is Jennifer Fraser. She is 22 and an actress, but not a particularly good one.

She has a wide mouth, sensitive eyes and a reasonable figure – her behind is the best part of her anatomy – and Hanley got to know of her through an incredible piece of good fortune. A publicity agent on a film had persuaded the newspaper for which Hanley worked to do a 'Day in the Life of . . .' and Jennifer was the subject. During a photo session at her flat, the photographer assigned had opened a wardrobe looking for fresh ideas and had seen displayed on a rack whips, canes, riding crops and straps; on the floor below were stiletto-heeled, thigh-length black boots. On a hanger dangled a pair of riding breeches.

Innocently enough, this lip-licking information had been relayed to Hanley who contacted Jennifer and told her all he knew. For her career's sake she begged him to say nothing. In return, she would flog him as often and as severely as he wished. She enjoys inflicting pain; she orgasms while administering corporal punishment. Hanley adores her and wants more than anything to go down on her. So far she has refused, but he still has hopes.

Peter Kemp is forty and married. He has a private income largely supplied by his wife's inheritance from her father who was killed in the Concorde plane crash outside Paris. He and his wife, Geraldine – they have no children for a reason to be explained – live a fairly amiable life, bearing in mind that he constantly wishes to dress in her underclothes. He adores frilly panties, pantaloons, briefs – even thongs (he adores those because they tighten his cock and balls), although to be truthful Peter hasn't much of a male organ to be tightened. On the rare occasions he can achieve an erection – even though it droops like Concorde with its nose lowered for landing – he cannot achieve orgasm even with his wife's knickers and other adornments clothing him.

She won't whip him, even though he points out that ejaculation would almost certainly follow. However, she allows him to visit Hanley's group, receive a whipping and afterwards display the resulting wounds to his buttocks when he returns home. Eyeing him, she masturbates, but he mustn't touch her or say a word.

Simon Cook is, perhaps, the most interesting of the group so far. Simon is just twenty and gawky. He likes being called gawky; he enjoys nothing more than to strip and have the rest of them pour scorn and derision on him. Despite his skinniness, though, Simon has a huge erection. It's over nine inches – it nearly got to ten one night as it was measured excitedly by the group in turn – but it's strong and, with the loose foreskin pulled back, the glistening knob is inviting enough for any of the group to kneel and close their lips around it. Simon is a product of the public-school system. He was introduced to sex at thirteen by another boy who initiated him into the delights of masturbation.

He was also initiated into the delights of caning when this same boy offered him money to accompany him to a long-neglected cricket pavilion at the far end of the school grounds. There he was ordered to take off his trousers and underpants and be whipped by the other with a bundle of birch twigs gathered especially for the purpose.

Later, as a chorister in the cathedral choir attached to the school, Simon took on a bet that he wouldn't appear in the choir stalls without his trousers and underpants beneath his cassock. During an interminable sermon, one of the boys who had placed the bet slid his hand under Simon's cassock and found him, indeed, bare from the waist down and with an erection which was then rubbed mercilessly against the rough material of the cassock. Simon ejaculated just as the sermon ended and stood for the final hymn, warm spunk streaming down his thighs. His overriding fantasy is to be clad in surplice, cassock and white underpants and to be led to the dimly lit altar by two cowled figures carrying whips; to be made to bend and prostrate himself willingly; to have the cassock lifted, the underpants dragged down and to be flogged while a distant, echoing chant adds to the eroticism. There are plans to help Simon fulfil his fantasy . . .

But how did he become part of this disparate group? Simple: Hanley was investigating aspects of disturbed clergymen to whom the sight of a boy, pure and innocent in cassock and surplice – never mind what might lie concealed beneath – would drive them to extravagant, risky excesses of behaviour, and he had met Simon in the course of his pursuit. A few innocent questions had convinced Hanley that Simon was masochistic. Brought to the 'gathering' one evening, he was flogged by Jennifer on the buttocks and subsequent fevered masturbation took but a few seconds to completion. Simon works as a messenger boy in Hanley's department at the paper where he can keep an eye on him. Hanley is not gay in the strict sense of the word. He has never had, nor indeed wanted to have, male sexual intercourse. But, like most, he delights in the sight of a slim, naked body, whether male or female. Perhaps Simon is a little too skinny, but he will grow, and his cock delights the ladies and, if truth be told, Peter as well.

He has never admitted this to the group or anyone else but his hungry eyes watching Simon being whipped tell their own story . . .

Hanley's 'bible', of which each member of the group has a well-thumbed copy, often precedes active sexual participation. Each member is, of course, already sexually excited in their different ways. They have adopted the usual informality of clothing. Harriet, for example, is wearing a pink slip which, tucked up, reveals loose, elasticated directoire knickers over her dark-brown stockings. Simon is particularly fascinated by Harriet's knickers and, on occasions, has been allowed to wear them and be humiliated and ridiculed by the others. Harriet, though, oddly, has never taken part in this particular aspect of sexual humiliation. As a young girl, she dressed in her mother's underclothes, including her tightly

7

elasticated knickers, and she knows well enough how Simon feels wearing them . . .

Jennifer is in bra and panties . . . French panties which hang loosely around her stockinged thighs. She stretches like a young, elegant cat on one of the long, black leather couches, and with deeply mascara'd eyes stares impudently at everyone. Peter is naked except for dark-blue briefs which, unfortunately display little evidence of sexual arousement. Hanley is muscular but slim in black boxers, erection plain.

And Simon? Simon is naked, sitting in one of the swivelling armchairs. His skinny legs are wide apart and his cock rises between them like a moist, ripe, pink, oversized banana. Behind them all, in darkness now but later to be spotlighted with red lamps, is a back-curtained stage on which is a flogging frame shaped like an old-fashioned school easel, tapering to the top from wide-bottomed, screw-plated legs for firmness. Straps hang from it at various points. On a pine scrubbed table nearby are set out a variety of instruments of punishment: heavily knotted whips; thinner ones with slender, red-tipped lashes; canes of varying thickness, carriage whips, riding whips and dog leashes of plaited leather; several bundles of birch twigs, the ends fashioned into rough handles with thick, black tape, complete the array of punishment tools. To one side is a replica of a flogging rack used in the Nazi concentration camps and copied from a photograph in the Ravensbruck museum. It is a curious structure: concave with a base consisting of a series of slats, and standing some two feet above the floor. Thick leather restraints dangle from the edges on each side.

Hanley began. 'I was reading the other day a book of Greek Myths – God knows why; it's not a subject that's ever interested me! – but it was in the office for review and I was glancing through it –'

'Oh, we know!' Jennifer cut in. 'Whenever you glance through a book anything beginning with "wh" or having two "ggs" makes you look twice!'

She grinned, a ringed hand creeping beneath the loose leg of her French panties.

Harriet snapped the elastic of her Dks. 'Well?'

'All right,' Hanley said, grinning, 'don't be impatient!' He reached for a notebook on a nearby table and flipped pages. 'I just thought this was interesting . . . apparently the Spartans had certain fertility rites – that would interest you, Simon, the young lads lined up once a year to see which would and could take a flogging to extremes!'

Simon was stroking his tightened balls, knowing full well that even to touch his cock would bring about completion. He didn't want to come yet – there was a long evening ahead.

Hanley smiled. 'Yes, I thought that would appeal to you. Anyway –' he consulted the notebook '– it says here, and I quote: "the victim was bound with willow-thongs to a sacred tree-stump, perhaps of pear-wood, and flogged until the lashes induced an erotic response, and he ejaculated, fertilising the land with semen and blood" unquote.' He closed the notebook and put it aside. 'What do you think of that?'

'You mean that anyone – even if they're not like us – can get it on from being thrashed?' Peter said, his hand moving urgently over the faint mound in his briefs.

'Only if they can take enough to realise it!' Harriet said harshly. 'And most of them can't – they don't know what they're missing! My God – Simon, you get ready; you're going to get it later! Just get yourself ready, you little, skinny bastard!'

'But before that,' Hanley interjected, 'I've a story to tell you. After I'd read that about the chap shooting his, er, well, during his whipping, I went down to the cuttings library – a lot of it still isn't on computer yet – and turned up the file on CP.'

'Oh, God!' Jennifer exclaimed. 'We've been all over that so many times ... the cat-o'-nine-tails, the whipping posts on the village green, the stocks and pillories –!'

'All right, all right!' Hanley held up a hand. 'Who wants to be spanked? If you don't listen, none of you will be! Now, I found an old cutting, dated around nineteen hundred and ten. I've never seen this story anywhere else – and, as you know, there aren't many books on corporal punishment I haven't read –'

'And masturbated over!' Jennifer sneered delightfully.

Her fist was clenched just as if, Hanley thought, she had the haft of one of the whips on the table behind her in her hand, ready.

He drew a deep breath. 'I'm going to tell you the story and I guarantee not one of you by the end of it won't be ready, willing and able ... Simon? Harriet? Jennifer? Peter?'

In their various ways they signalled their agreement. Simon's hand had reached the base of his cock, but Hanley gave him a warning shake of his head.

'Now, it's nineteen hundred and ten; it's November; capital and corporal punishment are widely awarded and carried out. In this prison outside London on this particular grey afternoon, a man is to be given fifty strokes of the cat for attacking a warder. The punishment has been confirmed. Now, listen ...'

1

Tales to be Told – The Cat Lover

The Assistant Governor came hurrying down the cold, stone corridor of the gaol. A mistiness from the outside seemed to have crept in; the oil lamps were faintly glowing, and dark shadows hung about the plain brick walls. All the seven hundred or so convicts were secured in their cells; it was always the same routine either when a man was to be hanged or, in this case, to be flogged.

They'd had their 'dinner' of cold sausage and bread washed down with blackish, bitter-tasting tea in thick mugs, and now they were confined for the next eighteen hours. Those nearest the punishment room situated on the first floor at the end of one of the wings would hear the strokes being applied. A sound unlike any other, a knotted, nine-thonged whip on a man's stretched, bare back. They would also hear his cries, ignored, as the whipping – administered by a warder from another gaol – was laid on with a will. The man, stripped to the waist, and with a thick, leather belt tightened across his waist to protect his kidneys from misapplied lashes, had his legs encased, and locked in a boxlike structure, while his arms were strapped to an upright post attached to the box. A warder stood by, as well as a doctor. A bucket of water was placed nearby with a sponge to wipe sweat from the man's back so that the flogger could see his target clearly as he completed the sentence.

The Assistant Governor was a small man, his peaked cap and high-buttoned uniform seeming only to accentuate his diminutive size. Like most men in those days, he sported a large, drooping moustache which, like his uniform, seemed ill suited. His cuffs, fresh on that morning, gleamed in the fitful light.

'Sir –' the Assistant Governor began.

'Take off your cap!' the Governor interrupted starchily.

By contrast, the Governor wore a black frock coat which, open, showed a waistcoat across which hung a thick gold chain. He was an ex-military man who, befitting his position, sported gold pince-nez. His wing collar was fronted by a black, silk cravat pierced by a pearl stick-pin. He was tall and gaunt faced.

His assistant removed his cap. 'Sir, the flogging this afternoon . . .'

'Well? What about it?' The Governor eyed him stonily, thrusting his hands beneath his coat.

'Sir, the doctor . . . I've just heard –'

'Heard what? Calm down, for goodness sake. Now, tell me.'

The assistant – his name was Carson – drew a breath. 'The man, Brown, to be flogged has a history; the doctor was in the same prison in the north when Brown was sentenced to be whipped for assaulting a warder. Apparently – apparently, he likes it!'

The Governor frowned and removed the pince-nez. 'What are you talking about? Who – likes – what?'

'Brown, sir . . . he likes being whipped!'

The room was silent for a moment. Then the Governor rose slowly and adjusted his black coat. 'What are you raving about? Are you telling me that this man likes the cat?'

Carson nodded. His face was crimson. 'The doctor said that in the other prison, he – Brown – had a, er, sexual emission during the flogging.'

The Governor shook his head irritably. 'Good heavens, man, that sort of thing isn't unusual! It's – it's muscular. I've seen men about to be executed with an erection!'

'Sir, but the doctor says that Brown has admitted he gains pleasure from being flogged. His assault on the warder in the other prison was minor, and the same for the assault the other day for which you have sentenced him to be flogged. He has told the doctor that – well, he wants to be naked for his whipping today, he –'

'My God!' The Governor wheeled round. 'What are you saying? This man gains sexual pleasure from being flogged? He wants it done naked? Who is he to say how it shall be done!'

'Sir, the doctor wishes to talk to you –'

'But I do not wish to talk to the doctor! At two-thirty, as prescribed, the man Brown will receive fifty lashes on his bare back – and with his trousers on. We'll see whether he enjoys it or not! Has the man arrived to do the whipping?'

'Yes, sir. He's in the usual accommodation.'

'Well, I wish to see him. Has he had flogging experience?'

'I – I don't know, sir. I presume so. At least he will have been given practice on a sack in the usual way.' (Any warder – and they were all volunteers – had to undergo training before they were permitted to administer corporal punishment. They had to show, by thrashing a sack of sand tied to a post, that they could, accurately and powerfully, lash correctly between shoulder blades and the lower back. The nine lashes had to be separated after each stroke to ensure that they fell evenly across the flesh.)

'I wish to see him,' the Governor repeated. His face was set grimly.

'Sir, will you see the doctor first? After all, he will have to submit his report to the Home Office following the punishment,'

'Oh, very well!' the Governor snapped. 'Send him in! But I warn you, he'll get short shrift from me.'

'I'll get him, sir.'

When the assistant had disappeared, the Governor went into the tiny bathroom adjoining his office, undid his tight trousers and fumbled for his cock. It was hard and moist. Slowly he began to masturbate.

He would, of course, be present at the approaching flogging and, as his hand moved up and down the stem of his none-too-impressive erection, he savoured the image of the man Brown being mercilessly thrashed ... maybe with an erection. God, the Governor thought, I've a good mind to allow his request to be whipped naked, then I'd be able to see! He ejaculated thinly into his long, woollen drawers, buttoned himself, washed his hands and left the tiny room.

Dr James was not one of the Governor's favourites on the prison staff. He had only been there for six months, but already it was clear he had his own ideas. He was young, too, which offended the Governor, and he clearly had his own notions of how prisoners should be treated whether punished with the cat or executed at the end of a rope.

When he came in, the Governor eyed his soft collar, his University tie, and gave a private sneer. 'Well, Doctor? What's this rubbish I'm hearing about Brown? The man committed an offence for which he is to be punished – what have you against that?'

'Unfortunately,' James said, 'nothing – under normal circumstances, although, as you're aware, I'm against whipping –'

'Yes, yes!' The Governor turned his head impatiently. 'I know your views.'

'But, Governor –' the Governor had always resented the fact that this upstart always seemed to treat him as an equal and never called him 'sir'! '– in this man's case, it's different.' He hesitated, then said, 'Do you know what a masochist is?'

'I don't believe I do,' the Governor said, fiddling with a paper-knife on his blotter, and not looking up.

'A masochist,' James said, 'is someone who derives sexual pleasure from suffering pain. It is not normal, but it exists. Out there across the river there are dozens of establishments which cater for men – and women – who want to be whipped, flogged, caned, birched, or any other means of giving them sexual pleasure. The condition, for some reason, is becoming more common as the years pass –'

'And this Brown is – what do you call him?' The Governor threw down the paper-knife and looked up piercingly.

'He's a masochist,' James said unemotionally. 'In the other prison he mildly assaulted a warder knowing the punishment. He was duly flogged and I treated his back. At the same time it was obvious he had been sexually aroused. He admitted it. He told me he had been birched at his elementary school, with his trousers and underpants down, in front of the whole school, and he had realised sexual pleasure. He'd made sure it happened again . . . with the same result.'

'The man's a pervert!' the Governor spat. 'He deserves all he's going to get!'

'But this is the point!' James broke in. 'He wants it! If you awarded him a hundred lashes instead of fifty, he'd have thanked you on his bended knees! Don't you see? You cannot have this sentence carried out on a man who is going to derive sexual pleasure from the punishment, it isn't – isn't –'

'Right?' The Governor curled his lip. 'Who's going to know, one way or the other?'

James stared at him. 'I will. I've told you the circumstances. The matter should be referred to the Home Office.'

'I will not be instructed on how to run my prison!' the Governor barked. 'You're a member of my staff and I will decide, under my own authority, what rules are applied. This, in case you have forgotten, is a house of correction. Brown has to be corrected. The whipping will proceed.'

'In spite of what I've just told you?' James asked incredulously.

The Governor had thrust a hand into his right trouser pocket. His cock was beginning to erect itself again, and he held it through the thick, tweed material. 'I understand from my assistant that Brown has had the effrontery to ask to be flogged naked.'

'That, Governor, with respect, shows the state of mind the prisoner is in. That, surely, is reason enough to consult a higher authority and postpone the punishment or direct it in another direction.'

The Governor gave a bleak smile. 'So, what you're saying, Doctor – if what you tell me is correct – that you wish to deprive this Brown of his, shall we say, enjoyment? Had I known this beforehand, I might well have sentenced him to double. The flogging will go ahead – I care not whether he enjoys it or not, but I shall request the flogger who has already arrived from another prison to lay the strokes on with particular strength and efficiency. We may be in a position to cure this man of his grossness!'

James met his gaze. 'And that's your final word, Governor?'

'That, Doctor, is my final word. I shall expect you, along with myself, my assistant and the Chief of Staff in punishment cell sixteen at precisely two-twenty-five. Brown will be brought in, suitably restrained; the sentence will be read out, and administered as prescribed by law. Anything else you wish to say?'

'Yes, Governor.' James voice was none too steady. 'The reason a man is flogged on his back is that it is not supposed to cause any sexual excitement. On the buttocks, which are an erogenous zone, whipping can induce erotic sensations. Brown is an exception – whipping his back induces as much sexual arousement as flogging his buttocks. For that reason, the punishment should not take place on moral grounds.' He drew a breath. 'If so, you might as well say that by sending him across the river to be whipped, caned or birched for his own pleasure is akin to what you propose to do for yours!'

The Governor gripped himself. 'Are you suggesting that I enjoy watching a man being flogged? I have seen them scream, beg for mercy, call on God to deliver them – and after only half-a-dozen strokes of the number ordained! Are you seriously suggesting that my motives are other than to see justice done? And to protect my officers from unprovoked assault?'

'Assault? The first one, in the other prison, had a slight cut to his upper lip! This latest one had a faint bruise on his cheekbone! If Brown had really wanted to attack them –'

The Governor interrupted. 'If a prisoner touches a warder in an attempt for assault he is deemed to have attacked that warder. As Governor, I have the authority to decide the punishment. It can be solitary confinement, a limited diet of bread and water or a flogging. In Brown's case, he will be flogged, and I suggest you attend to your other duties before being

17

present in the punishment cell. Now, I really must attend to important matters. As you're aware, an execution is due to take place in four days. Thank you, Doctor. Perhaps you'd be kind enough to ask my assistant to send in the warder from outside who will be administering the punishment to Brown?'

'Very well, Governor, but I warn you –'

'Don't threaten me, Doctor!' The Governor's eyes were grey and bleak. 'I shall take note of your suggestions to me this morning, which, I must say, seem to be absolutely beyond anything I have ever heard before in my long experience in the prison service, and include them in my report to Whitehall after the punishment has been carried out.'

'And I shall send my own report!' James was quivering with tension.

'That you are perfectly entitled to do,' the Governor said emotionlessly, 'but by that time Brown will have been flogged, so is it really worth your while? After all, you're a young man and a doctor can rise high in the prison service –' he paused, staring down '– provided, of course, he has sufficient senior members of the service to recommend him. It's really up to you – a man gets a whipping; whether he actually obtains satisfaction from the punishment is neither here nor there, and you have told me in confidence of your views on this particular prisoner. It need go no further, but if you wish to pursue it –' the Governor gave a theatrical sigh '– then so be it. This is nineteen hundred and ten; men are being flogged, hanged for crimes under which they are sentenced by law, sent to hard labour. They know their fate if they're caught.

'Doctor, you are tilting at windmills like Don Quixote. Your tiny demonstration will alter nothing; the law, as they say, will take its course. Perhaps in fifty years ... But not now, not at this moment in time.' The Governor stood straight, his hands on the desk, the knuckles white. 'Brown will be flogged at two-thirty, and now, if you will be so kind, ask my assistant to send in the warder who will administer the sentence.'

James turned in soldierly fashion and left the room, closing the door quietly. The Governor smoothed his half-erect cock beneath his black trousers; even more now, he wanted to see Brown whipped.

The warder who had volunteered from a prison to the south-west stood before the Governor. He was a tall man with a bushy moustache, dressed in familiar, high-collared dark blue. His buttons glittered.

'Your name?' the Governor asked, having seated himself ceremoniously behind his desk, his starched shirt-cuffs shining in the gloom, as he clasped his hands together on the pale-green blotter.

'Johnson, sir.'

'You've administered corporal punishment before?'

The Governor watched the man's prominent Adam's apple twitch twice.

'Yes, sir, and had training on the sack.'

'Have you given fifty strokes?'

'Yes, sir, up to a hundred, twice.'

The Governor hesitated deliberately. Then, moving the paper-knife around the green blotter, he asked, 'Have you seen a prisoner, while being punished ... ever display any kind of sexual, er, pleasure?'

Johnson appeared to ponder, stroking his chin, eyebrows down in a frown, then said finally, 'Well, sir, there was one – I couldn't be sure, of course, because they have their prison trousers on – but this one seemed, while I was whipping him, to be trying to ease his trousers down around his hips, like. And he was, sort of, thrusting himself out, if you see what I mean.'

'His, er, lower half?' the Governor queried.

'Yes, sir, almost as if he was – well, I didn't like to think what he had on his mind, as you might say.'

'How far into the punishment did what you say you saw occur?'

'Well, sir, it was only after about eight or nine strokes. Usually by that time they're already pleading, sir, you know: "stop, I can't stand it!" but this one was gasping, and I noticed, as I moved to one side to keep the lashes evenly spaced, that he had a grin on his face and his head was up, eyes closed, and there was this bulge in his trousers. I couldn't help noticing, sir. I thought it rather odd.'

The Governor's lip curled. 'You thought it rather odd, did you! And what happened after he was unstrapped?'

'Well, sir, I put the cat in the water, you know, to soak off the sweat –'

'No, with him! What did he do? Right after?'

'Well, sir, the doctor attended him and –'

'Did he appear to be suffering?' the Governor asked, his voice grating.

'I can't say as he did, to be honest, sir. Most of them are groaning, half-conscious like, but he, well, he seemed to be enjoying it. Funny you should ask that, sir; it's just come back to my mind.'

The Governor felt his groin responding. 'But you're ready to flog the man Brown this afternoon?'

'Oh, certainly, sir, it's an extra thirty bob and we've got a kiddy on the way. I'll do my duty, never fear, sir!'

'And what about you? Do you enjoy it?' the Governor asked and cleared his throat.

'Enjoy flogging a prisoner, sir? No, I don't say as I

20

enjoy it, like. But somebody has to do it, and, to me, sir, it's just a job of work'.

'You feel no – no pity for the prisoner upon whom you're causing intense pain and scars which will probably never fade for the rest of his life?' The Governor was gripping the edge of the desk, willing himself to keep his stiffening cock under control.

'Sir, he'd committed an offence; he knew what the punishment was likely to be. It's like an execution, begging your pardon, sir, 'cos I've talked with a hangman. He'd put the noose around dozens, probably hundreds of necks. He said to me, "It's just a job. I get it done as quick as I can." Sir, I do the same with the cat – deliver the strokes to the best of my ability. I'm never going to see the poor fellow again, thank the Lord, and I do as I'm told. Yes, sir, I'm a volunteer, but I look at it this way: if I give a man who deserves it a good thrashing and I get another thirty bob, then I'll take the money. It's as simple as that, begging your pardon, sir.'

'Thank you,' the Governor said coldly. 'You'll go through the usual processes, testing the whips, making sure –?'

'Yes, sir, you can rely on me. I'll make sure the apparatus is prepared.'

When Johnson had left, the Governor took a half-bottle of brandy from beneath a pile of old papers in the bottom drawer of his desk, and took a long swig. He replaced the bottle and sat back, brooding. He had a sense that the punishment this afternoon would be like no other.

Hanley broke off his narrative and looked at his audience. Harriet had a hand under the elastic of her knickers; Jennifer was openly masturbating, smilingly attending to herself; Simon's erection throbbed, but

21

his hands were firmly on his thighs; Peter had slipped his briefs to his knees, but his cock still flopped tiredly to one side over his empty-looking, baggy sac.

As for Hanley himself, from as long as he could remember, the words had for him an overwhelmingly erotic ring to them. 'Whip', 'flog', 'cane', 'birch' – as Jennifer had said, mockingly but with truth, he could read a page of any book, magazine or periodical and immediately his eyes would come to a halt at a word which immediately travelled like an electric current from eyes to brain to cock.

He coughed gently. 'Er, would you like me to continue, or shall we interrupt the recital for a little practical application?'

Harriet's voice was unsteady. 'As far as I'm concerned, I'd prefer to hear the end. Simon knows I'm going to whip him and I know he'd prefer to build on the expectation.'

'Jennifer?' Hanley asked, his heart rate increasing.

She gave him a lazy smile. 'You're going to be flogged anyway, so let's wait, shall we? Don't worry – I won't come. I'll keep myself on the brink, until . . .'

'Well, Simon, you know your fate,' Hanley said thickly. 'What about you, Peter? I see little signs of any excitement at your end, if you'll excuse the expression.'

Jennifer gave a throaty giggle.

Peter reddened. 'I – I've brought some pantaloons and vests. I'd like some humiliation and punishment . . . but let's hear the rest of the story.' He glanced round at the others and the looks of contempt on their faces managed to make his cock stir at last.

'Fair enough,' Hanley said, 'we seem to be agreed, so I'll carry on . . .'

* * *

Dr James, despite the Governor's warning, had frantically been trying to get through to the Home Office. The telephone system was perfunctory, to say the least, as each time he had to return to the switchboard and wait to be reconnected; time was passing amazingly quickly. Besides which, James had no idea who he could talk to and be advised as to his next move. He was embarrassed because the Home Office telephonists were, surprisingly, mostly women – a foretaste of the Suffragette Movement soon to blossom – and James could hardly mention the words 'whipping' or 'flogging' to them! So he kept talking about 'judicial punishment' and the women simply didn't understand. In despair, playing his last card, he asked to be put through to the Home Secretary.

The Home Secretary was away, and one of his senior civil servants wasn't much help. He, apparently, almost dropped the receiver – judging by the clicks and bumps – when James mentioned flogging.

'My dear fellow – who did you say you are, the Medical Officer? – well, my master has no authority over, er, matters of that kind. His concern is with listening to appeals for a reprieve of the death sentence.'

'I know that, sir.' James was trying to be patient, although patience had worn thin over the past 45 minutes. 'But, surely, if a man is to be flogged and is going to relish every stroke, isn't there something – something immoral about that? Aren't we, as representatives of the law, pandering to his unnatural lusts? We're not punishing him; we're being, with respect, akin to prostitutes who flourish south of the river and who are paid handsomely to whip a consenting adult!'

'I hardly think –' the senior civil servant began.

'I beg your pardon, sir,' James apologised, 'but time is pressing and the man is due to receive his punishment – if that's the right word in this case – in less than an hour-and-a-half.'

'But my dear fellow, what on earth do you expect me to do? To be perfectly honest, I have to say to you that, from what you've told me, the man's damn lucky to be in a position to enjoy his whipping! I think we'd better leave it at that. Good-day to you!'

James slumped in the hard, wooden chair in his tiny room and stared bleakly at the smeared window panes criss-crossed with netting and horizontal, rusty bars. Then a sudden thought gripped him; he tried to wriggle from the grip but it refused to let go. How would he feel watching a man being flogged, knowing the man was being sexually aroused the longer and more fiercely the lashes were being applied? The thrust of the idea took his breath away. How would he feel? He had to be there.

He'd watched flogging before and felt little except a medical man's assessment of the injuries being inflicted and the state of the man's heart and respiratory processes. He had never, ever conceived that a man might go eagerly to the whipping frame, thrilled at being made to strip to the waist, thrilled even more at being bound tightly, and then ecstatic as he eagerly awaited the first stinging, spreading lashes across his shoulder blades.

Perhaps the civil servant had been right when he'd said, in effect, 'if the man enjoys a whipping he's damn lucky'? Why interfere? As a matter of medical science, it might be interesting to see the sexual reaction, but there wouldn't be a lot to see. The man's thick prison trousers would be on, and beneath harsh, cotton drawers. What would be visible? Very little, James thought.

Even at the end of the punishment when he would clean and apply soothing ointment to the weals on the man's back, he'd have no real conception as to his sexual state. Unless . . . James sat bolt upright: unless the man's request to be flogged in the nude could somehow be granted! Then evidence of sexual arousement would be plain to see . . . but that was nonsense! Even to suggest it to the Governor could result in dismissal and a huge, damaging blot on his subsequent career, whether or not he decided to stay in the prison service.

As a matter of fact, the Governor had arrived at his own conclusion. On the face of it, it seemed simple. Brown would have to rid himself of any sexual feelings before the flogging took place. In front of a witness, he would have to indulge in self-abuse. (The Governor rejected the word masturbation because that, in itself, suggested a sexual connotation.) He would have to show that all sexual involvement was absent when he was tied to the whipping frame, his back bare.

The Governor took out his watch (a farewell gift from the staff of his last prison). It was nearly one p.m., an hour-and-a-half to go. He proceeded along the first-floor corridor, smelling with his usual distaste the odours of cooking, sweat and urine. God, when would prisons be modernised and brought up to date with proper sanitary facilities?

On the way, he took along the chief officer on that particular corridor, and, when they reached Brown's cell, the Governor said, 'Unlock it, and wait a few feet away. I have something confidential to say to the prisoner. I shall give you a triple tap signalling you to open the door.'

'Yes, sir.'

The warder turned the heavy key and the door swung open. The Governor took a step inside and the door clanged resoundingly behind him . . .

* * *

Hanley broke off and looked up. He smiled inwardly. They were all rapt, faces flushed. Even Peter's cock seemed to have strengthened. 'Now,' he asked softly, 'have you got a picture of Brown – the one to be flogged – how you imagine him? What he looks like? Remember, I've given you no description, on purpose. Harriet?'

Harriet shifted slightly and spread her legs, the long knicker gusset stretched between her ample thighs. 'I think he's a small man, lower class, very lower class; probably uneducated; doesn't realise what his feelings are, can't understand –'

'No, I don't agree,' Jennifer broke in. 'I think he's tall, perhaps quite elderly – at least fifty – who has, well, come (if you'll forgive the expression!) to terms with his problems. I've no idea how he found himself in his situation, but obviously he wants to be whipped.'

Peter cleared his throat. 'Yes, but if he's some kind of intellectual –'

'I didn't say that!' Jennifer cut in sharply, giving him a murderous look.

'You said he'd, er, come to terms with his problem. That means he thinks, and if he's fifty, as you imagine –'

'Simon?' Hanley asked.

The youngster hesitated, shaking his head. 'I don't know. He could be seventy, his life virtually over, and doing what he's doing to get some excitement. 'You told us about the old woman in the Russian camp whose whole existence centred around being punished and humiliated, maybe this man was . . .'

Hanley smiled thinly and turned a page of his book. 'You're all wrong, as a matter of fact, but that's understandable. You're imagining this man as a bullet-headed convict, some kind of intellectual, a frustrated seventy-year-old – you're all wide of the mark. Brown was twenty-four. His psychological profile – oh yes, even in nineteen ten they had those – showed him to be a repressed individual suffering from a mother complex. Apparently his mother had wanted a girl, but got a boy instead. His father was killed in the Crimea. The mother became fixated, believing her child to be a girl. He was dressed in lace and ribbons and, when he didn't achieve her expectations of him, she whipped him. Eventually he was sent away to school – she wanted no more of him – and, there, he found a surfeit of corporal punishment, the birch and cane. He loved his mother, and every flogging he received he imagined it was her wielding the birch or cane. So, out of the window goes your bullet-headed convict, your intellectual, your aged craver after punishment.' He glanced around the intent faces. 'Now, you have a young man, beautiful by all accounts. There's a crayon of him here somewhere, done by some unknown artist – I'll find it later for you – he couldn't seriously attack a warder if he tried! He did what he did to be punished.

'Now, do you want to hear what happened next, when the Governor entered his cell and the door was closed?'

'You don't mean –!' It was Peter surprisingly, his eyes alight, his cheeks burning.

'I don't know what you mean by what I don't mean!' Hanley said teasingly. 'But listen, and you'll see if what you think happened is right. Either way, you will be corrected!'

Hanley turned a page of the book . . .

The Governor confronted Brown who was sitting on his narrow, straw-mattressed bunk. He had a thin, pale face with big eyes; the prison uniform was too big for his slender frame and it sagged and sank,

27

bulged and drooped, the too-long sleeves hanging over his thin, white hands. Something inside the Governor stirred.

'Brown, your punishment is taking place shortly. I have to ask you if you have anything to say which might mitigate, might persuade me to change my decision?'

'No, sir, thank you. I deserve what I'm going to receive, and –'

The Governor interrupted quickly. 'But you want it, don't you? You want to be flogged! Am I right?'

'Sir, I deserve the punishment you've sentenced me to. I attacked one of your staff.'

'I know all that!' The Governor stared at the thin legs encased in the prison garb. They were twitching slightly. 'But you attacked Parsons on purpose, knowing you'd be sentenced to a whipping! Am I correct?'

'Well, sir –'

'Never mind about "well, sir"!' the Governor rasped. 'Am I correct? Before you answer, let me tell you I know about your, er, condition. So, I'm going to put this to you – if you're prepared to, er, rid yourself of sexual feelings before your flogging this afternoon, I will reduce the sentence to twenty-five strokes. If you do not comply, I shall increase the strokes to one hundred. If necessary, I shall make sure that all sexual feeling is absent prior to your being flogged.'

Brown looked at the Governor meekly. 'And – how would you do that, sir?'

The Governor's groin crawled. 'You will be strapped ready for your punishment. Then, you will be, er, stimulated until you ejaculate. The doctor will be present to certify that sexual completion has taken place. The flogging will then begin immediately, as I said, one hundred strokes. If, on the other hand, moments before the punishment is due, you bring yourself to completion, then I shall reduce the sentence.'

Brown stared at the floor, his thin hands clenched. He was trembling. Then he looked up. 'Sir, I'm not going to masturbate myself. It's – it's demeaning. I'd rather have it done once I'm strapped –'

'And receive a hundred lashes?' the Governor interjected, curiously moved.

Brown stared at his hands. 'Yes, sir.' He looked up. 'Sir? Who will make me –?'

The Governor wondered to himself. Then he said, 'A prisoner called Grey; he's due to be flogged next week for attempted sodomy.'

'Oh, I know Grey, sir! Yes, I'd love him to –'

'If he agrees, I'll reduce his punishment,' the Governor said.

'Sir, can I have my trousers and underpants right down if Grey agrees?'

'Well,' the Governor said, clearing the thickness from his throat, 'I suppose they'll have to be down, but they'll be pulled up and the protective strap applied before you're flogged!'

'Very well, sir,' Brown said meekly.

The Governor drew his breath in sharply. 'If you agree now, in front of me, to take your trousers and pants down and make yourself, er, ejaculate, I'll make sure the twenty-five strokes are given lightly – as lightly as possible.'

'But, sir, you don't understand – I want the punishment. I want to have someone make me ejaculate, and then have my hundred lashes.'

'Very well!' The Governor turned on his heel. 'It will be as you said. I shall approach Grey and put the suggestion to him. But, if he disagrees, you'll take your punishment as prescribed.'

Brown grinned faintly. 'Grey won't disagree, sir.'

Outside the cell, the Governor watched the wing chief officer approach.

'Everything all right, sir?'

'You heard nothing?' the Governor demanded.

'Nothing, sir.'

The Governor nodded. 'Very well. Which cell is Grey in? On this wing?'

The chief officer consulted a sheet drawn from his top pocket. 'Grey, Grey ... Ah, yes, Edwin Grey. Yes, sir, on this wing. Number sixty-six.'

'Take me to him.'

As he followed the squat figure of the chief officer along the narrow, railed corridor, the Governor's mind was in turmoil. He knew he was allowing his sexual needs to supplant his duties. But he wanted this! He wanted to see Brown masturbated, tied to the whipping post and then flogged. First he had to persuade Grey; then his assistant and the doctor. James would be no problem.

Outside the cell, the chief officer unlocked the door and swung it open. 'The Governor!' he barked. 'On your feet!'

The young man who rose from his bed in his baggy uniform was pale with big brown eyes. He wasn't unlike Brown, the Governor thought as he strode in.

'Very well, you may stand at ease.' He turned to the chief officer whose bulk was blocking the cell doorway. 'All right, chief, wait along the landing.'

When the door was closed, the Governor looked Grey up and down. 'I informed you yesterday of your punishment? Thirty lashes.'

Grey's eyes widened with a hint of panic. 'Sir! Not today –'

'No,' the Governor said, keeping his voice steady as best he could, 'and not at all if you pay attention. Sit down.'

Grey obeyed.

'Brown is to be whipped this afternoon,' the Governor went on, looking at a point above Grey's head. 'He is known to be sexually aroused by corporal punishment –'

Grey gasped.

'He was offered the choice of either relieving himself sexually prior to his punishment or being sexually relieved while restrained, in which case his punishment would be doubled. He has elected to be relieved while restrained, thereby incurring the extra number of strokes. Someone has to stimulate him to, er, completion, and he has asked that it be you.'

Grey's eyes widened even more. Instinctively, his hand went between the thighs of his trousers.

'Stop that!' the Governor warned.

Grey's face had gone white. 'Sir, you mean you want me to toss him off before he's whipped?'

'If that's the slang for making him ejaculate, yes,' the Governor said. 'You will lower his trousers and underpants – he will already be fastened to the whipping post – and you will stimulate him until he sheds his sperm. It has to be seen to be done. Will you perform this, er, task, in return for the postponement of your own flogging?'

'Of course, sir.' Grey's face had gone from white to crimson in a second. 'And if I do this I won't be whipped?'

'That's what I said,' the Governor confirmed. He shifted slightly, his cock taut against his tight trousers. 'Of course, you will say nothing of this to anyone. If word gets out around the prison, the information can only have emerged from your lips. In that case, you will be punished with the utmost severity.'

'Yes, sir, I understand. When?'

The Governor consulted his gold hunter. 'In about three-quarters-of-an-hour's time. I have some other arrangements to confirm. You agree? You will be escorted to the punishment room. No words will be exchanged. Brown will be strapped. You will lower his trousers and underpants and do what is necessary.'

'May I – may I watch the flogging?' Grey asked faintly.

'No!' the Governor barked. 'You will obtain your satisfaction in your own way! Isn't that enough – and that you are spared a whipping yourself?'

'Sorry, sir.' Grey bent his head contritely.

'So I should think!' the Governor spat, and knocked three times on the cell door, adding, 'And don't take too long about doing it when you start!'

'I'm determined,' the Governor said, facing James in front of his desk. 'If you wish to make a protest, then you will have ample opportunity. In the meantime, Brown has made his choice. 'Had he decided to stimulate himself, the sentence would have been reduced. As he has decided otherwise – and wasted a good deal of time – he will be flogged accordingly. He made up his own mind upon the matter. All you have to do is observe that Brown's sexual excitement has been reduced. It will be you and I observing. The officer administering the punishment will be outside the room until called in to do his duty.'

'Sir, this is turning the matter into a sexual charade!'

'Not at all,' the Governor contradicted him. 'As I've said, Brown has been given the choice. Which would you rather witness – the prisoner punished and deriving sexual pleasure or receiving his sentence as it is intended to do and deter further attacks on members of my staff?'

'But, sir, need it be done in this way? I mean –'

'What do you mean?' the Governor demanded coldly and leaned forwards, his fists clenched on his green blotter. 'Are you telling me you would object to seeing a man being masturbated by another man prior to being whipped? You have an interest in corporal punishment – I have a sense about that. So, you will attend to your duties and allow me the responsibility. No one else need know. Johnson, the man who has volunteered to do the flogging, will be outside the cell until Grey has finished what he has to do. He will then leave by the inner door. Johnson will enter and, to all intents and purposes, see Brown strapped and ready and, no doubt, dreading what is about to befall him.'

'Yes, sir.'

'You will conduct your usual routine examination prior to a man being flogged and report to the punishment room in twenty minutes.'

The Governor arranged for his assistant to make an inspection of the prisoners' working area at the time the punishment was to take place. He wanted him out of the way. James, he knew, he could rely on. He'd seen the gleam in the doctor's eyes . . .

Johnson was examining the three cat-o'-nine-tails to see which he would choose. It was now to be, he had been informed, one hundred lashes instead of fifty. In that case, he reckoned, he would need two whips as one would become clogged with sweat and grime. The whips were standard Home Office issue, made by a firm of leather-makers in the West Country. The handles were of oak, covered in plaited leather. The lashes, nine of them, were knotted at intervals down their lengths, Held at waist level, the tips of the lashes reached the ground. The flogger had to position himself in such a way that the lashes spread evenly over the back and did not curl and rip into the victim's chest and stomach area, as this involved the possibility of internal damage. After the whipping, the medical officer had to examine the victim's back and report on the expertise with which the 'cat' had been applied.

In his cell, Brown thought of the approaching ordeal with a mixture of emotions. His last flogging had been while he was sexually aroused. This time, he would have the pleasure of being masturbated, but then have to endure the whipping. However, he was confident that his excessive sexual energy, during the punishment, would bring him back to the euphoric state he usually felt while being thrashed.

Grey was in a mixed mood. A homosexual since the age of thirteen, he had masturbated both boys and men – but never one about to be flogged. Some had stripped naked; others, in dark alleyways, had merely opened their buttons and allowed him to stimulate them. He knew how to bring a man, or boy, 'on', pause and then bring them 'on' again until they were pleading for fruition. He had sucked many an erect cock in his time and felt the warm spread of spunk over his tongue and down his throat. This would be something new, something to regale his mates with back in the slums of Southwark. But not for a year, or until his probation came up for review. In the meantime, he could constantly relive the experience about to occur with frequent exercises in masturbation.

Brown was 'sounded' by James. Nothing was said. A warder escorted Brown along the deadly silent corridor to the punishment room. Brown hadn't seen it before. An open box stood in front of a frame of wood with two arms stretching out horizontally, attached to which were thick, leather straps.

Brown was told to remove his shirt and position himself in the box which clamped around his thighs and was bolted tight. He was ordered to stretch his arms ahead of him and they were secured by the straps. Brown was now helpless, unable to move either the upper or lower areas of his body.

His erection swelled beneath his loose trousers and coarse underpants. A warder placed a bucket of water and a cloth next to the whipping frame and left.

The Governor appeared with James, and at the same time another warder entered with Grey who stared fearfully at the sight awaiting him. Brown twisted his head and saw a pale young man with big, staring eyes meeting his gaze. The Governor closed the heavy door with a thud and closed the peephole.

'Very well,' the Governor said with a glance at James and Grey, 'let's get on with it.'

'Now, sir?' Grey asked in a whisper.

'Now', the Governor ordered, 'and no talking!'

Grey approached and looked up at Brown. Their eyes met and Brown gave a brief nod. Grey kneeled in front of his victim and, with his long, thin fingers, unbuttoned Brown's loose prison trousers and dragged them down to his knees. Next, he took the waist of the coarse urine-stained undergarment, and pulled it over Brown's rigid cock which throbbed, the foreskin pulled back tightly, the balls tight beneath the rigid shaft. Brown tried to open his legs but the box prevented them moving; however, he was able to bend his knees a little and thrust his cock out as Grey took it in his right hand and, with his left, cupped Brown's taut scrotum. Brown gave a groan.

'I said no talking!' the Governor rasped.

Moving his hand to the top of Brown's cock, Grey began to rub slowly, squeezing Brown's balls as he did so. His hand moved smoothly – the result of long practice – varying the pace and strength of the hand gripping Brown's shaft between finger and thumb. He was watching Brown's face, twisted in ecstatic pleasure, and his hand moved faster, running up and down the shaft, using a forefinger to tickle the exposed, moist tip. Then Grey's hand became a blur of movement and the sound of squelching, moistened, tormented flesh was loud in the room. Brown arched his head, thrust outwards, and, as Grey turned his head aside, a spurt of thick spunk shot out of Brown's cock and, as Grey forced the foreskin back, more emerged, splattered to the floor and then dwindled to a thin dribble. Grey continued to rub gently as the cock gradually reduced in size. Then he let go, and stood. Brown hung, head down, his breath a rasp.

'Pull his underthings and trousers up,' the Governor ordered. He hadn't looked at James.

Grey did so, buttoning him up with shaky fingers.

'All right, you can go. Through that door there and back to your cell.'

'Did I do all right, sir?' Grey asked unsteadily.

'Just go,' the Governor said, and, as Grey scuttled out, the Governor hurried to the main door where Johnson was waiting, two whips in one hand and with a thick leather belt in the other. 'Come in here,' he said, 'and do your duty. One hundred lashes – and lay them on hard!'

The belt was secured around Brown's waist. Johnson removed his uniform jacket and rolled up his sleeves. He dropped one whip on the floor beside him, grasped the other, ran his fingers through the knotted lashes, measured his distance with an experienced eye and brought the whip slashingly across Brown's prominent, skin-tight shoulder blades.

'One!' intoned the Governor, a catch in his voice.

Brown pushed his back out into the path of the cat. As the lashes cut his body, he felt comforted by the remembrance of Grey masturbating him, the sudden shock of his ejaculation, strapped to the whipping post. The lashes he could stand; there was only a limit of pain; after that, the flesh numbed. Now Brown, his body thrust into the wooden base of the whipping frame by the strength of the flogging, prayed for the familiar tickle in his groin; the sense of a swelling in the deep-rooted base of his cock; the sensation as the shaft grew, and the foreskin stretched lazily back.

He heard the count – 'number twenty-four' – and eased himself into the flogging. It was best to accept the strokes as they were administered; stinging lashes whipped into his naked back. He thought of Grey masturbating him with firm, authoritative hand movements and the satisfying eruption of spunk . . . Now, he would come again!

The lashing continued, and gradually Brown spread his legs a little and bent his knees as far as the locked box enabled him to. His trousers were loose around his hips and beneath the rough underpants he felt his cock rising. 'Thirty-eight!' The flogging continued. Brown's cock rose to its fullest extent and he bent his legs. He heard himself groaning – at least, he supposed it was him, long expulsions of breath as the knotted lash continued to thrash into his back.

Now, suddenly, he felt the familiar stir, deep within his loins. A message, a sudden 'itch' in the base of his cock; a feeling surging upwards through the distended shaft.

'Whip me!' Brown moaned aloud. 'Flog me! I want it!'

The lashes fell. Sweat trickled down his lower back, heightening the eroticism. 'Flog! Flog!' He braced himself and, beneath the sagging trousers and tickling underpants, he thrust his cock out. He felt the spurts of spunk into his pants and the muscular reaction seemed to continue indefinitely. The whipping continued relentlessly. Now, Brown felt nothing but pain; agonising pain ripping into his back. He tried to think of other things: of Grey gripping his cock in such a familiar way, as though he had done it before, and was conscious of Brown's cock and its reaction to his smooth handling of it.

'Eighty-five.' He heard the count. Another fifteen – he could take it! His cock was stuck to his underwear. In silence, he endured the last fifteen lashes. The silence in the punishment room was palpable. The only sound the drip-drip of sweat from Brown's flogged back on to the stone floor.

The Governor drew a deep breath. 'Very well. Doctor, would you see to the man?' He nodded at Johnson, who had the cat-o'-nine-tails still in his hand. 'You may go. I'll sign your release and you'll be paid in the usual way. You've done your duty.'

Brown was unstrapped. His legs were unsteady. James turned him gently on to his stomach on a leather-topped bench and proceeded to dab at the weals which extended deeply from his shoulder blades to his lower back. In places, they had formed into thick ridges on the pale flesh.

'This man needs hospital treatment,' James said, turning to the Governor who stood motionless, his legs oddly close together.

In a strangled voice, the Governor said, 'You can deal with him; it's just the result of a normal corporal punishment.'

'It isn't, sir!' James protested, while applying ointment. 'This man has had a hundred lashes!'

'Are you saying you are incapable of treating him?' The Governor raised his eyebrows as James stared up at him.

Brown's head was down. He hadn't uttered a word.

James shook his head wearily. He was in two states of mind: he had to admit to himself that seeing Brown strapped to the whipping post, trousers and pants down and being masturbated, had affected him in a strange way. He had been aroused. But watching the merciless whipping Brown had been subjected to afterwards robbed him of any sexual feeling. He had seen Brown ejaculate, had seen the telltale muscular spasms as a man spurted his spunk, but the continuation of the flogging had disgusted him. It was as if an animal was being flayed alive purely for the butchery involved.

This had been a sexual orgy, in his view. Across the river, brothels catered for this kind of thing: corporal punishment given with extremity, to the extent the customer was willing to pay. That was their concern, the clients: if they wished the skin to be flayed from their backs and buttocks, that was their affair. They went home sore, and, presumably, satisfied – until their weals had faded to some extent and they were ready for more of the severely applied whip, cane, birch or riding crop with the whipper dressed in knee-length knickers, corselet and riding boots, preferably with glinting, cruel-looking silver spurs attached to the highly polished heels . . .

Hanley snapped the book closed. 'Now – who wants to be Brown?'

Eight eyes stared at him. Simon was first to break the silence. 'You mean whipped – after –?'

Hanley nodded. 'Not on the back, though, on the buttocks.'

Simon's face was a picture. 'I will –'

'Of course he will!' Jennifer put in. 'He'll do anything for a thrill!'

'I thought that's what we're all here for,' Hanley said reasonably.

'And what are we supposed to get out of it?' Jennifer sat up, her long legs apart and her knicker gusset tight over her pudendum.

'Watch, and then flog me!' Hanley retorted.

'You bet I will!'

'Can I be Grey – that was his name, wasn't it? – who made Brown come when he was tied?' Peter said hesitantly.

Harriet spread her legs. 'If we're going to do this properly – and personally I think it's a superb idea, always supposing Simon can take it – he should be wearing something on his lower half to be pulled down. Why not my knickers? They're loose, like the sort of breeches convicts wore – I've seen pictures. Simon?'

'Oh, please!' Simon was standing, his thin legs shaking, his erection pulsing.

'Well.' Hanley looked round at them as Harriet was already slipping her knickers off. 'Let's play!'

They 'played'.

When they met again, Hanley had another tale ready . . .

2

Tales to be Told – The Man Who Drew Too Much

Tony Simmons had been visiting one of his five mistresses – this one in Gloucester Road not far from the Park – all of whom paid him well for his services, when a taxi, cruising on the wrong side of the road to swoop on a possible fare, hit him from the rear as he crossed the wide expanse of Gloucester Gate . . .

'We'll find out what happened next in a while,' Hanley explained, watching Jennifer drawing the knotted lashes of her favourite whip languidly between her long fingers, 'but first it's necessary to know a little more about the man in question.'

He read on, watching their eyes . . .

Tony Simmons, a thirty-year-old bachelor, was a successful creative designer with an up-and-coming advertising agency. He dressed well, ate well and lived well – the flat he rented in Maida Vale was financed partly by his salary and his freelance work, and partly by the willingness to be dominated, humiliated and punished by rich, bored women who were either unmarried, divorced or separated. Whichever, their sexual lives were enhanced only by having a tall, slim, young man obey their every whim, serve as their slave and then be punished for minor faults deliberately committed. They demanded excessive sexual favours, oral and anal stimulation and, naturally, sexual intercourse in a variety of ways to their bidding with his cock and various dildo devices. He was required to escort them to dinner and to functions, and to be extremely attentive all the while. They paid him! He'd found it difficult to believe when Helen had first told him of this new, unknown world.

He had been masochistic from the age of sixteen or so when he'd realised he had been aroused during a caning administered by a senior prefect at his public school – he was forced across a desk, his trousers and pants taken down and given the traditional 'six of the best'. But, after the first three stinging blows, he found the sensation not unpleasant. He discovered he was erect and, the punishment over, he took himself to the nearest bog and masturbated. He'd never ejaculated so quickly and so thickly! Now, instead of handing over substantial amounts to have his tastes catered for, he was being paid handsomely himself! Mind you, he had to perform some tasks outside even his wide experience – but what the hell! He got his money and it was only afterwards that he sometimes thought how degrading it had become. But then his twice-monthly bank statement convinced him otherwise.

As an accomplished artist with pen and ink, crayon and black chinograph, Tony was able to translate his fantasies on to thick pads of drawing paper. He kept the results of his efforts hidden well away, but, while artistically rendering his desires, images and graphic representations of his suppressed needs, he would become extremely aroused sexually, although he would restrain himself until the drawing was finished.

He had carried the drawings around with him, secure in a large, black artist's case, everywhere he went. He had, of course, other, more conventional examples of his creative ability, and these he showed to creative directors at various advertising agencies. One had invited him to dinner at his flat, but the invitation for a meal soon turned to an urgent invitation for other things – such as Tony stripping naked and bending over. If it had been for a whipping, he would have gladly acquiesced . . . but it wasn't for a whipping! The man already had his trousers and pants down and was bringing himself to a full erection when Tony took a swing at him and ran for his life.

He hadn't got that particular job – naturally enough under the circumstances – but the third agency had hired him on the strength of one drawn picture. It was a black crayon and he had done it one night after returning home after a conventional session of corporal punishment.

He hadn't really known what he was aiming to do when he took the thick pad on his knee and started to sketch. There were trees, naked branches against a wild, windy sky. The branches were thin and threatening. As he drew, he felt he could almost feel the sting of their lashes against his face as he – presumably a lost traveller on this stormy night – blundered through the storm to some kind of lighted haven.

It was a picture he looked at often, and he finally decided to include it in his portfolio. It gave nothing of his sexual inclinations away – except to him – and could have a totally different significance to anyone looking at it from a creative point of view. Tony knew well enough, though, what those thin, naked branches represented: they were birch twigs and they weren't lashing his face; they were stinging his buttocks. The various 'mistresses' he visited for punishment were not equipped with birches. Whips, canes and riding crops could be bought; birches had to be made. Tony didn't know a birch tree from a maypole, but he studied a book, took a journey into the countryside, found a wood and soon found birch trees. He cut the long, thin twigs into bundles, keeping a wary eye open for any casual walker, took them home and fashioned them into instruments for the infliction of pain.

He was helped in this by studying a woodcut in a Victorian novel. As with most Victorian novels, a lengthy section was always devoted to school punishments. This picture displayed a begowned and mortarboarded master punishing a boy. The birch depicted as about to be brought down on the boy's bare bottom was a thick bundle of twigs, and, his own bundle thus fashioned, the ends bound together with tape, he took them along to one of his more mature ladies, and was duly flogged, much to his satisfaction. And once a week without fail.

Meanwhile, the agency to whom he had last shown his portfolio had taken him on; and in six months he was the star of the department. He could draw swiftly with the minimum of strokes (of the pen!), conveying an urgency to the subject which even the camera was unable to convey.

The agency won a new account for ladies' underwear. A fashion house in Paris was preparing to open a salon in London, and they wanted full-page ads in the quality papers and magazines; nothing suggestive in the obvious sense, but compelling enough to persuade the more mature woman to consider their designs.

Tony enjoyed drawing maturer women in their underclothes. They had rather a condescending approach to their modelling. They looked sideways down towards him, cool; their corsets, bras, slips and knickers seemed to be a privilege they were agreeing to wear.

Tony often achieved an erection while he was drawing, and one woman in particular aroused him the most. She could have been anything between forty and fifty, and was heavily bosom'd, with substantial thighs and long, surprisingly slender legs. Her name was Helen Forman and at one time she had been an actress. Tony found her intriguing. He had fantasies about her dominating him, punishing him and afterwards burying his face in those ample breasts and sliding down to urge his tongue between her thighs and into the sweet-tasting softness beyond.

On this particular day, she was modelling pantaloons: tight, cotton knickers down the thigh, with three bands of frilly lace instead of elastic. Tony drew swiftly as she stood, one leg forwards of the other, showing the sleek line of the knickers. His cock rose so hard he almost could have used it as a stand for his drawing pad. He wanted to feel those knickers on his own body and at the same time be flogged by this Helen!

They hadn't exchanged many words during the five or six times he had drawn her in various styles of underwear, but this particular day – after he had drawn her in those enticing pantaloons – they emerged from the studio at the same time. Tony held the door for her respectfully. She had on an expensive-looking suede coat with a fur collar and beneath black leather trousers which 'broke' over gleaming, pointed shoes, or boots – he couldn't tell at that stage.

'Thank you,' she said, but with no hint of a smile. 'I've seen some of your drawings in the ads; you're good.'

'Thank you,' Tony said humbly, moving sharply to the outside of the pavement as they walked towards Oxford Circus. He wondered what sort of knickers she had on now – it wouldn't be those heavenly pantaloons which clung so enticingly to her thighs in the studio!

'Do you like drawing women in their underclothing?' She glanced sideways at him.

'It's part of the job, I –' Tony said.

'Yes, but that wasn't what I asked!' Her voice was sharp and a thrill ran up his spine. 'Do you enjoy it?'

They were at the corner. It was noon and the traffic was heavy in all directions.

'Well,' he said, 'it's always a pleasure to draw beautiful women.'

'So, you're saying that you do enjoy it?' Her chin was up imperiously.

His cock was growing. Tony nodded. 'Yes, I do, especially when I draw you.' There, he'd said it! Would she leave?

'Have you another assignment?' Her chin was still raised.

Tony shrugged. 'I was going to have a quick bite to eat then go back to the office. I have to get my sketches ready –'

'So you have an hour or so?' She'd had to raise her voice because at that moment four buses in line, like elephants nose to tail, raised a crescendo as they revved through the lights. 'Very well.' She raised an arm and a taxi appeared like magic, though Tony hadn't seen one with its light on. They climbed in. She said to the driver, 'The Bistro, Dean Street.'

'Lady, it's quicker to walk!' the man whined through the open panel. 'I've got to go all the way down Regent Street, up Shaftesbury Avenue and then do a double turn –'

'I don't want to know the route, just get us there!'

Tony thrilled to her commanding tone. Oh, he thought, if only she had those pantaloons on still! He could imagine her, in some medieval time, accusing the taxi driver – although, of course, he'd have been driving a horse and cart – of being insolent and having him flogged at Newgate, or wherever they did such things in those days. His cock seemed to agree, and became even more upright.

The taxi took its time, but she didn't seem to mind. Tony kept glancing at her set profile and its sternness aroused him even more. He could feel the head of his cock sticking to his tight, dark-blue briefs. Eventually, the taxi made its manoeuvres and came to a halt. She got out quickly and paid the driver. Tony followed her meekly into the restaurant. It was all marble floor, gold fittings and white table cloths. Tony hadn't been in that particular restaurant before, but he recognised it for what it was. Expensive. High class.

They were seated in a corner, a banquette, and Tony sat on her right. She removed her suede coat, revealing a black sweater through which the prominent bulge of her white brassiere showed clearly. They evidently knew her there, and the service was lavish. She chose the meal and the wine without hesitation or consultation with him. Tony didn't care; by this time he was obsessed with her. This magnificent woman was the one he'd been drawing earlier in her lace-edged pantaloons and now she was buying him lunch! When the Chianti came and was tasted and approved, she raised her glass. 'Here's to a successful future.'

Tony wasn't sure what she meant by that, so he nodded vaguely and sipped his wine. 'Thank you.'

'You may have more to thank me for before very

long,' she said, putting down her glass. 'Does women's underwear arouse you?'

The sudden question, out of the blue like that, left him breathless for a moment. Gathering his thoughts, he managed to say eventually, 'Er, what sort do you mean?'

'You know very well. The sort I was wearing this morning. Long ones, knee-length.'

He drew a deep breath. 'Yes, they do.'

'Hmm.'

The anti-pasta arrived, together with warm rolls. There was a heavy silence. Tony watched her eat delicately, noticing for the first time a heavy gold ring on the little finger of her left hand.

'You like to be dominated?'

This question, so out of the blue, astonished him even more. 'Er – dominated?'

'Told what to do ... ordered.' She put her fork down and wiped her mouth. 'Would you do what I told you to do, without question?'

Tony sipped his wine. 'Yes,' he said finally, 'anything.'

'When did you last have a whipping?' Her voice was low, but every word was distinct.

My God, he thought, is it that obvious? But he played it safe. 'A whipping? I don't think I've ever –'

'Nonsense! I can tell from experience what a man likes sexually! You're a masochist! It shows in your every gesture, in every look. I would guarantee that if I took your trousers and pants down this minute your behind would be covered in welts!' She poured more wine from the basketed flask with a steady hand. 'Well?'

'Yes. But –'

'But – nothing! How recently were you punished?'

'Two nights ago,' Tony said.

A warm, sensual glow was spreading through him and his erection jumped spasmodically. He felt he was sinking into a delicious dream world and hoped he wouldn't find himself waking up.

The main course arrived and more wine was brought. Tony found himself, oddly, unable to look at her; all he remembered was that body clothed provocatively in that clinging underwear.

'I presume by a mistress whom you had to pay?'

'Yes,' Tony said, 'but I can afford it.'

She leaned forwards. 'But how would you like it if you were being paid for your services? Paid to be dominated, humbled and punished?'

Tony dropped his fork and lifted his eyes to meet hers. They were steady, unflinching. 'How – how do you mean?' His voice sounded distant as though somebody over his right shoulder had answered. He swallowed hard.

She leaned more closely across the table and he saw a slight smile at the corners of her lips. But it wasn't a warming smile: it had a sense of menace to it. 'I know several women – women in society whose names would astonish you if you read magazines like *Queen* or *Vogue* – hard women, brought up in the country, ride to hounds, bored with life in general. They lead separate lives from husbands too busy in politics or industry to bother very much. Women whose children are away at boarding school most of the time, but whose sexual appetite for the unusual has grown. They crave young men, good-looking young men such as yourself, to please them in various ways.'

Tony felt his face flushing. 'What sort of ways?'

He drank some wine to ease his parched throat.

'Can't you guess? I said they're hard women, around horses a lot, leather, riding crops – they need to take their frustration out; to relieve their humdrum lives; a plaything with whom, within reason, they can enjoy their tastes – and pay well!'

Tony glanced around, but the table nearest theirs was now empty. 'You mean – whipping?'

'That, of course, and other things – servant work; allowing them to satisfy their particular whims. Oh, you'd be able to negotiate; nothing would be forced on you – on the other hand, the more you were prepared to satisfy their needs, the more you would be paid. I have two other young men in my stable – if you'll forgive the expression – much like you, in fact, who are well satisfied with their situation. The assignments would in no way interfere with your professional life; they take place at night or at weekends and total confidentiality is, naturally, assured. After all, their secret is of much more value than yours, to put it bluntly. And they pay in cash.'

Tony pushed his plate away. His erection was giving him pain now; it was like an overripe fruit about to burst and he had to return to the office – a world which seemed a million miles away at that moment. 'Is this serious?' he asked.

'Of course. But if you're not in favour of the idea then it will be forgotten, and no more mention will be made. My clients – for want of a better word – require absolute co-operation. They're prepared to pay well and they expect their money to be well spent. After all, you're paid well to do your job . . .' She left the sentence unfinished and raised her finely pencilled eyebrows.

The overripe fruit burst, and Tony felt his underpants flooding. He tried to keep his expression bland as the eruption of spunk continued. He bet there'd be a telling stain on his trousers, but he didn't care. Even though he'd come, an erotic wave of excitement overcame him. Easing himself on the leather seat, praying that nothing would leak through, he said, 'I'd like to – yes, I would. What happens now?'

The waiter cleared the table. Coffee was brought. It was gone two now, and Tony should have been back. But he was in good standing with the company – nobody could draw like him, especially of mature women wearing stretching pantaloons!

'It's necessary, of course, to test you, to have an interview,' she said. 'Only this will be no ordinary interview, as you will imagine. You'll visit my home at a date and time to be arranged. I shall expect you to demonstrate your sexual performance, and I shall flog you severely. If I then feel you are competent to be passed on to my clients, we shall arrange the first meeting. Is that agreed?'

'Of course,' Tony said thickly, 'What sort – sort of things will they want me to wear?'

'That will be their choice. Some like you in women's underwear –'

'What sort?' Tony interrupted eagerly. 'Like – like the sort you had on this morning?'

'Possibly. Others favour directoire knickers – you're familiar with those?'

'Oh, yes,' Tony confirmed, 'my mother used to wear that sort. I, er, sometimes put them on myself.'

'It all depends on their mood at the time,' she said and waved a hand for the bill. She took a card from her handbag. 'This is my very private number. Ring to make an appointment. When I answer say "Bond" – that will be your code word.'

She paid with an American Express Gold Card, and they got up, Tony slowly and carefully. On the red leather seat there were thankfully no stains. However, looking down, he could see a patch on his crotch but luckily he was wearing a dark suit.

Outside, he said, 'Thank you for the lunch and –'

'I hope we can do business together,' she cut in.

As if by magic, a taxi appeared and in a swirl of suede coat she was gone.

Tony made a thoughtful way back to the office. On the way, his cock was beginning to harden again. What she was suggesting, quite simply, was that he become a prostitute! Like the women he visited and paid for their services, he, in turn, would be paid for his. But what? She had indicated these were hard, tough women, who were frustrated, wanting something new to sharpen their jaded appetites. A thrill ran through him as he thought of how it would be to venture into the unknown, to meet someone new and discover what they wanted from him! Older women, always more attractive because of their experience, their special tastes – and willing to pay! Probably eager to pay: to get a sight of his body, his genitals, his buttocks, which would be smooth and white but which would bear the evidence of frequent CP.

Helen had said he would have to pass tests – fucking her? he wondered. Going down on her? Drinking her? In any case, she had warned him that she would flog him severely. Well, Tony thought, as he dodged the traffic across Piccadilly Circus and made his way westwards along Piccadilly itself. He paused at the windows of Swayne, Adeny and Brigg. They sold riding gear – saddles, leather straps with buckles which glistened, crops, boots and breeches. He thought of what Helen had said and imagined the women she had mentioned in tight, white jodhpurs, knee-length glistening boots, a high-buttoned white blouse and over it a cutaway tunic; and in gloved hands would be a menacing, thin, red-tasselled riding crop. He would have to unzip her breeches . . .

His eyes strayed to a corner of the window. There, on a metal stand, was a black-handled whip with –

yes, he counted them – nine thin lashes spread enticingly on the floor. He stared, unable to believe his eyes. This, surely, wasn't riding equipment! A crop, or a dressage whip, yes, just to flick its hocks down and again, but not a nine-thonged whip!

But there it was. Tony looked at his watch. The early afternoon had grown perceptibly duller. His watch, which he had bought in Zurich during a visit to the agency's Swiss branch, had complicated dials and looked more like the control panel on the flight deck of a 747 than something merely to tell the time of day. It was two-twenty. He looked at the whip again and, drawing a deep breath, entered the leather-smelling interior. An elderly man with thinning white hair stood behind a glass-topped counter. Tony was conscious of gleaming steel brasses, thick straps, bridles, a row of crops dangling invitingly.

'Yes, sir?' the white-haired man asked. He looked pink and benevolent.

Tony coughed. 'I saw in the window a, er, a whip . . . the black one with lashes. I wondered how much it was. It's odd, I have a friend –' he was improvising brilliantly '– he's a theatrical producer; you wouldn't know his name, but he's putting on a play at the Tricycle Theatre in Kilburn, amateurs, but they get some good reviews, and in this particular play –' he swallowed hard '– they need a whip, you know, a proper whip, and I just saw that one, and I wondered –'

There was no reaction. 'Certainly, sir, I'll get it for you. I won't keep you a moment.'

Tony stood irresolutely, praying no one else would enter the shop. The old man had unlocked the partition to the window and now was bringing out the black whip almost delicately. He closed the partition and brought the whip in both hands, holding it before him like some kind of ritual sacrifice. 'There, sir.'

Tony stared at the whip, the lashes spread on the mirrored counter. Close up, it looked formidable. The handle was of fine, plaited leather; there was even a leather strap at the top of the haft for hanging it up.

The old man said quietly, 'As a matter of fact, it's the only one in stock at the moment. They're made, you know, for export – to Africa, I believe. This was left over from the current supply. It's sad, isn't it, in this day and age these kinds of things are still used in some parts of the world?'

Tony nodded. 'I – I agree. How much is it?'

'Thirty-six pounds, sir. I know it sounds a good deal, but it is made of the finest quality workmanship. Indeed, the firm which makes these whips, in the East End, used to make the cat-o'-nine-tails used on prisoners. I'm sure your, er, theatrical friend would find this most satisfactory'.

'I'll take it,' Tony said, fumbling for his wallet, then producing a credit card.

He wanted to get out, away from the smell of fresh leather. He was worked up as it was, and also confused. The old man's words had probably been innocently spoken, but, in the state he was in now, everything seemed to be underlined with a special significance. The whip, lashes curled, was packed into a white box and wrapped in brown paper tied with white string.

Tony returned to the office and put some final touches to his sketches of Helen in her knickers and handed them over to the etchers.

He left as soon as he could and took a taxi straight home. There, he stripped naked, unpacked the whip, dangled the lashes over his long-aroused cock and began rhythmically flogging his buttocks. He was determined to go ahead with Helen's idea. All that remained for him to do was to convince her that he was capable of meeting the requirements. He thrashed himself until his buttocks were swollen and livid. But he didn't ejaculate. He decided to punish himself in that way even though his rigid cock was begging. He had to rehearse what would be happening in the future – and he knew from experience that mature women liked to see a man powerless and desperate to masturbate. It somehow evened up, to them, the injustices of sex to which they had been subjected. He cleaned the lashes and then tied several knots in each of them, pulling them tight.

Like in the olden days, Tony would be the 'whipping boy' to a prince, or other noble youngster, who had been found to be disobedient. A servant boy endured the resultant flogging instead; Tony was to suffer in the cause of female equality!

I wonder, Helen Forman thought, as she poured herself a vodka and tonic, if he'll phone. She badly needed another young man, handsome and slim, to add to her stable of studs. They had to be remarkable young men, she realised that, able and willing to cater for every need that her circle of women demanded.

Helen received fifteen, sometimes twenty, per cent of the fee for the introduction and in some cases this could amount to a hundred pounds or more. It depended if the lady in question required the young man to stay all night – which meant from somewhere around six in the evening until nine, or later, in the morning. During those fourteen or fifteen hours, he would be totally in the client's control. Within reason, she could demand anything of him – and in some instances he could make his own demands on her, which were usually accepted. The money was paid in cash and so far Helen had experienced no problems in that area.

But two of her clients had expressed boredom at what she had to offer and needed something fresh, and they were, as it happened, two of her best.

Hilda Maidment was 55 and single. Where her money came from, Helen didn't know, but she always paid on time – and sometimes more generously than the hitherto agreed fee. One of Helen's young men had been Hilda's particular favourite. His name was Philip Scott. He was 24, but looked like a schoolboy: fresh faced and innocent. But he was far from that. Oddly, despite his fetishes, his needs for punishment and his desires to do some punishing himself given the opportunity, he was also religious.

At least, he was religious to the extent that he was fascinated by why Jesus Christ elected to defy both the High Priests of Jerusalem and the Romans, knowing he would be flogged and then crucified. Philip had studied manuscripts and read medical journals. He had become convinced that Jesus was a masochist who desired to suffer. He knew what fate awaited him, Philip argued, while Hilda masturbated him gently.

She loved to hear about suffering. And loved the practice as well as the theory. She was a woman of medium height, but with a face which seemed to foretell anguish. Her eyes were deep set and somehow expressionless, her skin strangely smooth and unwrinkled. When she and Philip had first made love – she protesting she was a virgin – he had found it incredibly easy to slip into her with no problems. She hadn't felt like a virgin and his cock, with the foreskin drawn back, had thrust itself like a well-oiled machine.

She loved to hear how victims of Roman crucifixion met their end. Firstly, Philip explained, after the sentence they were taken into a courtyard, stripped naked and chained by the wrists to a tall, column of wood or stone. Two Roman soldiers then took up special whips preserved solely for pre-crucifixion scourging. The whips had leather thongs of varying lengths, some plaited together, and with small pieces of metal or sharp fragments of sheep bones sewn into them. The victim would be flogged on the back, buttocks and legs, each lash producing deep lacerations and loss of blood. Each soldier would alternate the strokes.

Then, the man – already in extremis – would be swung to face his torturers, and be whipped on the chest, stomach, genitals, thighs and calves. Philip had discovered that, through some metabolistic process, men thus being whipped would involuntarily experience an erection – in which case the hardened cock would be thrashed to ribbons. If the victim could still stand, he was then forced to carry the heavy cross-beam of the cross to the execution site – some mile or so away – being whipped as he staggered along and being jeered and spat at by crowds gathered on each side of the Via Dolorosa, 'the way of the Cross'. Once on the site, he was tied and flogged again before being nailed and raised spread-eagled to suffer his demeaning death, exposed in all his nakedness and bloodiness to the assembled crowds who would have bets with shekels or stones on how long it would take the man to breathe his last.

'I want it, I want it!' Philip would moan as he strained while Hilda teased his erection. 'I want a Roman flogging!' But it had never happened.

They had whipped each other many times, but Philip had met a priest who had introduced him to a monastery, secluded and strict in its regime, and he had taken the lessons and the vows, and was now firmly installed. And Hilda wanted another like him. It was as simple as that.

Helen's second problem was with Fiona Trench. She was an out-and-out masochist, wanting no more than humiliation and punishment, usually with a cane while she was dressed in navy-blue school bloomers. In a room at the top of the house which she shared with a lesbian partner in Chiswick, there were several old-fashioned school desks, ink stained and with names carved by long-ago pupils, a blackboard and easel. There, her humiliation would take place as she failed to answer the simplest of questions and as a result her gymslip would be lifted as she lay across one of the desks, her knickers lowered and the punishment begun.

Her lesbian partner would chalk on the blackboard as each stroke was administered. It wasn't exactly a game, because pain was involved – but there was, always had been and always would be a thin line dividing pain and pleasure.

When Helen heard that Tony had been knocked down by the 'fucking taxi!', she panicked. 'Yes, I'm his sister; how badly hurt is he? Oh, fractures . . . but he'll – live?

'When can I see him? We're very close; there are no other relatives. I see, in about twenty-four hours . . . and which ward? Yes, thank you.'

At first nobody noticed anything. Someone had phoned 999 and Tony had been picked up off the roadway. On the way to St Mary's, Paddington, he was monitored by the ultra-efficient, calm paramedics who placed an oxygen mask over his face and, after ripping open his shirt, taped ECG monitoring pads on his chest.

He was handed over, signed for in A&E like a package and wheeled to a curtained cubicle, where a sister began to undress him. Lowering his trousers, she discovered that he was wearing voluminous, siken directoire knickers, a roll-on girdle and stockings. Then, exposing his buttocks, she found recent weals. Other marks of corporal punishment were found on the backs of his thighs.

The nurse was Jenny French. She was 22 and had only just been assigned to A&E. She was single and lived at home with her widowed mother in Belsize Park. She was alone in the curtained cubicle and Tony lay unconscious, his head to one side, a bleeding gash on his forehead which she soon attended to, and then awaited the trolley to take him away for X-ray. She'd taken his soaked trousers off, and he lay sprawled, the long knickers draped around his thighs. Her mother wore that sort; she'd seen them often enough hanging out to dry or airing – but why did this attractive-looking young man have them on: and why were his buttocks scored with what were obviously marks of punishment?

She'd vaguely heard of masochism – it had been mentioned but only in passing during a lecture on sexual psychology – so this young man was a masochist! With the curtains round the cubicle tightly drawn, she gingerly lowered the waist of the knickers, displaying his thick, brown pubic hair and then the cock hanging limply over the tight balls. Within her tight, white panties, her groin stirred and an itch developed inside her moistening pussy. What did she want? He'd been whipped! Had that limp, yet powerful-looking cock been towering as whoever it was had flagellated him? And why the knickers – that particular sort? From what little she knew, she'd gathered that, if men wanted to wear women's underclothes, they usually wore lacy panties or briefs; not bloomers!

She heard the rumble of the trolley and hastily covered the genitals with the knicker silk.

'Blimey!' One of the orderlies had arrived. He was about nineteen, already balding in front, thin faced and with rabbit teeth. He'd asked Jenny out more than once, but she'd always refused. 'What's this, then? Right bloody pervert, this one!'

His older colleague – a man who looked drawn and grey in the job of transporting mortally injured to X-ray, or shrouded bodies to the morgue below – said, 'Shut it!' He looked at Jenny with a sympathetic eye. 'Sorry you had to see this, love.'

'It's all right,' Jenny said, and smiled thinly, trying to sound experienced. 'He's got marks on his, er, behind, I don't know . . .' Her voice tailed off.

'Never mind,' the older man said consolingly, while the other gaped, 'we'll take care of it. If you'll just sign this.' He handed her a clipboard and indicated where to sign.

When they'd gone, Jenny sat on the rumpled bed. There was so much she had to learn! About people, and the way they were. She felt tears flood the backs of her eyes and she sniffed, taking a small handkerchief from her uniform pocket.

They say that when a man is drowning, or near death, his life flashes before his eyes. Tony's last thought before being struck by the errant cab was: Oh, Christ! I've just been –

Now, he had no idea where he was as he sluggishly regained consciousness. He could see bright lights, and blinked in the glare. His first impression was that he was in some kind of heaven; he'd had that split-second feeling when he knew the taxi was going to hit him. It was inevitable; there was no way he was going to avoid it. He stared at the lights. He knew he was partially unclothed because he could still feel the roll-on, stockings and the knicker elastic tight on his thighs. Also, his buttocks smarted. Where the hell was he? He sank into a kind of coma with images darting like streaks of lightning through his befuddled brain ...

This particular 'mistress' had been Donna. He'd visited her several times before and always enjoyed the two hours for which she paid handsomely. She was around 35, he guessed, and very thin, with an angular, high-cheekboned face upon which no makeup was visible. The first time he had gone there, he had been disappointed at first sight. The woman looked too scraggy, too dried up to be of any use. He'd met women like that before, he thought, who only wanted to wield a whip or cane to compensate for their frustrations; who had flogged him and then coldly dismissed him with a brief nod, while he went away frustrated, hard as iron and desperate to masturbate.

With a sinking heart, he had expected Donna to be like the others. But Donna wasn't, no way! Thin as she might look, she had a luscious body with small but firm breasts, and down below, amid the fine, silky hair, the lips and entry of an exceptionally juicy pussy. It oozed sweet-tasting moisture as he grovelled between her thighs which squeezed his cheekbones as he explored with his tongue.

Unlike his other 'clients', she wanted to whip him after she was satisfied. She had him strapped up naked and upright chained to a wooden post in her cellar, watching his cock rise with each stroke, before finally witnessing the shuddering climax as he spilled his spunk on the floor at his feet. Then, as she was aroused again at his anguish, he was down on her again, relishing the wetness as she moaned, 'I'm going to flog you to death . . . one day . . . one day soon!'

That's where he'd been. Now, in these unfamiliar surroundings, with his thoughts making his cock elongate under the thick silk of his knickers, he lay supine, revelling in the humiliation. Hurt as he was, bruised and aching, his natural masochism blossomed at the thought that he was being exposed in women's underwear.

'Good God!' a male voice said. 'What on earth –?'

'Sir – hadn't we better get these things off him, whatever they, er, are?'

The other voice replied, 'Well, yes, take his, um, knickers off and all the rest of what he's wearing.'

Deliciously, although still confused, Tony felt himself being undressed. The long knickers were pulled down and off; the stockings and corset undone (he had the feeling that whoever was undressing him hadn't had the experience of women's solid underwear before!) and so he lay there, eventually naked as the day he was born, with the difference that his cock rose in moist salute.

He felt his body being turned gently.

'Look at his bottom, sir!'

'That's got nothing to do with the accident,' the other voice said, with some contempt. 'He's been whipped, for God's sake! And, if I'm not mistaken, with a cane and a riding crop – see the difference in the weals there, and there, and there.'

The first voice asked plaintively 'But what do we do, sir?'

'He's a traffic accident – we treat him as such; that's our concern. Now, wheel in the equipment, and let's see how many bones have been broken.'

'But look at his –'

'You look at it – I've got better things to do,' the other voice answered sternly.

Helen was on the phone to Donna. 'It was virtually outside! Didn't you hear anything?'

'Darling! I was, er, otherwise engaged. He does turn me on!'

'Did you whip him?' Helen asked impatiently.

'Of course.'

'What was he wearing when he left?' Helen demanded.

'Well, he had his long knickers on, as usual, and his roll-on and stockings –'

'And now he's in hospital, being stripped and examined.'

'Well, dear,' said Donna languidly, 'I'm sure he'll enjoy that. I know I would!'

Helen drew in an angry breath. 'He might talk! He'll be asked questions!'

'Well, he'll be a fool if he talks,' Donna said, 'and, anyway, what possible crime has he committed? He visits a friend for an evening of mutual enjoyment – what he wears or what marks might be on parts of his body are no concern of anyone.'

'How much did you give him?' Helen interjected.

'Money? Three hundred as usual – a pound a stroke –'

'Cash?' Helen interrupted again.

'Yes, dear, in fivers. Why?'

'Can't you see?' Helen hissed. 'If you'd given him a cheque, your name –'

'Of course, darling. Good point. Listen, why not come round for an hour?'

'No!' Helen almost shouted, and slammed the phone down, angrier than ever.

She wandered from room to room restlessly, arms

folded across her bosom, feeling the nipples hard under her thin brassiere. Thank God it had been cash!

The next thing Tony knew he opened his eyes to blurred, white curtains. Instinctively, he knew he no longer had on his corset, stockings and knickers. Gingerly, he ran a hand over himself. It was some kind of nightgown with tapes at the back. His lower limbs and genitals were uncovered. His head ached and there was a pain in his lower back. Exploring a little further, he found bandages on his upper thigh and the right forearm. His behind stung – but that was different.

What time was it? What day was it? How long? Then he remembered the money, the wad of notes Donna had given him, but how long ago? And what was going to happen next? Sweat trickled into his groin, beneath his armpits and across his forehead. He vaguely remembered voices, but nothing now made any sense. Lying rigid, not daring to move, listening to the vague sounds outside this plastic he seemed to be encompassed in, he closed his eyes and an eager hand sought his flaccid cock beneath the high-length nightgown thing. What could they do to him? He'd committed no crime – was it an offence to wear women's underclothes and have flogged buttocks? He thought vaguely of the agency, but then surrendered to the delights of bringing himself slowly to a climax . . .

He was bubbling ready to come, when a side curtain was drawn aside abruptly and a middle-aged woman in a severe blue dress with white cuffs and a starched collar stood there. Her dress, over thick black stockings, reached below her knees. Her calves were thickly muscled. On her grey hair was a white cap with lace edges. Her face was grim; not thin, but muscular; her lips broad and unpainted. She wore steel-rimmed spectacles through which her black-buttoned eyes were magnified.

Hurriedly, Tony withdrew his hand from his cock and pulled up the flimsy sheet. His balls ached and there was a sharp itch in the distended shaft. He had been on the brink of ejaculation.

'Mr Simmons! I am the Matron here! I wish to know the meaning of this.' She moved to the side of the bed and, from a crumpled pile of clothing which Tony hadn't noticed, produced the directoire knickers he'd been wearing, holding the waist elastic by her ringless fingertips so that the legs dangled in front of her. 'And this?' Letting go of the knickers with one hand, with the other hand she picked up the corset, the stockings still drooping from the suspender clips. 'You were wearing these, er, items when you were brought here, and, from my report, your buttocks appear to have been, shall we say, beaten?'

Tony nodded. Nothing else he could do, really. Under the sheet, his cock was rising like a tentpole and he pulled up the thin blanket.

Matron's thighs were thick and there were ridges along her thighs which might have indicated a variety of underclothing . . .

'You have, of course, every right to be here as a result of your accident. You are established on the National Insurance computer, and apparently you're up to date with your income tax.'

'How – how?' Tony pulled himself up in the bed, releasing his cock. He was angry, and yet oddly excited by this big woman, dominating, severe, used to being authoritarian; she had seen his knickers and his flogged buttocks and no doubt his cock as well.

She stood, fore-square, arms akimbo, her lenses gleaming. 'We are required to ask questions.'

Tony looked at her. Beneath the thin sheet his cock towered. 'But what you've just said has nothing to do with my accident.' He swallowed hard. 'Whatever I was wearing or the, er, state of other parts of my body have nothing to do with the accident.'

'That may be your opinion!' She raised her chin.

'And what's yours? May I ask?' Tony challenged her.

She looked away at the curtain, her mouth set. Now he could clearly see, as she turned her ample thighs, the unmistakable ridge of underwear! 'I shall put in my report, as I am required to do.'

'But your report can surely only concern my injuries as a result of the accident!' Tony stroked his cock gently. 'What I was wearing at the time or anything else unrelated to the medical reports of the accident can surely have no bearing on your report.'

She turned her head. 'You think not?' She was twisting ringless fingers between her capable-looking hands.

'I think not,' Tony said, meeting her eyes, still fondling his growing cock, not caring if she saw the movement beneath the cotton sheet.

She did, and for a moment didn't turn her eyes away. Then she said, 'You need psychiatric help.' She raised her chin again, this time staring down at the chart hanging from the end of the bed on its hook.

'I didn't realise this was a hospital for the mentally ill,' Tony said non-committally, 'so why are you so interested in my private life?'

She gave a sniff. 'It isn't. Even so, it's not natural for a man to wear, er, women's underthings and obviously get enjoyment from being, well –'

'Why don't you say it?' Tony suggested softly. 'Enjoyment from being whipped!' His cock was hard now. 'How would you know what's natural? What experience have you had in that area? How would you know what a man feels when he is subjected to pain? You condemn without knowing the facts!'

'The nurse was extremely upset, seeing you like that, with those things on.'

'I'm sure she's seen worse – after all, they were only knickers, a corset and stockings.' He hesitated, then said, 'I'm sure you wear the same kind of under-clothes.'

She drew herself up. 'How dare you! What I wear has nothing to do with this – this situation!'

'Then, neither,' Tony pointed out levelly, 'does what I wear have anything to do with this – what you call – situation. And, what's more, if I get satisfaction from being flogged, then that has nothing to do with the situation either!'

Her face flushed angrily. 'I won't stand here and be insulted in this way! I've said what I had to say –' She turned to draw the curtain aside.

Tony began masturbating gently. 'Matron, what sort of knickers do you wear. Why not show me?'

'Oh!'

She almost ripped the curtain aside before hurrying out and closing it behind her fiercely.

Equally fiercely, Tony lay back and masturbated, thinking of Matron's powerful thighs encased in elasticated knickers, and with a pliant cane in her hand, standing over him . . .

Matron went to her office, closed the door and sat down heavily. She was damp between her thighs and her mind was in a turmoil of conflicting emotions. On the one hand, her professional training tried to persuade her that what she had witnessed was a man with truly psychological sexual problems and it was her duty to make a report. Her duty? Why? As he'd said, reasonably enough, what he'd been wearing at the time of the accident, and the state of his buttocks, had nothing to do with the traffic accident.

But, despite her medical training to be completely impersonal, she was intrigued. A corset, stockings and long knickers . . . and a bottom covered in welts! Clearly of his own choice! Beneath her girdle and knickers something stirred deep down and rose almost to choke her. He'd been whipped! Dressed in those – those things! A woman – or perhaps a man? – had flogged him as he accepted the punishment! Her own knickers – of cotton – were cheap; but the ones he'd been wearing were of heavy celanese with a double gusset; thick and well stitched around the elasticated hems. Even at school, and for some time afterwards, she had worn navy serge knickers with long legs. She'd been taught to be modest. She was a virgin. You, Mavis Jones, she told herself, are a virgin at forty! Her career was set. A good reputation with the Governors and respect, even fear, from her staff.

So why was she so absorbed with an attractive young man who clearly enjoyed dressing up and being whipped? Did she want to wield the lash herself, or have it on her own behind? At the thought, her ample buttocks seemed to twitch. She could almost feel what she imagined would be the sting of corporal punishment. To whip – or be whipped? That was the question. Perhaps, she thought, why not both? She'd noticed his keen eyes on her thighs, looking for the knicker ridge. With a glance at the glass-panelled door, she surreptitiously drew up her skirt to the edge of her white pantaloons, crisp on the thick wool of her black stockings.

After pulling her skirt down decorously, she attended to paperwork. But the image kept interceding of the young man, bent over, knickers down, and her flogging him; or, even more vividly, of herself being humiliated, ridiculed, in front of the hospital staff, uncovered, her buttocks bare, waiting for the whip.

Of the two images, the second brought a thumping heartbeat to her throat and a flood between her legs. Would he know how she could achieve this – this craving for humiliation which was rapidly engulfing her?

Again, she tried to concentrate on her work, and again she failed. What was wrong with her?! But she knew, deep down, well enough. It was the young man in the cubicle with his whipped bottom – and his knowledge. That was the thing: his knowledge! She wanted to find a way into this mysterious world of pain and pleasure. Scanning her notes, she realised that on his admission form there were two blanks needing to be filled. She picked up the folder, stood up, smoothed her skirt and made her way to the cubicle where, possibly, the solutions to her problem might lie . . .

But only possibly. She slowed along the gleaming lino-covered corridor to the assessment unit. What was she doing? She was Matron of a large hospital and had signed in her early days a declaration that, within the confines of any hospital in which she served, she would have no relations, sexual or other-wise, with a patient except in the course of her duties. She paused by the long windows and stared down at the gardens. In the sunshine, walking patients were gingerly making their way along the paths between beds of flowers and shrubs, accompanied by nursing staff, watching their every move whether they were on crutches or walking sticks. This was her world: the world to which she had dedicated herself. Now, like a volcanic eruption, her perceptions had been turned about. She wanted to know! At least, that! She was curious like someone penetrating an unknown world, moving cautiously, not knowing what to expect next; but with a tingle up her spine at the exploration.

Could she trust him? That was a thought! Blackmail? She knew of his desire for women's underwear and his obvious sexual pleasure in being whipped ... But she didn't want it like that – no threats!

She stood irresolutely staring down at the innocent activities in the garden below, drew a deep breath and continued on her way along the glistening lino with a steady, determined tread ... towards what?

Tony had 'come' – a large patch on the sheet was evidence enough of that – a highly satisfactory ejaculation preceded by images like videos running through his mind. But the image which insisted on projecting itself before all the others was ... the Matron. A dominating figure! He loved the way she showed such contempt for him! Standing there imperiously: those blue-skirted thighs with interesting ridges beneath them; her ringless hands. What had made him spread his spunk eventually was the thought of her – having given him a damned good session of corporal punishment; ordering him to strip her naked; go down on her; and, when she was moist and oily, thrusting himself into her, his bottom lancing with pain as he took her, with all his strength and urgency, to completion.

She would know about men, the size of their cocks, every intimate detail about them. Now she knew all about him! And he relished the thought. It was like exposing himself in public wearing his silk knickers. The crowds would jeer and pelt him with rotten fruit (he had a woodcut of a man in the stocks, or the pillory, from somewhere around the sixteenth century, hands and feet through holes, bending his head as the onlookers threw whatever came to hand at him).

Therefore, he was surprised when the curtain was slid aside and she appeared. He was even more surprised by her first words: 'I'm sorry.' Her hands were folded in front of her skirt and he noticed they were shaking slightly.

'Sorry?' He looked at her; it was odd to see her in person after the fantasies.

'I – I understand – I think.' She met his gaze. 'About the – er – punishment and the items of clothing. I should have realised.'

'Realised?' Suddenly he felt in control. It was as if he was playing chess – and he was a good chess player – and he could see, two moves ahead, a chance to trap the Queen . . . 'Realised – what?'

He lay back; although he'd just come, his cock still wasn't entirely flaccid and he tantalised it with one finger up and down the shaft.

'That you like it.' She paused and looked away.

He sensed her discomposure and relished it. Let her be abject! This powerful woman! 'Would you like to –?' He left the sentence unfinished.

She drew a breath. 'Not here.'

He had her! And a great pulse of excitement surged through him. 'Where?' he asked softly, his finger tracing the swelling vein in his shaft. 'And what would you like –?'

'I'd like – like to beat you. That's what you want, isn't it?'

'And other things,' he said, keeping his voice calm.

The ridges along her blue-stretched thighs seemed more apparent. Perhaps she'd been to the loo and pulled her knickers up more tightly than she realised.

'What?'

'What sort of knickers do you wear?'

'Oh, you wouldn't be interested –' her face had flushed '– not – not the sort young men like, I'm sure.'

71

'Tell me,' he said. His cock had hardened. 'Or show me.'

She glanced round at the closed curtain. 'Very well,' she whispered, 'but only for a moment.'

His heart thumped as she lifted her skirt and he saw the edge of white pantaloons and, through them, the long-boned lower edge of her roll-on biting into her thighs, and the broad band of suspenders. He swallowed hard. 'Higher.'

Her skirt came up to her waist and he saw the full flow of her pantaloons. She held the position and then let the skirt drop. 'There!'

He wanted to come again! 'How long,' he asked, struggling to keep his voice steady, 'do you think I'll be in here?'

She smoothed her skirt. 'Two days – your injuries are only superficial. We need the beds.' She eyed him. 'Of course, you could always stay with me for a few days . . . nobody need know. I have leave owing to me . . . I could look after you.'

'And?' he countered.

'Other things – if you want.' She looked away.

'But, Matron,' he said teasingly, 'I thought you disapproved!'

'I've – I've changed my mind. Life is passing me by. I – I need –' She broke off, her face twisted. Suddenly she looked rather ugly, pathetic. She pulled out a handkerchief and blew her nose.

'What do you need, Matron?' Equally suddenly, he felt sorry for her. He wanted her. Perhaps she might, in time, join Helen's team – but on the other side, as it were! Many men, he knew, would be sexually aroused by having a Matron, in full dress, spanking them, maybe treating them as babies . . . scolding them, making them dress –

'Whatever,' she said simply.

He pulled the sheet away. 'This is whatever,' he said, holding himself out invitingly towards her.

There were all kinds of possibilities . . .

3

Tales to be Told – A Whipping at the Cart's Tail

'I'm taking you back four centuries,' Hanley said.

He'd been flogged by Jennifer, and Harriet had had her whipping. Peter and Simon had mutually masturbated watching: even Peter had managed a respectable erection with Simon's expert hand and fingers!

'It was sixteen sixty, six years before the Great Fire of London', Hanley began . . .

In Newgate Gaol where now stands the Old Bailey, in a narrow cell with stone walls which leaked moisture and through which little was able to penetrate as a result of the dirty panes of glass and the rusty iron bars, a man awaited his fate. Next morning, he was due to be tied to a cart-tail, stripped to his waist and flogged through the streets of London to Tyburn, now London's Marble Arch. As he was urged forwards, the cart pulled by two innocent horses, the lashes would fall on his bare back each signalled by a drum-beat.

From Newgate, where the whipping would begin, to Tyburn was a distance of some three miles. And, during that time, Amos Lang, convicted of rape and malicious assault, would probably receive some three hundred strokes, dealt by a flogger armed with whips knotted and soaked in brine. At Tyburn, he would be dragged back through the streets on a rough sled made of blackthorn which would add to the pain of his flogged back, and again incarcerated until it was deemed his punishment fitted the crime.

Lang couldn't wait for the punishment. He wanted to feel the lash, craved it. But, looking through the bars of the cell at the glowing, menacing London skyline, he wondered if this strange, unnatural phenomena was somehow connected to his lust. The angry sky with its dense smoke-filled clouds tinged crimson by a fiery bloom seemed to make his back sting already from the whipping to come. He was aroused oddly. In his shabby prison clothes of a foul shirt, stained drawers and knee breeches loose around his thighs, his cock rose as he predicted the next morning with the crowds gathered – crowds always gathered along the dirty roadways between Newgate and Tyburn when the proclamation of a cart-tail flogging was announced on poorly printed parchment posters along the route.

Lang didn't know this, because he could barely read let alone write, but even before Henry VIII introduced the Act Against Vagrants (known as the 'Whipping Act') in 1530 whipping at the cart's tail was long established. The Act, though, stated categorically that vagrants were to be 'carried to some market-town nearby ... and there tied to the end of a cart naked and be beaten with whips (throughout the town) ... till the body shall be bruised by reason of such whipping'.

'Vagrants' covered a multitude of sins, but the populace with few delights to entertain them would line the streets for the event. Mothers would bring their children; oranges and sweetmeats would be sold by vendors, along with gravy-dripping meat pies; and the avaricious crowds would run alongside the slowly moving cart, through the dung-filled cobblestones, as the bare-backed and bare-footed victim securely lashed to the tail-gate of the truck trod in the dung and received the strokes. How many depended on the speed of the animal drawing the cart. The famous – or infamous – political agitator Titus Oates had received three hundred lashes on his way to Tyburn and much the same number on his return to Newgate. He survived the punishment which, according to an observer, 'so flayed the poor wretch's bodie that he would fain have scream'd the length of his torture had his throat not been sore'd by his miserable agony long before it was done'. Of late, owing to the numbers of women who thronged the streets to watch, it had been decreed that the victim was no longer to be naked, but stripped only to the waist and wearing loose-fitting breeches to the knee or below.

Lang wanted to masturbate, but waited until his 'supper' was shoved through a narrow trap-door. Traditionally, a pint of porter in a pewter tankard was given to a prisoner on his last night before punishment, along with the so-called luxury of mutton going green, gnarled, virtually uncooked potatoes and dried-up leaves of cabbage.

As the tin plate containing these luxuries was slid to him across the uneven floor, speckled by rat and mice droppings, a voice called, 'Enjoy it, friend! There'll be no breakfast, but you'll get a taste of something, never fear!'

Raucous laughter echoed and died along the corridor and a heavy door slammed.

Lang drank most of the porter, leaving a little for later, and picked at the mutton, nibbling with his decayed teeth at that slim portion of the meat untinged by mildew. He had no desire for food; his hunger was for the physical punishment to come. He longed for the exposure, and, as he masturbated slowly, taking his time, he thought how his loose-fitting breeches, as he wriggled, might slide shamefully down revealing his rigid cock to the crowds, and how they would scorn and jeer even more as his revealed buttocks received the attention of the lashers. He ejaculated and, after stripping naked, lay on the rough straw of the so-called bed, turning this way and that, longing for the morning, smelling the stench of acrid urine, excrement and other basic prison odours. Earlier he had heard screams from below, female screams, as yet another flogging of a prostitute took place.

Amos Lang was 25, but looked at least ten years older. His face was thin and lined, his fair hair scanty, showing a dirty scalp. He had no recollection of any parents. All he recalled was growing up in a mixed household of two rooms in and out of which people seemed to come and go as they wished. The door to the street was always open. He ate what he was given, knowing nothing of where it came from, and, as he grew, so he was thin and emaciated, like the other ragamuffin kids in the street. Gangs of them would roam through the narrow, infested streets around Mile End and Stepney, occasionally venturing as far as Aldgate in their quest for food and pockets to pick. Punishment was harsh, age no consideration.

At the age of eleven, Amos was caught stealing a loaf. Up before the 'beak' in Clerkenwell Court, he was sentenced to thirty lashes. Next day, in public, he was roped to the whipping post in the centre of Mile End Road, his soiled trousers lowered – he wore nothing underneath – and he was thrashed on the buttocks, his legs spread. Oddly, the pain translated itself into a glowing arousement such as he had never felt before. He felt his small, thin cock rising as the flogging continued. He was excited by the watching crowd, exposed, being hurt. Back in the courthouse, he felt sore but was filled with a thin kind of lust, and, as the physician who treated him afterwards handled him roughly, a strange sensation flooded through him.

From the age of fifteen, he had worked in a bottle factory by the Thames where empty flagons were thrown into the stinking mire and boys had to strip naked and jump into the turgid water to retrieve them. At the end of the day, the tally-master would count the number each had recovered. The boy at the bottom of the list was birched in front of the others as an example to do better. Amos often made sure he was last. He relished being made to bend across a wine chest and feel his breeches coming down, followed by the stinging delight of the birch lashes across his behind.

The others would watch silently when he rose, his cock hard, and restored his clothing. Later, some of the boys would indulge in mutual masturbation. It was their only relief from the twelve-hour day of toil and filth. The food was meagre but each was allowed a tankard of wine which had gone sour.

Finally, the tally-master recognised Amos's addiction to the birch and he would be disregarded when he continued to foot the list. The tally-master, who had a distinct bulge in his velveteen breeches when he flogged, wanted no boy who clearly enjoyed being thrashed. He wanted those who cowered fearfully when their names were called and who pitifully screamed as the birch twigs fell on their twitching, bony bottoms.

Seeking other means of satisfying his lust for pain, and it had become a thirst which thickened his throat and made his thin body tremble with urgency, Amos met Meg. Meg was twenty and worked for a mistress in the notorious Bankside Brothels on the south shore of the Thames, near 'The Clink' prison, who ran one of many 'houses of pleasure'. As in succeeding centuries, the desire for flagellation as a means of arousing sexual desire was widespread. Indeed, apart from its sexual connotations, physicians would recommend a sound thrashing with stinging nettles as a means of making blood pump more quickly through turgid veins. Titled personages and those in the common parliament – whose faces would have been instantly recognised had there been newsheets at the time – flocked to Meg's for sex, sodomy and flagellation. The mistress, a Beth Trenchard, was some fifty years old and knew all the tricks of the trade. She engaged young girls only too anxious to make a few silver coins and submit to the indignities of the clients: if some of those indignities went a little too far and got out of hand – well, then, the river wasn't far away and one more unidentified body would cause little or no concern to the scant constabulary of the time.

Meg introduced Amos to sex not far from the river; beside an abandoned row-boat on the shingle. When she lowered his breeches to take his cock in her rosy lips, she noticed the scars on his buttocks and thighs. Questioned, he admitted his desire for punishment, at the same time allowing Meg to guide his cock into her. After it was over, she pulled up her shabby drawers and told him that Mistress Trenchard would like to meet him. She explained a few things to him and he was eager for the meeting to take place as soon as possible.

Beth looked at Amos and curled her lip in disdain. He was unkempt and he smelled. His clothes were indescribable. But, when on her order he stripped, she noted his slimness, his unmarked genitals, and then she saw the scarred buttocks. How many times had he been flogged? How did it feel? How much could he take – if necessary? She had clients prepared to pay good money to watch a boy of his age receive a whipping. They were not floggers themselves – although many were – but wanted to see a young man cruelly lashed. He would be paid enough to buy food and, if he wanted, a bed in the attic at the top of her establishment. But, first, he would have to be bathed and cleaned, and given fresh clothes. Then, she told him, she would give him a sound flogging herself to see how much he could take. If she was satisfied, she had the very customer that evening.

It was the first time he had been in a real bath, soaking all over, and the soap, slippery in his hands, was sweet scented. He emerged and put on a long, embroidered gown and was then told to make his way to a room two doors along. Inside, heavy, red-curtained drapery covered the room, lit by four-branched flickering candlesticks in each corner. In the centre of the room stood a stout pillory and whipping post, with holes in the cross-beam for the victim to be secured. He knew such apparatus well. The massive centre post was stained, dark blotches against the pale wood.

Madame stood naked, magnificent, thick thighs, a huge clump of dark-brown pubic hair. She was wielding a thick, three-thonged whip and motioned Amos to the post. Eagerly, pulses racing, cock stiffening, he obeyed. She bound him with leather thongs, stepped back and flogged him on his back, buttocks and legs.

'I shall be doing this when my rich friend watches,' she said to the rhythm of her strokes.

She thrashed, and Amos bent his body to the punishment. He ejaculated spurtingly, his body on fire from shoulders to calves, moaning his pleasure.

'Very well,' she said, 'not bad at all. But my customer might wish to see your, er, organ flogged. Have you any objection? I shall make you erect first, and then whip it. Could you bear that?'

Amos nodded, his face flushed, his cock flopping. 'Yes, Madame,' he said, 'anything.'

The man was about forty with a high forehead and powdered wig. When Amos entered the whipping room, Madame stood high corseted and black stockinged with a heavier whip in her hand than she had used on him earlier. Amos's cock rose. He was naked, the marks of his earlier flogging starkly etched against his white skin.

'Here he is, sir,' Madame said obsequiously with a slight curtsey.

The man removed his brocaded jacket and stripped off his satin breeches. Beneath, his cock was hard. He still had on white, silk stockings and buckled shoes. He looked at Amos thoroughly, back and front. 'Very good,' he said finally, 'strap him and whip him: his back, buttocks and down his thighs to his knees. I want to hear him scream for mercy, to beg, grovel and plead! And then we'll see about that!' With a quivering finger he pointed at Amos's erection.

'Yes, sir,' Madame said.

As she bound Amos to the whipping post she whispered, 'You'll have to take it. He'll have no half-measures – but you'll be well rewarded.'

He braced himself for the lashing. As usual, the first strokes were agony. But, perhaps, feeling a little sympathy or understanding, she concentrated on his buttocks, arousing him so that whatever else was to befall him he could tolerate and even indulge the pain. He had no idea how many strokes had been delivered when the voice ordered, 'Stop it, Madame. Now, turn him, and take his organ, and hand me that lash there.'

Amos turned, still bound, and, as Madame took his shaft tightly, holding it outwards, m'lord, legs apart, knees slightly bent, manipulated himself with his left hand and thrashed Amos's cock with the lash curled in his right. He whipped expertly, flogging the tender tip and all the way down to the base of the pulsating stem. Finally, he stepped back and masturbated himself to a climax. It was over.

'Very well,' he said, 'you're a good lad.' He nodded at Madame, produced a purse and tipped several gold coins into her hand. 'A week today,' he said, watching as Amos was unthonged from the whipping post, 'I may have a lady with me who might wish to indulge.'

He waved a negligent, lace-handkerchief'd hand and Amos left for the attic to relish his pain and bring himself throbbingly to a violent completion which shuddered through his entire body convulsively.

He was the star. His reputation spread amongst the gentry. Men and women alike chose him for flogging. Strapped to the post, he would be sucked by a kneeling woman while his body was being punished.

But then, after two years, he was thrown out, on to the streets again. His body had suffered too much, ironically; the eager sadists wanted to see unmarked white flesh being flogged. Amos's body was scarred beyond healing. He was no use to the aristocrats any more.

All he had were a few copper coins and a body which craved punishment as an alcoholic craved the bottle. He was birched several times for minor misdemeanours. But it wasn't enough. Cunningly he found out that by rape and abuse he would be sentenced to flogging at the cart's tail. He chose Meg – not assaulting her but begging her to report him for the alleged offence. And thus he was sentenced . . . and now he lay on the rough straw, willing himself not to masturbate again, denying himself the need, saving it for what was to come . . . in every sense of the word.

It was morning. A dull, grey morning. Amos urinated and defecated in the bucket in the corner of the cell. Looking through the barred window he could see in the courtyard the horse and cart drawn up ready, loose ropes attached to the tail-board to which he would be bound. His pulses quickened. His breeches were loose and ill fitting, baggy around the knees. In place of a fly, there was an opening in the rough cloth gathered by a series of thin leather cords. He loosened them so that, if his wish was fulfilled, his erect cock might thrust itself through the gap and the breeches would sag revealing his buttocks, thereby giving the flogger another target to lash. He wanted his breeches to fall and his appearance jeered and spat upon by the crowd as he shuffled along, the lashes falling pitilessly upon his back and, hopefully, lower down as well.

'It's time, Lang, take off your shirt.' A gaoler stood in the doorway.

Amos removed his shirt and at the same time loosened his breeches. As he left the cell he felt them slide to his waist, caught by his stiffened cock.

Outside, the cold bit Amos's back and he shivered. He was led to the back of the cart in front of which the horse snorted and stamped, and his wrists were bound tightly to the tail-gate. The sentence was announced: 'You will suffer whipping through the streets at the cart's-tail in accordance with the sentence . . .'

The man who would flog Amos on his journey was a burly fellow called Jack Star. He came close to Amos, spreading the whip-lashes between his fingers. 'I'll not lay it on too hard, lad, but I musn't be seen not to be doing my duty. You un'erstand?'

'Lay it on,' Amos said, his heart thumping, 'and, if my breeches happen to slide down, thrash my arse, and don't pull them up!'

A drum rolled. The cart jerked forwards as the man in the driving seat snapped the reins and cracked his whip. At the same moment the first lash bit into Amos's willing, bent back.

By the time the cart had hauled up the slope and turned left into what is now High Holborn, Amos had received a dozen strokes. Few people here watched the spectacle, but, as the slow procession moved westwards, the crowds became thicker, either jostling on the muddy pavements or leaning out of overhanging windows, some throwing down oranges, others more daring emptying their filled pots on to the roadway.

But, as time passed, the crowds grew even more festive, and so did Amos's cock. The lashing had by now spread a familiar glow throughout his body as he tramped obediently, whipped to the drum roll, splashing through horse dung and urine which soon covered his bare feet. He eased his hips cautiously to allow the waist of his loose breeches to fall below his hips and, at the same time, a thrust brought his erection through the thin opening and into the air.

Lash after lash drove him onwards. Sometimes the drum roll indicating the next stroke would be de-layed; at others, two came in sharp succession. He could hear Jack Star's grunts as he flogged, and longed for his breeches to slip even further. At the Temple it was traditional for the procession to pause and the victim be given a tankard of ale. Amos wasn't untied. The ale was tipped down his throat and he coughed. Then his breeches slipped and his buttocks were plain to see.

On the move again, the flogging party entered the area of St Giles, noted for pimps, prostitutes and gangs of 'dippers' (pick-pockets). It was here that the local vice girls gathered to see the whipping. With Amos's breeches now nearly to his knees, his tread became a shuffling travesty, his feet slipping on the filth sticking to his soles. But now, Amos's cock was high, and the girls shrieked their delight. Some, ignoring the top-hatted constables in attendance, raised their voluminous skirts tantalisingly showing their loose drawers; others, more daring still, raised the skirts to reveal nothing beneath.

Amos had dreaded his breeches being pulled up, but there seemed no intention on the part of the escort to do so, and Jack Star began to flog the buttocks with what seemed increased vigour. Amos eyed the faces as the cart trundled by. On some was written horror; on others lust. Some mothers shielded the eyes of their young ones, while taking a coy peep themselves.

Amos eventually ejaculated at a point which might now be Oxford Circus. He could hold on no longer. A strumpet had eased out of the crowd and run to him, fingering his cock before disappearing. He shot a solid bolt of spunk ahead of him and trod in it as he passed. Star had returned to lashing Amos's back and, now, he could feel, sweat trickling down to join the dribble from buttocks and thighs. Amos's erection dwindled and he braced himself for the final stage of the flogging.

But it had been worth it, by God! Instead of remaining static at a whipping post watched by the curious crowd, he had seen a myriad of faces as he'd passed, a new audience every few feet: watching, gloating, aroused, eyeing his thrustful cock, his sagging breeches and the lashing, the unrelenting lashing.

At Tyburn, an officer of the gaol awaited the cart. As it swung and dragged to a halt, he stepped forwards. He inspected Amos's back and then turned to Star, who was still holding the whip. 'Why were this man's breeches down?'

'Your honour, sir, they come down natural, like,' Star said hesitantly.

'So you whipped his buttocks! Your orders were to punish his back! This will be reported and an inquiry held. You may find yourself in a good deal of agony yourself before this is at an end!'

Unstrapped, Amos was placed face down on a sled of cross-branches of birch. His back and buttocks were dabbed with salt and vinegar which made him wince agreeably. Turned on his back, a dirty, shroud-like piece of cloth was wound about his genitals and he was dragged back the way he had come. But, by now, his progress had no fascination for the multitudes who had flocked to see his punishment – and his ecstasy. The streets were no more full than usual. They'd seen the whipping and they'd gone, prostitutes and all – no doubt fired by the sexuality of seeing a man's cock exposed as he was whipped along the street. Maybe their own birches would cut more deeply into the willing flesh of their clients as a result!

4

Tales to be Told – The Mother-in-Law

It was two weeks later when the group met again. Once again, Hanley was 'in the chair' as it were. They'd been treated to an exhibition of self-flagellation by Simon who, naked, had whipped his buttocks until he ejaculated, while the others did their own thing . . .

Hanley, having been pleasured by Jennifer, asked, 'Mothers-in-law? What crude things are said about them by those who know nothing! The thrill of a mature woman – we had the Matron in the last tale – but this is different . . . a man about to be married but having met his future mother-in-law . . .'

James fell in love with his future mother-in-law before he was really in love with his future wife! Jenny was 24; her widowed mother 44. Her husband had been killed in a rail crash a year after their daughter was born. The mother's name was Winifred, which somehow had an erotic tingle to James. He liked old-fashioned names and mature women who looked as if they knew what a man had inside his underpants!

He'd longed for his own mother to be sexy after a boy at school had told him in a whispered conversation in the lav that he wore his mother's underclothes when she was out. He masturbated in them. She caught him and caned his bum! He'd loved it . . .

James had desires which he couldn't fathom at that age. But as he progressed in age and experience he realised that what his mother hadn't given him – she was frail and old for her age and had been separated from her alcoholic husband for several years – and what he needed was discipline! Not to be sent to his room without any supper: something more intimate; something to arouse those feelings which he was still unable to define. His schoolfriend, Nigel, had described to him in vivid detail how his mother had caught him in her pink knickers and stockings. The knickers were long and loose. Nigel, caught in the act, was forced to kneel across the double bed as his mother drew down the knickers and caned him.

'I got a hard-on!' he'd told James, his cheeks flushed. 'It was . . . well, I had her clothes on and she could see my cock – as hard as it is now! – and she was punishing me!'

'But didn't it hurt?' James asked. 'The caning?'

'Oh, yes! It hurt. But that's what I wanted! I can't explain it.' He shook his head. 'The harder she caned me, the more I wanted! When she'd finished, I stood up and my cock was hard as it is now.'

They were at the top of the sports field in an old, broken-down pavilion which was now derelict as the playing fields had been reduced due to increased ground rent.

Nigel had unzipped himself and brought out his erect, uncircumcised cock, the foreskin drawn tight. There was moisture on the tip. 'Show me yours,' Nigel said, his mouth half-open.

He was a year older than James, tall and fit looking. He'd got his colours for soccer and cricket and was a house prefect. He'd seen Nigel's cock in the changing rooms and had noted he was never shy of exposing himself as were some of the others, James included. Nigel's limp cock hung over his balls, curving and heavy. James, despite himself, had eyed it with a kind of hunger and curiosity – why wasn't his own like that, strong and masculine? He had erections, of course, but it seemed to him that even his erection was no larger than Nigel's in its flaccid state!

Fumblingly, James opened his trousers, dug into his white underpants and brought out his floppy cock. 'I'm – I'm sorry,' he said.

Nigel got up. 'Don't worry – I'm going to flog you! I want to see how you react.' From somewhere he produced a thin, yellow cane. 'Take your trousers and underpants down to your ankles and bend over. Touch your toes!'

James obeyed. The cane stung into his stretched bottom again and again. A wild recklessness surged through him as he felt his cock rise as it never had before. He ejaculated with a loud cry . . .

When he met Jenny at art school, James had already savoured the delights of being flogged by prostitutes. Since he'd learned that he could achieve ejaculation by having pain inflicted, he'd become a disciple. And – as a result of Nigel, who had taken him one day to his home while his mother was out and let him relish in her silk knickers – he'd developed a fascination for women's underclothes. He cut out advertisements from magazines: of corsets, suspender belts and stockings worn by disdainful-looking models. He wandered past windows displaying lingerie; then turned, and wandered back, his cock rising as he looked sideways at the feast of draped, silken garments, tight corsets and dangling suspender clasps.

He told Jenny nothing of his dreams and desires. Thankfully, they had little sexual contact and as a result he was able to disguise the welts on his bottom. She wore plain, white panties; he craved the more intimate, decadent directoire knickers which he'd worn at Nigel's. He found that the women he visited to be whipped invariably had one or two pairs of that particular style of underwear. He bought his own, too, and, once stripped, he would put on a pair and masturbate in front of the mirror on his dressing-table. His freelance work for a company making commercials for TV brought in enough money to allow him to live comfortably and to indulge his tastes.

He had these thoughts in his mind when Jenny took him home to meet her mother for the first time. She was understandably nervous and so was he – until he actually saw her! She was all in black except for a loose-collared white blouse. The black skirt hugged her substantial thighs and she had strong, dark-stockinged calves and high-heeled court shoes. Her hair was short and tinged, close cropped and with an angry-looking fringe which immediately reminded him of the lashes of a whip. She wore gold-rimmed spectacles and was without makeup. Her bosom wasn't prominent, but he'd never been turned on by breasts. He liked the lower half of a woman, the stomach and below, the fleshy swell and the inward curve to the triangle of hair and the tastes of various kinds within to be explored and relished.

He wanted her! That evening, during dinner, he found it difficult to take his eyes off her. As he was eating, he imagined her dominating him; he could see those thighs encased in riding breeches tucked into gleaming boots. He grovelling before her, being ridiculed, cruelly mocked, before the exquisite lance

90

of pain as she flogged him. And afterwards? Kneeling before her abjectly, lowering her underwear, then, spreading her thighs apart, thrusting his lips and tongue to satisfy her.

He wondered how long it had been since she'd had sex? Would that pink, creased-lipped opening be dry? Not for long! He found it difficult to keep his mind on the conversation which was mundane in the extreme. But at one point, while they were having coffee and liqueurs, he was sitting opposite and she crossed her legs – but not before he had caught a glimpse of stockinged thigh. What lay above? He had to find out. And soon. She filled his masturbatory fantasies. He wanted her to bully him; to be her slave. And then punish him. He imagined her going to the toilet, lifting her skirt, taking down her knickers and urinating. Afterwards, he would lick her . . .

Jenny, who was a fashion designer, had to make a trip to Paris for her agency. She would be away for five days. James decided to make his move. It was a risk – but what the hell! Her mother had often bemoaned the fact that she never went out to dinner so James invited her to one of his favourite restaurants. 'With Jenny away,' he said, 'I thought you and I might have a meal together. Future son-in-law and future mother-in-law?'

She hadn't sounded too surprised, which he felt was possibly a good omen, and they made an arrangement to meet the following evening. But she phoned later – why didn't he come to dinner at the house? She would cook a nice meal for him. He protested – he wanted to take her out for a change! No, she said firmly. She wanted to be at home in case Jenny phoned. She had hesitated and then said, 'You could always stay the night if you want to.'

Maybe, he thought lasciviously, that would be better ... If he was invited to stay the night, well, anything could happen. He said he'd be there the following evening at six. James went for a whipping to his favourite pair of women in Pimlico. He was flogged and humiliated, and he orgasmed twice under the persuasive strokes of their whips, canes and birches. He wanted to be marked for the next evening, well marked, so that she would have no doubt as to what he wanted. It would take some explaining – but that, in itself, would be a turn-on.

Momentarily, he considered the possibility that, if he suggested the things to her that he wanted to suggest, she might be profoundly shocked and tell Jenny; and that would lead to the end of the relationship. But, he thought, lying in bed that night and gently stimulating himself, the mother was drawn to his fantasies; he could have a relationship with her, and still continue with Jenny. The secret would be theirs. And, if the worst came to the worst, and Jenny discovered the truth, he was sure that the mother – having been reintroduced to the pleasures of sex both standard and perverse – might well be reluctant to forfeit them.

His thoughts the next day were of the evening to come as he edited a particularly boring commercial for washing-up liquid. What did these prancing idiots know of the joy of the whip? Of clinging, silk underwear? These unattractive so-called 'sex-objects' wore brief panties. There was no mystery. The mystery lay within the folds of sensuous Dks: hidden, waiting to be discovered with questing fingers ... and tongue.

He went home, took a shower and decided what to wear. He was tempted to wear Dks, but thought it might be pushing it a bit. Instead, he put on a brand-new, tight, white pair of briefs, a crisp blue shirt and cream-coloured slacks, tight enough around the groin to give firm indication of genital arousement. He took out his favourite suede jacket which, zipped, tightened around his behind. In a holdall, he packed spare underpants, a pair of directoire knickers – dark-blue, his favourite colour – and a thonged, knotted whip. Thinking he shouldn't hurry things, he also packed a thin cane. She might draw back from using the whip the first time; but the cane might be more amenable as a traditional instrument of punishment. He wanted to be a naughty boy, caught wearing her underclothes! He looked forward to leading the conversation round to the subject. He wasn't going to be brutally frank: 'I want you to whip me!' Neither was he going to hint at her type of underclothes. 'What sort of knickers do you wear?' No, it had to be subtle, teasingly subtle. She wouldn't, or mightn't, know what he was progressing to. A little hint here, a vague suggestion there; some compliments . . . how different she was from his own mother . . . how he wished – well, let matters take their course.

He drove to the house, a feeling of excitement mounting. He had no thoughts of Jenny now. His mind was concentrated on the erotic thrill of a, hopefully, sexual encounter with Winifred, the mother. His heart bounded when he saw her in the doorway, dressed in a stiff-collared, stiff-cuffed, white blouse, black skirt and stockings and high-heeled black court shoes. Her hair was short, as he liked it, and she smiled – a knowing smile? – as he locked the car and with his overnight bag went up the drive.

'You're punctual.'

Tempted to reply, 'I couldn't wait,' James said instead, 'The traffic wasn't as heavy as I'd thought.'

'All to the good,' she said, closing the front door, 'we'll have more time.'

James let her pass and lead the way to the lounge. What had she meant: 'We'll have more time'? Time for what? His scrotum crawled, watching her tightly skirted buttocks move sensuously. He could, in fact, see the ridge of her girdle below the swell of her behind.

'Put your bag down,' she said, turning to him. 'I'm sure you'd like a drink. What will it be?'

He was bursting for a pee and said, 'I'd love a glass of wine; I know you like it. But, first, may I, er, use the bathroom?'

An expression he couldn't quite define came over her face. She hesitated before replying. 'Of course, yes, you know where it is.'

He thought she was about to add something, but didn't. He went upstairs, into the combined bathroom and toilet, closed the door and, unzipped himself. Then he noticed an airing rack standing in the gleaming bath. Hanging on it was a white, panelled girdle – and two pairs of white, long-legged pantaloons with layers of lace at the bottom; sensual, provocative. James urinated, feeling his cock start to rise. When he'd finished and with difficulty bundled himself back inside his pants and trousers, he fingered the pantaloons gently, and then lifted a pair and sniffed the cotton-gusseted crotch. They smelled fresh, washing-powder fresh, but with a faint hint of an elusive perfume. Was the presence of these intimate items the reason for her hesitation downstairs? He stood for a moment looking at them, imagining a pair on her stockinged thighs, to her knees, as she commanded him, her slave, a whip threateningly in her grip . . .

He washed his hands and face, willing his erection to subside, and then went down.

'I'm sorry,' she said, handing him a tall, fluted glass of wine, 'there were some things of mine airing in the bathroom – I hope they didn't inconvenience you. I meant to put them in the airing cupboard.'

'Oh, no,' James said quickly, taking a sip of the cold wine which felt comforting on his parched mouth, tongue and throat. He wondered if the bulge in his trousers showed, and he cast a furtive glance at her thighs for any telltale sign.

'Let's sit down,' she suggested and indicated a chair identical to her own on the other side of an elaborate coffee table with a stack of magazines, an onyx ash tray and a gold Dunhill table lighter.

She crossed her legs, but he didn't look. She went on, 'It was kind of you of ask me out, but, when Jenny goes away, I like to be on hand, just in case. I'm sure you know what I mean.'

James nodded. 'Yes, of course, I feel the same.'

'There's nothing to be jealous about, you know,' she said unexpectedly.

James wasn't sure what she meant by that, so he gave a non-committal nod and stared at his glass. There was something in the atmosphere of the room which he couldn't define – or was he imagining it again? Was he putting into the atmosphere what he wanted to put into it, or was there something more? It must have been obvious that, at some time during the evening, he would have wanted to pee: so why hadn't she taken her underwear out of the bathroom before and into the airing cupboard where it would have been hidden from view?

She was talking again: 'Jenny loves you. I've heard so much about you from her. I don't think you need –'

James shifted and said into his glass, 'I'm not jealous – of her.'

She picked up the bottle and poured some wine into each glass. Even without her stretching too much, her breasts, shielded in a white brassiere, thrust against the starched blouse. The room was quiet. She put the bottle down gently on a silver-edged tray.

'Then, who are you jealous of?'

James turned the glass in trembling fingers. 'You,' he said.

What the hell! He could smell cooking and his saliva was thick, both from hunger and sex. Something was going on! He'd felt like this only once before in his life . . .

He was fifteen and had gone to stay in the country with one of his mother's sisters. Her unmarried daughter was not particularly attractive, but one afternoon, when the aunt was out shopping, the daughter had opened the door to his bedroom where he was spread, his trousers unzipped, underpants down to his knees, ready to masturbate, as he scanned the pages of a space cartoon comic, one series of frames of which showed a 'moon woman' whipping a man. He was tied to a post, naked. She, in boots and leather, stood behind him, her whip already landing on the helpless back of her victim. The detail in the drawing was vivid; James wished that the cartoonist, from another angle, had shown the victim's front. He was sure that he'd have had to draw an upthrust erection.

Visualising this, his hand creeping to the rigid stem of his cock, James was about to begin when the door opened . . .

She was wearing a bra, limp-looking panties and no stockings. She stared and closed the door quietly. 'What are you doing?' Her voice had a faint lisp.

James said, gripping the upper part of his cock, 'What does it look like? Do you want to try?' He let go and the erection towered, throbbing. 'Look at this.' He turned the page of the moon-whipping towards her and she stared blankly.

'What's going on?' she asked.

'Can't you see? This woman is whipping a man! He's naked!'

She looked from the page to his face. 'Is that why –?'

'Yes!' he said. 'Doesn't that do – do anything to you, seeing that?'

'Only that it must hurt terribly!' She gave a brief shudder which made the sagging breasts in her brassiere sway slightly.

'Of course it hurts!' James said. 'That's the whole point! Listen, look in my bag there and you'll find a leather strap. Get it out; wrap it round your hand and whip me! I'll show you what it does!' He got off the bed and bent over, showing his buttocks. 'Go on!'

'Oh – oh, I can't!' But she was already scrabbling in the bag, and she brought out the long strap, eyeing it fearfully.

'Now,' James said thickly, 'wrap it around your hand and leave enough loose. Then thrash me with it! Hard!'

He glanced over his shoulder at her. She presented rather a pathetic figure. There was nothing sexy about her as she doubtfully bound the strap. But he wanted her to whip him! To degrade him!

She'd never tell anyone, but the memory would linger in her mind, probably for ever.

'Do it!' he ordered.

The first stroke he barely felt.

'Hard!' he commanded, beginning to smooth his cock up and down.

The next was harder; the next harder still.

'Go on! Flog me!'

Now the lashes stung his buttocks and he began masturbating intently as she continued to flog him.

As he was about to ejaculate, he turned to her, thrust himself out and pumped thick spunk towards her. 'There!' he gasped, as more trickled and dripped. 'There! That's what a whipping does!'

James was lost in thought and Winifred's voice broke in sharply. 'What on earth are you talking about?'

He stared, trying to collect his scattered images. 'Sorry – I –'

'Jealous – of me?'

Then he remembered, and had to think for a moment. He considered his words. 'Well, you're an extremely attractive woman and there must be men –'

'Well, thank you for the compliment.' There was something in her eyes he seemed to recognise. 'But there hasn't been anyone since . . .'

'Oh, please,' he said quickly, 'I wasn't probing –'

'But – you do love Jenny?'

'Of course,' James said, 'but –' Oh, God, why had he said that!

She pounced. 'But?' She got up quickly, no sign of thigh. 'I must see to the meal. Help yourself to another drink.'

He sensed that there was a hint of something which she had picked up. The underwear in the bathroom; his mention of jealousy; could something be about to meld?

'It's all right,' she said, as she returned with two plates of pasta and sat down at the dining table; without crossing her legs this time, but the skirt was firmly at knee level. She gestured him to join her. 'Are you hungry? I'm sure you must be.' She took a drink and gave him a slight smile which, James thought, could have meant everything or nothing. 'You were saying – "but"?'

Was it too soon to take another bold step? He might be utterly wrong and that could lead to disaster if he pursued it. But, on the other hand, if . . . what might happen could unfold a dream-world.

'But,' he said, 'you – you are extremely good looking . . . you might have a, er, male friend . . .'

'And would that bother you?'

'Yes.' He couldn't meet her eyes.

'Why?'

He traced a pattern on the tablecloth with a fingernail and then looked up. 'Because . . . I love you!' There: he'd said it. And he braced himself.

'You love me? What about Jenny?' She had leaned forwards across the table.

He said hesitantly, 'I love Jenny – but in a different way –'

'What do you want from me?' Her voice was sharp, but at the same time curious.

He drew a breath. 'I want you – I want you to whip me . . . and I want to put your underwear on.'

She sat back and studied him. He kept his eyes on her face. 'And?' she asked.

'And?' he queried.

'What else?'

'I'd like to . . . make love to you after you've whipped me.' He knew his face was scarlet, but he didn't care. A wild feeling had overtaken him: it was all or nothing now.

'Do you realise what you're saying?' Her voice wasn't sharp; it was more seductive. It thrilled him.

'Of course I realise!' He'd spoken sharply. 'I'm sorry –'

'You may be sorrier before very long . . .'

He looked up. 'You mean –?'

She said, with what he felt to be complacency, 'You'll find out what I mean. Finish your food!'

He ate, watching her. She seemed to become more seductive even than he already considered her to be.

Her colour was high and she'd put on her gold-rimmed glasses. A sign of discipline to come?

'If – and I emphasis "if" – anything is to happen between us, between the two of us, it has to be understood that Jenny must know nothing. I will not have her hurt – and I don't mean in the sense you're interested in.' His heart thumped, as she continued. 'I'll thrash you if that's what you want and you can dress in my, er, underwear . . . I'm not sure yet whether I'll let you have sex with me – it's been a long time, as you must realise, since anything like that happened. I find you attractive; I always have, but I had no idea that you felt about me the way that you have said. It's been a shock, but I think I understand why. Am I a mother substitute? Answer me!'

His cock stiffened at her tone. 'I don't know –' he began.

'You know!' she interrupted contemptuously. 'You want a mother to punish you! Well, I'm not your mother –'

'You're better!' he broke in.

'You want me more than her?'

'Oh, God, yes!' he exclaimed, his excitement mounting.

'Why?' Her chin was up.

'I – I want you to punish me –'

'I know that! You've already made that plain. Have you ever worn your mother's underclothes?'

He pushed his plate aside, took a drink and wiped his mouth. 'Only once . . . I put on a pair of her, knickers, but it didn't do anything for me.'

'And if you wore a pair of mine – the ones you saw in the bathroom?'

'Oh, yes. ' He hesitated, his head swimming. 'but there's another sort –'

'Knickers?'

He nodded.

'Tell me!'

He cleared his throat. 'Well, they're long and silky with elastic down to the knee –'

'Oh, you mean directoires!' She smiled slightly. 'My mother used to wear those. I think I've still got one or two pairs somewhere. You like those? You'd like to wear them when I whip you?'

Again he nodded. He felt himself floating. Was it a dream?

'By the way, what am I going to whip you with?'

Without looking at her, he said, 'I – I brought a whip and a cane, just in case . . .'

'Just in case!' She surveyed him severely. 'You're a cool one!'

'And some, er, knickers,' he said, before adding hastily, 'But I'd rather wear your mother's.'

'Why?'

'I just would,' he said (please, don't come!), 'they'll be different . . . someone else's.'

'You buy yours?'

He nodded. His cock had never felt so stiff. 'There's a shop near where I live. They, well, the manageress knows me. I buy them and other things.'

'What other things?'

He was confident now, sensing that the line of no return had long ago been reached. 'Vests; a couple of corsets; stockings and, oh yes, some slips, or, petti-coats. I, um, dress up and whip myself.'

'Really!' Her colour had heightened even more. 'Get up – leave the dishes; you can do them later.'

He rose, his cock sticking out of his crotch. She gave it an amused glance and continued: 'Go up-stairs, the second door on the right. In the corner is a chest of drawers. In the bottom one you'll find some of my mother's underwear. Strip; decide what you want to put on, and wait. I'll find what you've brought in your bag and bring them up in a minute. Now, go!'

He hesitated. 'Are you really – really –?'

'Do as you're told!'

The spare room was musty. He switched on the light, went to the chest of drawers, and opened the bottom one. His heart thumped.

There were interlock knickers, thick and long in pink, white and blue; whalebone corsets; thick, brown lisle stockings. He drew the items out one by one and laid them on the coverlet of the single bed. He arranged them carefully: the knicker legs spread enticingly apart; the stout corsets and the stockings.

He undressed quickly, tremblingly, his cock thrust savagely upwards. The corset took some getting on, but that all added to the thrill. At first he'd tried to draw it down over his head and shoulders, but then realised it would be too tight. Then he drew it up over his shaking legs and lifted his erection to be enclosed by the stiff material. He drew the shoulder straps over his bony shoulders, the cupped brassiere material cutting into him. With difficulty, he sat and pulled on the thick stockings, bringing them up over his knees and thighs, then fastening them, after a number of false starts, to the six suspender clips. Then, the knickers! He studied the four pairs on the bed and finally decided on the pink, picking them up and dangling them against him. Then, urged on by his intense desire, he put his feet through the elastic legs and raised them slowly. God! The feel of the elastic biting into the stockings! The coolness of the restricting corset on his hot flesh. He adjusted the knicker waist and straightened and tightened the elastic at the tops of his stockinged knees. There was a small dressing table with an adjustable mirror and he crossed to it, slanting it so that he could see his lower half. The knickers drooped and he spread his legs relishing the feel of the heavy interlock material. God, he looked ridiculous! And he savoured the humiliation of his future mother-in-law seeing him dressed as he was.

As if on cue, her voice sounded sharply from outside. 'Are you ready?'

'Yes,' he replied, trying to keep his voice steady.

He crossed the room, the corset tight against his erection, the knicker elastic pulling seductively above his knees, and opened the door. She was standing at the head of the stairs holding the whip and the cane he had brought with him. She looked him up and down derisively.

'Very nice! Very nice, indeed! I wonder what my daughter would say if she could see you now. What an object. Do you like my mother's underwear? Her knickers? They look well on you; you're so stupid. Get in there!'

She pointed to a half-open door and he slunk in. A pink-shaded lamp on a bedside table gave the room an intimate glow, reflecting off the double-doored wardrobe with its two mirrors, and glinting off the dressing table with its array of hairbrushes, silver-topped cosmetic jars and manicure trays. The heavy curtains were tightly drawn. She closed the door, and put the whip and cane on the bed. Then, without taking her eyes off him, she unzipped her skirt and let it drop to her ankles. Her pantaloons, similiar to those he had seen in the bathroom, were lacily clasped just above her knees, and showing through the stretched, cotton thighs the heavy, suspendered edge of her roll-on.

'Very well.' She picked up the whip and shook the

thongs loose. 'I'm going to thrash you, and then – do you know what?'

He shook his head, his throat too full to make a response.

She moved forwards slowly. 'After I've whipped you, you're going to undress me . . . then you'll lick me from head to foot, back and front, every inch, and then you'll enter me and make love to me.'

His head swam. 'What about – about Jenny?' he muttered. He was on fire, as though he'd already been flogged.

'Jenny has nothing to do with this! This is between you and me! Do you intend to tell her?'

'Of course not,' he said, watching the whip lashes swinging gently in her hand.

'Take your knickers down; undo those back suspenders; push the corset up and lean across the bed on your hands. I don't want you flat on your face! Do you understand?'

He nodded and pulled the thick knickers to his knees; tremblingly he undid the back suspenders and folded the tough edge of the corset above his buttocks. He leaned forwards, supporting himself on his hands.

'I don't want to hear a sound, apart from the sound of the whip on your bare flesh, she said tersely, then exclaimed, 'My God!' She'd obviously seen the weals from the previous night.

Her first stroke was high and hit the edge of the corset, but then her aim became more accurate and lower, being guided, he thought, by the marks already there. She whipped hard and grunted as each stroke fell.

He was in a faraway land, relishing every lash. By turning his head, he could see glimpses of her in one of the mirrors: her pantaloons stretched, her arm bending as she delivered each stroke. Oh, God, he thought, don't let me come!

Luckily, his cock, gripped by the leading edge of the corset, was unable to react and lay imprisoned. But he ached to orgasm. He had no idea how many strokes she had given, but the flogging was suddenly over.

'That's enough – for now! Stand up and undress me! Roughly! The clothes don't matter; rip them off!' She kicked off her shoes and dropped the whip.

He pulled his knickers halfway up and kneeled before her. He took the waist of her pantaloons and tore them down to her ankles, ripping the legs apart to get them off. He was beside himself. He ripped the stocking tops from their suspender clasps and tore them in a frenzy. Now the girdle. It was tight, but he managed to ease it down her hips and drag it off. He could smell her: sex, sweat. Her thighs, thick at the top, showed only a hint of brown pubic hair.

She was shaking. 'The rest, the rest!'

He ripped the starched blouse down the front, the buttons flying, and she bent her shoulders to allow him to run it down her arms. He flung it down and took the front of her brassiere in both hands and wrenched it apart. It came away. Her breasts, large, tight nippled, brown ringed, sprang out. She was naked. Turning her, he flung her face down on the bed, then kneeled and thrust his tongue between the ample twin mounds of her unmarked buttocks. He found the anal opening and tickled it. There was an odd taste – he wondered how recently she had emptied her bowels. But he didn't care. He wanted to taste her. She was moaning and trembling. He spread her thighs apart and moved his tongue down, tickling her to her knees, along her calves to her feet, then, taking each toe in turn, sucked them greedily.

Now, roughly, he turned her on her back and she rolled unprotestingly, spreading her legs. He was there, the pubic hair rough on his lips as he sought for the opening. It was moist and he smelled her arousal. But, eagerly, he spread the lips with his tongue and began exploring. Now she was no longer silent. She was moaning and saying things he could not hear. He found her hard clitoris beneath its little hood and put his lips to it.

'No!' she whispered suddenly, urgently. 'Not yet!'

He withdrew his tongue. But it was the taste; the smell. Something ... intimate about a mature woman; perhaps not known for some years, and all the more mysterious for that and provocative! Areas where possibly no tongue had explored before. And this was the woman who had savagely flogged him; whose mother's underwear he had on, and with whom shortly he would be having unbelievable sexual intercourse. She'd wanted to be treated roughly – very well! He got off his knees, stripped off the knickers, stockings and corset, rubbed his cock up and down to bring it – unnecessarily – to its fully erect state, then laid himself above her, searching with his fingers for the opening to her pussy, ready to thrust as she begged, pleaded for his entry. He plunged himself in, feeling the tight pussy walls gripping him.

She screamed aloud, 'Oh, God! Further! Further!'

He was almost to the base of his shaft, but he continued to probe and twist as she moaned and thrashed her upper body, her breasts bouncing.

He could go no further. His pubic hair was brushing hers. They were as together as they ever could be. The tightness of her muscles around his cock had relaxed slightly and he felt the wetness now coursing over him. Had she come? He gave a final, urgent thrust, and ejaculated, pumping himself into her. There was a flood, a warm flood which seemed never ending. She gave a loud cry and her thighs gripped him so hard that he gasped. The head of his cock was trapped; still fairly erect, but sticking to her pussy wall. He didn't move.

It had grown dark in the room and, when she turned her face towards him, a chill ran up his spine. In the dimness, her features had softened: it might have been Jenny beneath him, the pair of them intimately connected! But his smarting buttocks told him otherwise . . .

He kissed her hard nipples and rubbed his tongue over them. He didn't know what to say. In films, the man – or the woman – or perhaps both – lit cigarettes and lay staring at the ceiling.

Suddenly, he knew he had to urinate. 'I've got to . . .' he whispered. 'I've got to go to the bathroom. sorry.'

She gave a deep sigh, but said nothing. Gently, ever so gently, he withdrew his cock from the warmth, the cloying moisture of that magic cave . . . that's how he imagined it: a softly lit cave full of treasures, and the further one explored, the more one found to be amazed at. He was out, and she gasped. He rolled to the edge of the bed and stood uncertainly, swaying in the darkness of the unfamiliar room. He saw a crack of vertical light and made for it. In the bathroom he tugged the light switch and looked down at himself. His cock, the foreskin folded way back over the stem, had a thin thread of what could have been the results of her orgasm or his ejaculation. It didn't matter. He took the pale, cream-coloured strand in his hand and licked it. Salty; strong, as he had tasted her before.

His cock was now back to normal size, and he was able to urinate easily and strongly as he stood over the bowl, legs apart, one hand guiding the pale yellow stream which had an unfamiliar, yet not unpleasant, odour to it. He washed himself and stared into the mirror. Should he have looked any different? Anyway, he didn't; perhaps, though, there was something in the eyes which hadn't been there before. He found a tube of toothpaste, squeezed some on to a finger and rubbed his teeth, rinsing his mouth thoroughly. Then, quietly, almost on tiptoe, he returned to the bedroom, his not altogether slack cock swinging gently.

She opened her eyes as he eased on to the bed beside her. 'What are we going to do?' she whispered almost plaintively.

'Now?' He smoothed her stomach, but she pushed his hand away.

'You know what I mean!'

'I don't know,' he said. 'I can't think at the moment. All I know is that I want – what we've just been doing to go on.'

'But – you and Jenny?'

He sighed. 'I didn't think anything like this would happen.'

'Neither did I!'

'But now it has, I couldn't imagine just giving it up . . . it's too – too good.'

'That's selfish.' She moved slightly and he felt her hand searching for his cock. He took her wrist and guided the fingers to their destination. 'But I know what you mean.' She was bringing him up slowly. 'D'you think we could . . . keep it to ourselves? Our secret?'

He savoured her hand on him. 'How? Eventually Jenny is going to see the whip marks.'

'But – say – without the whipping?' She was rubbing him harder – which, he thought, told its own story.

'That's part of it, isn't it?' God, it felt good! 'Whipping? You want it – I want it!' She moved her hand harder, more urgently.

'Yes, yes!'

She pumped, hurting him, but he didn't care. He spread his legs and she moved across and devoured him, moaning to herself, smoothing his inner thighs.

'I'm going to –' he gasped. 'Now!' And he thrust himself intensely into her mouth as he spurted over and over, his cock muscles jerking feverishly.

Her tongue was licking greedily. He smoothed her naked back and felt the warmth of her arousal, moving his hand down to the base of her spine and gently between her buttocks, seeking the opening. He slid a finger in – thank God he'd cut his nails recently! – and, as she had closed over his cock, so her sphincter closed over his finger as he probed.

She withdrew her mouth. 'No, this isn't right! It's not right!' She eased away and he allowed his finger to emerge. 'What are we doing? What the hell are we doing?'

It was the first time he had heard her use any kind of swear word.

He moistened his dry lips, staring at the shadowy ceiling. 'What we're doing is having a sexual relationship which neither of us thought possible. But it's happened . . . it's still happening. We can't stop now, – can we?'

He moved his hand and cupped her breast, a finger teasing the erect nipple.

'I – I don't know!'

He kissed the tight, smooth skin between her shoulder blades. 'Don't you?'

'No – yes – no!'

He ran his hand downwards over the curve of her belly to the damp pubic hair between her tight thighs.

She squeezed them together, effectively imprisoning his hand. 'Don't, please!'

'I love you,' he said.

'You don't know me!'

He tried to lighten his tone. 'Well, sweetheart, if I don't know you now, I never will.'

'It's not funny.' She was sniffing.

Gently he pulled her on to her back. Her eyes glistened and he kissed them gently, tasting salty tears.

'It isn't funny. It's serious. I love you!'

She sniffed again. 'I won't – I won't have my daughter suffer. It's not fair.'

'I love Jenny,' he said softly, 'but I love you, too.'

'You can't – you can't have it both ways!'.

A risque reply sprang to mind, but he resisted it. He felt so much more confident; so much more in control. What had happened had given him a new faith in himself. There wasn't much show of affection from Jenny, he had to admit that. Kisses, and a tentative hand on him, or his own fingers exploring beneath her tight pants, but nothing so momentous as this evening. Not in his wildest fantasies could he ever imagine Jenny whipping him; or seeing him in the sort of underwear – or any sort of women's underwear! – he'd had on earlier.

'Jenny,' he said finally, 'will have to go her own way. I want you. We're much better suited together, you and I. Don't you think so?'

She relaxed her thighs a little and he slipped one finger between, finding the silky opening. 'Don't you?' he demanded.

'Yes!'

The phone was ringing from downstairs. He tightened his grip. 'Don't answer it!'

'I must – it's probably Jenny.'

She pulled away from him and got out of bed. Naked, she crossed the room and slipped through the door. He lay back, playing with himself. There was the low mutter of voices. He stretched languidly. He heard the ping of the phone as it went down, and a moment later she stood in the doorway.

'That was Jenny. She's – she's staying on for a while . . . she's written to you. It's in the post.'

He smiled contentedly. 'Come back to bed . . . we've all the time in the world.'

5

Tales to be Told – The Card in the Phone Box

Hanley said, 'Simon, you're into self-fladge. You might be interested in this story. It's mentioned briefly, but only two paragraphs, on page thirty-eight of the book, but you all might want to hear it in more detail. It's interesting, because a policewoman – or I should say a former policewoman – is involved at some point. But we begin with a handsome, masochistic, nineteen-year-old called Andrew ...'

Andrew had taken the card furtively from a Paddington phone box which was plastered with dozens advertising call-girls and their various 'come-ons'. One had particularly interested the slim, rather shy, student who was in his second year of studying biology at Queen's. He was living in a bedsit in Kensington, not far from the Natural History Museum, and the allowance from his divorced mother allowed him to live reasonably enough. He also had a student grant which helped considerably.

Andrew was a confused young man, sexually. At school he had been worshipped by another boy who, though six months younger, knew a great deal more about sex than did Andrew, whose explorations so far

112

consisted only of solitary masturbation. The younger boy, Mark, had indulged in many more sexual activities than Andrew. He had, for instance, been seduced by a woman three times his age when he was only thirteen; he knew about homosexuality and described to Andrew the feeling of a male cock penetrating one's bottom. 'It's like having a crap – only backwards, if you see what I mean!'

What interested Andrew most, strangely, was Mark's story of how he had been caned on his bum by an aunt who had looked after him when his mother was hospitalised for a hip replacement. The aunt, who was single, was a tall, austere woman who usually dressed in black. She worked part-time at a reformatory for delinquent children up to the age of eighteen and she gave Mark a warning that she knew how to deal with badly behaved young men and that he would suffer if she ever found him disobedient.

He'd arrived home from school one day – to his aunt's rather gloomy house in Croydon – to find her awaiting him at the top of the stairs, standing threateningly in her long black dress. He'd not made his bed that morning (he had slept late and had intended doing it when he got home) and his clothes were strewn all over his room. She didn't allow this kind of behaviour where she worked and she didn't intend to allow it with her nephew with whose care she had been entrusted!

He had to be taught a lesson: it would benefit him, she was sure, in later years and she told him to come upstairs and into his room. She produced a cane, and ordered him to lower his trousers and underpants and bend over the unmade bed. She gave him twelve strokes on his behind.

'But,' he told Andrew, his face flushed, 'it hurt like

mad at first, but then my dick started to get hard! I actually wanted her to go on!'

When she'd gone, he said, he 'wanked himself off'.

The idea of punishment somehow being exciting had stuck in Andrew's mind. He'd never been beaten, never been hit anywhere, but now he wanted to be. Mark had said that his dick had become hard and Andrew, oddly, could feel his own strengthening and, even more oddly, he felt a tingle on his smooth, untouched bottom. Almost as if . . .

What was a caning like? How could he get one? Fortunately, or otherwise, he watched a film on television about the life of Christ. Towards the end, after Christ had been condemned, he was stripped and scourged. Andrew reacted to the sounds of the lash on flesh; little was shown as the result of the whipping but he had a good imagination. Had Christ got an erection? Perhaps he'd ejaculated during the scourging, spilling his precious seed on the sandy ground below the whipping post?

Well, he wasn't going to get that. But he wanted something. It was an itch within him. Then one evening he went into a Paddington telephone box and saw the array of advertisements: some crudely printed; others quite expertly sketched and lettered. He'd read somewhere that these cards were illegal and the police regularly toured the area and took them away. The one he liked best, as his cock rose, was of a woman in a short schoolteacher-type gown, with a mortarboard on her head and a cane in her hand. The artist had caught the compellingly intriguing image of the woman, and, below, the message read: 'If you've been a naughty boy, I'd like to meet you and you can tell me all about it . . .' There was a telephone number.

Tell her about it! He took the card and went home, all kinds of fantasies flooding his brain. A strange woman ... he'd have to undress in front of her, expose himself, and obediently bend over to receive his punishment! The telephone number seemed to grow before his eyes as he sat studying it. Then he picked up the phone and dialled the number.

It was engaged! Well, it would be, wouldn't it? he argued to himself. She was a professional, wanting to make money, of course! Many men would want her services – and it suddenly excited him to think that others had suffered at her hands. He rang again and it was answered.

'Hello?' The voice was curt.

'I've been a naughty boy ... I'd like to tell you about it,' he said.

'Very well! It's eighty pounds for an hour – if you want more we can discuss it. Cash, though.'

'I accept,' he said thickly. 'When can I –?'

'This afternoon?'

'Yes,' he said meekly.

She gave him the address in Pimlico. 'It's the second bell up. Don't ring any other! If you have to wait, well, you'll anticipate your discipline even more, won't you?' She put the phone down.

He had sixty pounds and could get more from the cashpoint. He decided to get another twenty as he made his way. Firstly he had a long, hot bath, soaping himself everywhere, before drying off and applying lotions. Then he put on a pair of brand-new, tight, white briefs, straight from the packet, a white shirt, tight jeans and a pair of Wrangler, thick-soled shoes. He pulled on a suede jacket, checked his keys and wallet, and left the flat, his heart thudding.

He wanted it, but he was scared: the unknown! And that, in itself, was arousing. He'd be at the mercy of this unknown woman. Would she tie him up to be punished? The tight underwear kept his cock somewhat under control, but he was still aware there'd be a telltale bulge as he rang the second bell as instructed.

'Yes?'

He jumped. The harsh voice had come from a sound grille at the side of the door.

'I, um, phoned earlier.'

'Second floor, door facing you.'

There was a buzz and the door swung open a degree. Ahead was a narrow hall and stairs. It smelled musty and of cigarette smoke. He trod the stairs and saw a door ahead slightly open. Before he could knock, a woman appeared: a small middle-aged, woman with a ginger fringe. She was wearing a dark-brown skirt and green sweater. Her stockings looked loose, wrinkled around her thin calves. Andrew's heart sank. Surely not . . .

'Come in, dear,' she said, opening the door. 'Madam's engaged at the moment, but if you'd like to wait . . .' She showed him into a small room with a sofa and two easy chairs. On a glass-topped, smeared table there was a pile of magazines. 'She won't be long. I'll tell her you're here.'

Andrew sat down gingerly, wondering if he shouldn't just get up and leave, now! But the excitement was too strong. Then, from somewhere, he heard a sound, a steady, rhythmical sound, inexorable; like . . . He flushed deeply. He was hearing a whipping in progress! Someone nearby was having a flogging, and he was next!

He picked up one of the well-thumbed magazines from the table and leafed through it. Images of naked women exposing themselves: pubic hair, breasts, faces, mouths open in acted lust. One made him pause: a naked man strapped to a frame, spread-eagled, helpless, a woman behind him, naked except

116

for thigh-length black boots, about to deliver a lash with a long-thonged whip. The man's backside and back were already scored with reddening welts.

He realised as he put the magazine down that the sounds of punishment had ceased. He heard a door, a mumble of conversation, then the slam of another door.

After a moment, the little ginger-haired woman entered. 'Madam will see you now if you'd like to come this way.'

It all sounded so formal! He followed her along the corridor; she opened a thickly panelled door and swung it back for him. He walked in and the door clicked heavily behind him. There was a spotlight directed on to a wooden crossbeam in the middle of the floor, and she stood facing him, wearing – he was surprised to see – ordinary clothes: a dark-grey skirt, white blouse and court shoes.

'Hello,' she said with a friendly smile, 'are you the one who's been a naughty boy?'

He nodded, feeling weak at the knees.

'Well,' she said, 'and what do you think should happen to naughty boys? By the way, can I have the money?'

He fished into his pocket, egress somewhat hampered by his solid erection, and pulled out eighty pounds in tens. He'd brought a hundred, just in case. She took it, counted it and laid it aside.

'Now,' she said, eyeing him. 'I think – I may be wrong, of course – but I think you should have the birch. I like the idea of taking your trousers down and, of course, your underpants if you're wearing any?'

He nodded, the excitement running like an electric current through him.

'And I'll birch you. Do you wish to be tied?'

'I – I leave it to you,' he said uncertainly.

'If you wish me to be your school mistresses, then you shouldn't, of course, be tied. Is that what you want?'

'Please!' His balls ached agonisingly.

'Then take down your trousers and underpants to your knees!'

As he did so, he watched her remove the skirt and blouse and don a short pleated gown. She placed a mortarboard on her head, adjusted it and took up a thickly bundled collection of twigs, bound together.

'Lift your shirt-tail and bend, you wicked, wicked boy!'

He thrust his buttocks out and received the first stinging blow. There followed regular lashes, agonising, but at the same time thrilling. As he bent he fondled his cock, stimulating it gently as the flogging progressed.

'Thirty!' she said finally. 'Stand up!'

He straightened painfully. The agony was exquisite and he wanted more. 'Please?' he begged.

Putting the birch down, she shook her head. 'No. Don't you ever whip yourself? To get satisfaction?'

He shook his head, conscious of his position, his cock begging.

'Then you should. Self-flagellation is overwhelmingly arousing because you can regulate the punishment yourself.'

'But how?' He was puzzled and excited.

'How?' She was divesting herself of the mortarboard and gown. Now, she stood in tight, black knickers which bulged around the pubic area. 'You get a whip, or a pliable cane, and you thrash yourself! That's how!' She eyed him. 'Do you have any more money?'

'Twenty,' he acknowledged.

'I've a client due shortly who enjoys self-flagellation while I watch. She –'

'She?' His cock twitched.

'An ex-policewoman – dismissed from the force for reasons I won't go into – she visits me twice a month and flogs herself for, what she calls, her sins. But she whips herself to a climax. So, how would you like to watch from a little room at the back, through a spyhole? Perhaps that would teach you how to punish yourself. She brings her own whip. Well?' She raised her eyebrows.

'I'd – I'd like that.'

'Give me the money.' She held out a hand.

He groped in his hanging trousers and brought out the extra.

'Put it here,' she said, pulling out the waistband of her knickers. He thrust the money in, feeling the warmth.

'I'll show you where.' She opened the door and called, 'Hilda!' The ginger-haired woman scuttled into sight. 'Take this gentleman to the other room – you know where.'

'Yes, Madam.' She glanced at Andrew as he was pulling up his pants and trousers.

He followed her a short distance into a tiny room, windowless and dimly lit. Hilda led the way to the far wall and slid aside a small partition. 'Look in there, sir.'

Andrew put his eye to the aperture. He could see the room he had just been in as if in a film, every detail clear. His punisher was stacking away the birch she had just used to flog him.

Hilda said, 'The lady'll be here in a minute. Just you wait! She's regular – regular as clockwork! I watch sometimes and I wet my knickers. I don't mind telling you that – you're a nice young man. Let me feel you . . .'

He undid his trousers and a small, cold hand caressed his erection.

'Beautiful,' she whispered. 'I want to show you my knickers.' She released him and drew up her skirt. She had drooping, pink interlock bloomers down to her knees. 'I just thought I'd show you. Now I must wait for the lady. See that?' She pointed to a small knurled knob on the wall. 'Turn that up and you'll hear everything.' She dropped her skirt and was gone silently from the room.

Andrew pulled out his cock and waited. He heard the buzz of the doorbell, and a moment later Hilda was ushering in a woman of about thirty, Andrew reckoned, dressed in jeans, coat and sweater. She had a holdall, which she dropped to the floor as Andrew's punisher moved towards her. He turned the knob and voices sprang out from some hidden loud-speaker.

'So, you've come.'

'Yes.' The other woman bowed her head.

'Prepare yourself.'

The woman bent, unzipped her case and brought out a blue tunic and skirt. She stripped down to her briefs which she hurriedly pulled off. She had on a black suspender belt and black stockings. Then she donned the tunic and skirt, which hung just above her knees.

'Take out the whip!' The order was harsh.

The woman bent and brought out a short-handled whip with long, knotted lashes. Andrew's heart began to pump.

'Madam, will you lift my skirt?' It seemed part of a ritual.

'Very well.'

Andrew's punisher pulled the other woman's skirt up to her shoulders and fastened it there with some device Andrew couldn't see. Now she stood, buttocks and legs naked, grasping the whip.

'Flog yourself! Punish your body for your sins.'

The woman turned slightly and Andrew could see, even from a limited viewpoint, the ridges of whipped flesh on her bottom. Skilfully, she swung the whip around her body and lashed it into her behind. He heard her gasp. Then another stroke and now she was steadily flogging herself with grim determination, her eyes down, frowning slightly in concentration.

The whipping sounded loudly in the room, and Andrew was slowly beginning to masturbate. Suddenly, Hilda was beside him, grasping him. 'Let me.'

She pressed his hand to her side and he realised her skirt was up and he was feeling her knicker elastic. He watched the flogging going on through the peephole as Hilda stroked his cock. The self-mortification never seemed about to cease, but finally the whip fell to the floor and the sufferer masturbated savagely; at the same time, Hilda's sensuous, experienced hand on Andrew's cock brought him to violent fruition.

How could he, he thought afterwards, have let a little old woman like Hilda bring him on, and feel her knicker elastic? But, as he walked slowly home, reliving the experiences of the last two hours, he realised that any woman of any age or any size was sensual. The mystery was always there.

He needed a drink and went into a pub on the corner. He hadn't been at the bar more than a couple of minutes when, looking round, he saw 'the police-woman' sitting on her own. He'd just watched her whipping herself! And seen her masturbate! Beside her was the bag which he knew contained her uniform and her whip.

He asked for his vodka and tonic to be doubled and, taking his glass, crossed the saloon bar towards her, a new wave of erotic need swamping him.

She gave a sidelong glance as he sat at the next table on one of the leather benches just a few feet away. It was extraordinary to be sitting there, seeing the thighs under her tight jeans and knowing what he knew! She shifted slightly and he saw her wince. He knew why, too! Her bottom was sore from the thrashing she had given herself and he felt that warm swell within him, that sense of going into the unknown. He leaned towards her.

'May I buy you a drink?'

She shook her head irritably, as if a fly was buzzing around her.

'Oh, sorry I spoke,' he said, keeping his voice casual. 'I expect you're waiting for somone. I apologise.'

He began to shift away, sliding along the leather, feeling his own buttocks pulsating.

'I – forgive me,' she said in a low voice. 'That was rude of me. I'm sorry.'

He thought, I'd love to make you sorrier. He imagined whipping her as she bent obediently to receive the punishment. 'I'm sorry, too,' he said, 'for bothering you.'

'No.' She looked at him and he saw her face close up for the first time: wide eyes, a sensual mouth which curved, lipstickless, in a shy sort of smile. 'I was thinking of other things. I'd – I'd like another drink, thank you.'

'What was it?' He knew when he stood there was going to be a telltale bulge, so he played for time. 'I'm having vodka.'

'Well,' she said, 'I think I'd like the same.'

'Doubles?' He started to get up, turning his hips slightly away.

'Oh, I –'

'Yes,' he said, now on his feet. Luckily he had tight

122

underpants on and his cock could scarcely pull itself upright.

He went to the bar and looked back. She was eyeing him and looked away abruptly. He took the drinks back and sat down closer to her. 'Cheers,' he said, raising his glass. 'It's funny but I'm sure I've seen you before.'

They clinked glasses and drank.

'That's an old line, isn't it?' she said mockingly.

'No!' He tried to sound convincing. 'Honestly, it's just that you've got a memorable face, if you don't mind my saying so.'

'Memorable!' It was a half-snort, half-laugh. She was twisting the glass in long, lean fingers. 'I don't believe anyone has ever called me that before!'

'But,' he said, 'you have a face that people remember, I'm sure. It's unusual. I notice faces; I'm studying biology.'

She looked at him directly. 'How old are you?'

'Twenty,' he said, 'and a bit.'

'How old do you think I am?' Her eyes were still fixed on his.

He thought, I've seen you nearly naked, whipping yourself and – but he said, 'I'd be very tactless to make even a guess.'

He'd nearly finished his vodka and the desires inside him were mounting.

She uncrossed her legs and shifted her bottom. Ah, he thought, I know how it feels: the welts are beginning to harden, and every movement is a mixture of pain and pleasure. Her legs were slightly spread, and the mound of her crotch was very tight.

'I'm thirty,' she said, 'thirty-one in two months. I should be – oh, never mind!' She shook her head briefly and drained her glass. 'I don't want to burden you; I don't even know you.'

'I know you,' he said. 'I recognise something – something we have in common.'

He hadn't meant to say that, but it was too late now.

'What do you mean?' She stared, her pale cheeks a little flushed.

'Another drink?'

He got up, still hard. The bar had darkened and other people had filtered in. But their right-angled table in the corner was a sort of oasis in the tables around them.

When he returned with the drinks, she said, 'Thank you. I don't know why you're doing this but what did you mean – we have something in common?' She raised her rather thin eyebrows. They were brown – the same colour as he had seen earlier down below when she was . . .

He cleared his throat which had thickened. 'It's funny,' he said, making it up as he went along – unusually fluent for him – 'biology is partly the study of the chemical reaction between creatures, human and animal: some find a good reaction; others don't. Two dogs of the same breed, for example, will meet and immediately make friends; on the other hand –'

'What about humans?' She was studying him over her glass.

'Same thing,' he said. 'I, um, well, I saw you and I thought – maybe I'm wrong – but I thought I recognised something, as I said.'

Should he tell her he'd seen her flagellating herself? No, string it out a little longer . . .

She said, head down, 'I don't think I recognise anything in anyone any more. I've –' She took a drink. 'Well, I've been stupid and now I'm suffering for it.' She coughed and reached in the handbag beside her for a tissue.

He swallowed. 'It sounds as if you're punishing yourself for something.'

Her head turned abruptly. She was wiping her nose. 'What on earth made you say that?'

Keeping his voice steady, he said, 'Well, you said you've been stupid, and now you're suffering for it. It sounds to me like punishment – of some kind.' He extended the pause in midair.

She screwed up the tissue and dropped it into the empty ashtray. 'Of some kind?' Her voice was harsh. 'What would you know! You're twenty – sorry, and a bit! – what do you know of punishment?'

'Some people punish themselves for sins they haven't committed – as a sort of penance?' he said.

'What are you talking about?'

He noticed her fingers around the glass gripping it so tightly that the knuckles were white. He sat back and crossed his legs. Damn these pants! They were wrapped around his erection and made his balls ache.

'There's a religious group in South America,' he said. 'I've read about them –' he cleared his throat again '– and every Good Friday they march through the streets, um, flagellating themselves, stripped to the waist –'

'I've seen it on television!' Her voice was sharp. 'They use what looks like leather, but it's only for show!'

He noted the word 'leather'. 'Well, maybe this is a different cult. They actually, er, flog themselves properly. An act of contrition.'

'Do you believe it's an act of contrition or is there, well, some element of, er, sex involved?'

He drew a breath. 'How do you feel about punishing yourself?' It was all or nothing.

'What?' Her eyes were wide.

'I saw you this afternoon whipping yourself. I was

there. I'd just had a flogging myself – that's the way I am. Are you, too?'

She looked away. 'You saw me?'

'Yes,' he said, 'I saw you.'

She took a long drink and coughed again. 'And did it excite you?'

'Very much,' he said, 'very, very much.'

'Why?' She gave a stealthy look round, but the bar was noisy now and their corner was still secure.

He leaned towards her. He could smell no perfume, but there was something. Chemical? He said, 'I've never seen anyone whip themselves before – especially an attractive woman. I've often done it to myself when no one else was available, but I prefer an attractive woman to flog me.'

Their eyes met. She drained her glass with a positive gesture. 'Let's get out of here. I can't stand cigarette smoke.'

She picked up her bag and brushed past him. He walked behind her to the door watching her buttocks move sensuously beneath the jeans.

Outside it was drizzling and the streetlights were on. Looking at him, shielding her eyes against the glare of passing cars, taxis and buses, she said, 'Would you like to talk about this some more?'

'Talk?' he asked.

She looked away and energetically signalled a free taxi as it glided, its sign glowing, through the murk. They remained silent in the darkness of the cab as it threaded its way through the red, brake-blinking traffic and the now driving rain splattering on the windscreen and the windows. The wipers grinded as if most of the rubber had been worn off. He'd heard her say to the driver, 'Fourteen, Barkston Gardens, Earl's Court.' Oddly, he knew the area. It was a small square off the Earl's Court Road, surrounded on four

126

sides by flats, and there was a central, railed garden with a gate and a key, to which only mortgaged tenants were entitled. He'd lived there for six months in a dingy bedsit room, which smelled permanently of leaking gas from the nasty, blue-flamed, two-barred fire under a scorched, brown mantel which dripped evil-smelling creosote.

She paid the cab and they mounted scrubbed white steps to a glazed front door. She produced a bundle of keys, which jangled like a prison warder's, and opened the door into a dimly lit hall.

'There, to the left!' she whispered, giving him a nudge, none too gently.

The oak-panelled door stood high in the lofty hall. It had a menacing aspect which somehow excited him. Moving beside him, she jangled the keys and undid two locks before swinging open the heavy entrance. It was dark. She moved an arm around him and a light sprang on. The hallway was long and narrow. He stood as she closed the door and locked it. The sound made him want to take all his clothes off. He was in her power!

'Go down to the end,' she said. 'I won't be a minute.'

She went through a door to the left and a moment later he heard the sound of her urinating. He imagined her sitting on the toilet seat, her jeans round her knees, then rising and wiping herself. Meanwhile, he was at the door she had indicated and he paused. The streetlamps from wide windows at one end illuminated a narrow lounge with couches, a glass-topped coffee table which gleamed in the orange glow and shadowy bookcases along one wall. She was suddenly beside him, a hand cupping his buttocks. 'I'll put a table lamp on,' she said. 'I hate bright light.'

She moved quickly and bent slightly to click on a red-shaded lamp on a side table. He blinked. Now, he could see the room clearly. As well as the bookcases, there was a television set, video recorder and a hi-fi stack alongside a shelf of tapes.

'Take off your jacket,' she said, 'and give it to me.' He did so and she went to the door. 'Help yourself to a drink; the cabinet's over there. And pour me one – whiskey, neat. Large!'

He thrilled at her tone of command. The cocktail cabinet had double doors and he fumbled for the catch. A mirrored shelf sprang forwards and a light shone, displaying glass-topped shelves with a myriad of bottles and glasses winking in the glare. He felt weak at the knees, but his cock had hardened. He sought out a bottle of Johnny Walker, Black Label, and poured two measures into chunky, cut-glass tumblers standing in array on a lower shelf.

As he turned with the two glasses, she was in the doorway in a white blouse and black tights tucked into high-heeled, black boots. He gasped involuntarily.

Taking her glass from him, she said, 'Sit down.'

He eyed her buttocks as she made her way to the far side of the room. He could see no VPL, but imagined the weals beneath. She took a cassette from the deck and pushed it in, turning up the volume. At first, there was a faint sound of a door closing; then, sharply, the unmistakable sound of leather on flesh. It continued, regularly, and she stood, one hand resting on the shelf, watching him. He squirmed in his chair. It was the most exciting sound he'd ever heard! The lashing ceased, then there were gasps and throaty grunts. Finally silence.

She switched the machine off and sat opposite him on a high-backed, adjustable black leather chair, legs crossed, swinging gently, enticingly. 'Well? What did you think of that?'

He took a drink. 'It made me – made me want to take my clothes off!' He'd blurted the words without thinking, and felt his face reddening.

She nodded slightly. 'That was the first time – the first time I whipped myself and you're the only other person who's ever heard that tape.'

'I feel . . . privileged,' he said uncertainly, watching her.

'If you want to take your clothes off, you can,' she said calmly, 'but do it in here, and keep your underpants on. I presume you're wearing underpants?'

'Oh, yes!' he said eagerly and, after putting his tumbler down carefully, stood and stripped off his shirt, then bent to remove his shoes and socks before sliding off his jeans. He looked down at himself; not embarrassed, revelling in the exposure. The tight pants bulged and there was a visible stain.

'Sit down. No, pour us both another drink. I want to watch you.'

He walked stiff legged to the cabinet, keeping his muscles tight, his back taut. He could almost feel her eyes piercing into his swaying behind like a laser beam. He took his time refilling their glasses and then turned, a glass in each hand. He knew now that his cock must be like a tentpole, but he didn't look down. He handed her glass to her, and stood before her.

She eyed him keenly. 'Have you come?'

'No.' He shook his head. 'It's just that – I'm excited.'

'So you should be! Sit down opposite me and spread your legs apart.'

He did so, feeling his erection almost screaming to get out.

'I have a friend,' she said, running the rim of her glass along her lower lip ruminatively.

129

He didn't know how to reply to that, so he said nothing.

'A female friend.' She shifted and went on, 'More than a friend – if you catch on. Have you ever seen two lesbians making it?'

'No,' he confessed, confused now but just as excited. Lesbians! Two girls doing . . . well, whatever two girls did together.

'You might – just might – be what we've been looking for.' She nodded towards his crotch. 'Show me!'

He put his glass down carefully, his fingers shaking, and drew down the waist of his underpants. His cock, seemingly thankful to be released, stood to attention. He could almost hear a 'twang' as it vibrated in time to his heart. He wasn't holding it. He kept his hands away and let it speak for itself!

'Hmm.' She didn't get up, but just took a sip of her drink. Then she leaned forwards conversationally. 'You know, people aren't all a hundred per cent one way or the other. I was fired from the police when they found out I was having an affair with my friend – the one I've just mentioned. She was involved in a drugs racket and I managed to keep her name out of it. But some bastard split on us both; there was an inquiry and I got the bullet. I began to feel guilty, not for myself, but for her – her name's Audrey, by the way. Come to think of it, you don't know mine. It's June, and you're –?'

'Andrew,' he said, watching her with compulsion.

Her cheeks were flushed and she was drinking quickly.

'Let me get you another.' He stood, leaving his underpants halfway down his thighs. His cock bobbed as he walked.

She said, 'This friend, Audrey, she wants to meet a young man – with me, of course, but we've never

130

been able to find one who looks right. I think you do – but it will be up to her as well.' She accepted the refilled glass. 'Thank you.'

He indicated himself. 'Shall I –?'

For the first time, she smiled. It transformed her face and a surge of desire speared him. 'No,' she said, 'I want to see how long it stays up!'

It was strange; he no longer felt shy. Nor had he when he'd been whipped earlier; it was as if all his inhibitions had been released, a barrier broken, a door unlocked. 'Do you think I might pass?'

'I've seen your bum – you can certainly take punishment and your cock is quite beautiful.'

'Thank you,' he said, feeling himself flushing.

'But,' she said, and his heart sank, 'it's up Audrey. If it was my decision I'd say right now –'

'Can't we?' he broke in quickly. 'I mean, the two of us –?'

She shook her head. 'No. I feel obligated. She's – she's been good to me in many ways.'

'But so have you to her!' He felt his fingernails digging into his palms and tried to relax.

'We're lovers!' she said emphatically. 'She and I. I had no idea before –' She paused and drained her glass. 'Get me another, and take those pants off. I can give you a pair of knickers to wear if you want them! Audrey likes to see a man in women's knickers! And so do I.' She lowered her voice. 'Long, baggy silk ones like your grandma probably wore!'

'No,' he said and stripped the soaking underpants off. Now he was nude and felt excitingly vulnerable. 'When will I be tested?!'

'I can call her now and she can be here in ten minutes – if that's what you want.'

He poured the drinks. 'That's what I want,' he

said, his throat thick. 'I used to – to wear my mother's knickers – that sort. Can I?'

'Of course.' She got up, took the glass he proferred her and gulped the whiskey; she handed it back and left the room.

He stood, naked, staring at the wall blindly. His balls ached. He wanted to come, but at the same time wanted to deny himself. It was extraordinary . . .

One summer afternoon, the blinds down against the heat, he had crept into his mother's bedroom while she was out. He was looking for her knicker drawer. Earlier, in the bathroom, he had seen pink knickers hanging on a clothes horse. On impulse he'd felt them, smoothing the silkiness; they were damp.

Later, when he went to bed and made himself come, he imagined wearing them: the tight elastic at the top of his knees, the gusset silk caressing his erection. That afternoon in the dimly lit room he'd gone instinctively to the drawers in her dressing table and opened them one by one. In the lower one he found what he was looking for, and drew out a pair of light-blue knickers with sagging legs. Tremblingly, he stripped, fondled himself to stiffness and drew the knickers on. He gasped. The feeling was incredible! The elastic gripped his kneecaps; the baggy silk stroked his erection. His mother's knickers! Would she arrive back and catch him? What would she do? He imagined her discovering him: her disgust; strong words; making him take them off and then bend over to receive the cane . . .

June was back. 'What are you thinking about?'

He shook his head, bringing himself back to the present. His cock and balls were like solid wood. He wanted to pee, but knew it was impossible in his present state.

'Here.' She handed him a pair of navy-blue, silk knickers, holding them by the waist.

The legs drooped and fell to tight elastic. He took them and, with some familiarity, drew them up over his calves and thighs. He snapped the waist; already the moist head of his cock was thrusting eagerly at the sweet-smelling material encasing him.

'I'm going to phone Audrey,' she said peremptorily. 'Have you any objection?'

'No,' he said breathlessly, hands at his sides smoothing the thigh-clinging knicker silk. 'Please – bring her round!'

She gave him a brief up-and-down look, straight faced. 'I will,' she said, and picked up the green telephone on the coffee table. 'Hello, it's me. I may have a candidate . . . here now. What?' A laugh. 'Oh, yes, I think so. In fact, I'm sure! Yes, he's standing here . . . got you-know-what on. What? Not bad . . . nice one, I think you'll like it. He's pretty close. OK, see you in five? Yes, my sweet, of course.' She replaced the receiver.

'Do you like the knickers?' she asked.

'Oh, yes. What'll happen when she comes?'

She gave a brief giggle which made her suddenly sound more girlish. 'When she comes? That's a long way ahead, believe you me. This could go on all night – always assuming, of course, she likes you.'

'And if she doesn't?' he asked meekly.

'I'll flog you and then you'll go, but, if she finds you satisfactory, then, my boy, you're in for a night you'll never forget! And one of many!'

'But I'll still be whipped, either way?' His throat was dry. 'I don't have a lecture in the morning.'

She looked at him with a thin smile. 'Just as well! You'll be whipped – both ways! Pour us large drinks and have a bottle of Campari ready – she adores

133

Campari; she likes the colour. I'm going to put my uniform on. Relax – while you can.'

When she'd left the room, he sat, legs apart, the knicker elastic on his kneecaps. His cock felt almost numb; it seemed to have been hard for ever. He could feel pressure at the base, a swelling strength, which he knew, with a few rapid hand movements, would bring him to a climax. But that musn't happen! When Audrey arrived he had to be hard and pass inspection!

June reappeared in her uniform tunic and skirt. God, she looked severe! In her hand was a pair of gleaming handcuffs which she swung gently, erotically, menacingly.

'Where's my drink?'

He got up and handed her the glass.

She stood before him, skirt stretched. 'When she arrives, you'll do exactly as she says. What we may do with each other before we get to you is our concern. She might agree to you watching – but she might not. It depends on her mood. Even I sometimes can't predict how she's going to be.'

'Has there – has there been a man before?' he asked hesitantly.

'Just the one,' she said, 'but he was useless!'

He cleared his throat. 'In what way? This?' He thrust his hips out and the silk tentpoled.

'No,' she said, 'he couldn't take the punishment. His cock was big enough, but his bum wouldn't stand what Audrey was dealing out. He begged, pleaded, but it was no good. He offered money – quite a sum, in fact – but money doesn't play a part in this. If it is to be the three of us, what we do is for our pleasure – that's reward enough.'

A doorbell buzzed.

'That'll be her,' June said, putting her drink down, then making for the door.

He stood, readying himself, heart thumping. There was a murmur of voices and then June entered the room followed by a tall woman in riding breeches and boots, with a suede coat over a black silk blouse. In her hand was what looked like a sports bag. Her black hair was short, well groomed and her face without makeup was pale, the cheekbones high, her eyes seeming to have an upwards slant to them, making her catlike, inscrutable.

'This is Andrew,' June said.

'So, this is Andrew.' She let the sports bag drop and moved towards him, staring at the bulge in his knickers. She took hold of him through the silk and squeezed. He gave a gasp. 'Pain – or pleasure?' she demanded.

'Both,' he said.

'And when did you come last, eh?' She squeezed the head of his cock and he gasped again. This woman knew how to hurt and give pleasure at the same time.

He said weakly, 'This afternoon. I watched June –'

'Flogging herself?'

He nodded.

'Pull your knickers down!'

He obeyed, spreading his legs.

'Turn around!'

He obeyed again, and her hand ran over the welts on his behind. He twitched, watching June who stood silently watching the scene.

Audrey gave him a slap. 'All right, pull your knickers up, and kneel down.'

He sank to his knees.

Audrey turned away and moved close to June, putting her arms round her and kissing her full on the mouth. A hand smoothed up and down June's blue-skirted thigh. 'Well, my love,' Audrey breathed, loosening her lips, 'how's my severe policewoman tonight? Is she going to discipline me? Take me to the cells? Handcuff me to the wall, and –?'

'Tell me!' June said huskily. 'Tell me!'

'No, *you* must tell me!' Audrey's hand was under June's skirt now and Andrew could see the shape of it sliding upwards. 'I'm your victim tonight, and we have an audience, too.'

June moaned. Andrew knew where the questing hand had reached. He could imagine the feeling of wetness and heat . . .

Suddenly, Audrey said sharply, 'Into the bedroom! Both of you!' She pointed at the kneeling Andrew. 'You, on your knees!'

Audrey had her hand on June's back, guiding her to the door. Andrew, crablike, followed in their wake, the knicker elastic tugging voluptuously. A soft light shone from a room to the left along the corridor and Andrew shuffled towards it. He could hear vague sounds, soft groans, the telltale shuffling of things happening. Still on his knees, his kneecaps already sore under the knicker silk, he reached the doorway and froze. June was on her back on a Queen-sized bed, naked from the waist down, her skirt and panties on the floor. Audrey, her riding breeches and a pair of silk panties round her knees, was half-kneeling and burying her face between June's thighs.

June's head was towards the ceiling, her eyes closed and she was saying repeatedly, 'Do it! Do it! Tongue fuck me! I want it! I want it! I'm going to whip you – so make the most of it! I'm going to flog – ahh – flog you raw, you bitch! Oh, God! More, more! I'm – yes! – I'm – Oh. Christ! There, with your tongue! A little – yes, there! Jesus! Harder! Bite it! Fuck me! Fuck me!'

June convulsed in a tangle of arms and legs, a fury of completion. She let out loud rasping sounds and, incongruously, also broke wind. Andrew stayed where he was, transfixed. He'd never seen two women together before: nor two men, for that matter!

Audrey's head came up and from her lips dripped white orgasmic juices. She turned and looked at Andrew and ran her tongue around her mouth. 'This,' she said softly, but threateningly, 'is just the beginning! Crawl back to the lounge – crawl, mind! – open my bag and take out the riding crop, the one with the crystal handle, the leather strap and the chain with the gold heart. Bring it here!'

As he turned and swivelled on his sore knees, Andrew looked back. Audrey was greedily licking the insides of June's spread thighs and lowering her breeches and panties to her ankles.

In a misty numbness of unreality, Andrew started back down the corridor. Already, his buttocks were quivering in anticipation of what he imagined to be the next scene in this erotic theatre of fantasy steadily becoming reality!

He unzipped the bag and looked in. There were some silver chains bound in places with bright-red leather. He found a slim white box which he opened gingerly. Inside, on a bed of velvet, lay a black rubber dildo. It was circumcised and the head bulged. It must, he thought, have been at least eight inches long. It was thick, deadly looking, but at the same time almost pulsating with eroticism; and from the base curled satin, studded straps with gold buckles. He'd seen a dildo before, but nothing like this one. He closed the box and saw the gleaming haft of the riding crop. He pulled it out of the bag and stared. It was ornate; the grip sparkled. It was long and tapered to a leather tag. Attached to the handle was a gold chain with a heart attached. Without getting off his knees, he whistled the whip in the air and shuddered with excitement at the sound. He guessed that, beneath the polished, smooth erotic odour of the leather, there was whalebone or cane. Whatever, it could inflict punishment of a high order – and who was destined to receive the baptismal strokes? Because it appeared, as far as he could tell, that it had never been employed for what it had been designed and manufactured for.

Still on his knickered knees – the elastic had slid caressingly down – he grasped the whip, turned and made his painful way back along the corridor to the bedroom.

'You've been a long time! What have you been prying into?'

Audrey was naked, sitting on the edge of the bed, her breeches and knickers in a heap on the floor. Her nipples glowed; her skin glowed; her thighs were smooth and between them there was a hint, just a hint, of pubic hair. June was handcuffed to the rear bedrail, her arms stretched backwards. She too was naked, and her legs spread wide. She gazed at Andrew, but he could tell nothing from her expression.

'You can stand up! Hand me the whip!'

Andrew rose painfully, the skin on his kneecaps smarting – but what was that compared with what he anticipated? Audrey took the whip and made it whistle. June, in her bondaged position, gasped and gave Andrew another sharp glance which he was unable to interpret.

Audrey said, 'Take those stupid knickers off! Now, you're going to fuck June and I'm going to thrash you while you're doing it. She's orgasmed once, and you're going to make her orgasm again! You'll get that – that thing of yours into her; pretend you're raping her! I want to hear her groan, scream and screech! Make her suffer!'

138

Andrew shed the knickers, shaking off the elastic clinging to his feet, and moved to the bed. He stood over June, his cock jumping. She stared into his eyes, but said nothing. Awkwardly, he lowered himself on to her, wriggling for the right position.

She whispered, 'Let me.'

He felt a cool hand gripping his cock and guiding him.

'Move forwards . . . a bit more . . . now . . .'

Suddenly he was sliding into a juicy cavern.

'Slowly,' she whispered, 'not too hard at – first!' She gave a groan. 'NOW!'

At the same time, as Andrew slid further and further into this dark wonderland, the first sting of Audrey's crystal-shafted whip stung into his stretched bottom and over his thrusting hips. It was blackness, in a sense. But stars appeared and they seemed to coincide with the thrust of his love-making and the even, almost impersonal, lash on his buttocks. He thrust; the whip stung. He thrust more, and June groaned; the whip descended remorselessly. By now, his buttocks were afire, and so was his cock. He had to come; he'd kept it back for as long as he could – like someone dying to pee and searching desperately for somewhere to relieve himself – but the combination of the whipping and the searching, tingling probe of his cock between those heavenly, amorously gripping walls of greedy flesh was too much.

He ejaculated stunningly. A great surge from the base of his cock; it hurt with the strength and power of it! This wasn't the normal 'come' he'd experienced on his own! This was mammoth: he was scared by its scouring of the vein upwards to the head of his cock. He held his breath: then, the full flow, feeling as if it was tearing the slit apart; hot, stinging, and he emptied himself, thrusting, pushing, wanting to hurt?

The whip fell on his buttocks, but he didn't care. He lay pumping his life into her . . . and the whip fell and fell and fell.

'Stop!' It was a command.

He sank his head into June's breasts, warm and enclosing. He could feel her heart pounding. He wanted to stay as he was for all time: his cock still hot, and partly stiff, inside her. She'd made no move. Her head was to one side and it appeared that at least one eye was open, staring blankly at the curtains. It was as if the two of them were together, alone in their intimacy; but he was aware – was she, as well? – that behind them stood a woman with a poised whip.

What now, then? He heard a movement and felt the whip stroking his back gently. 'Are you through?'

'I – I think so,' he said. He had cramp in his calf and he turned his leg which pulled out his slackened cock on to his thigh. He felt the drip.

'Good! Get up!'

He did so slowly and glanced at her. Stony eyed, she studied him. She really was magnificent, he thought. Strong and tall. The light shone on her oiled thighs; her flat stomach and pink-nippled breasts. She tapped the crop on her bottom.

'You don't, for a moment, imagine that's it for this evening?'

'I hope not,' he said, feeling a little weak at the knees.

'Your *lover*!' She emphasised the word. 'Your lover! Look at her, handcuffed, her legs apart, "come" on her bush! Look at it, glinting in the light. She's had her pleasure – now, the sacrifice.' She looked at June. 'You understand, honey?'

To Andrew, the word 'honey' sounded out of place. It was more like the dialogue in an American sitcom. This was far removed from that! He knew, with a beating heart, what was about to happen.

140

'I – I understand,' June said faintly.

Audrey nodded curtly at Andrew. 'Here.' She gave Andrew a strange-shaped key. He stared at it puzzled. 'For the handcuffs!' she said scathingly. 'Release her!'

It wasn't easy. The key twisted in his wet hand and he had to turn it twice before the clasps opened and she was free. She lay on the bed rubbing her wrists which were red from the steel which had been biting into her.

Audrey leaned forwards. 'Hello, angel.'

June gave a slight smile. Andrew thought it was one of those enigmatic smiles he had seen before. How long had this been going on? It felt, already, like days. Surprisingly, he found he still had his watch on. In the dimness, the green, luminous hands pointed to a quarter-to-nine. Was that all? The same day? The tiny window on the watch face showed the date, denying his belief that more than 24 hours had passed.

June struggled to her feet. 'I've got to pee. I'm dying.'

'Do it on him!' Audrey said, giving a nod in Andrew's direction as he stood uncertainly, not knowing the script.

But, maybe, this was unrehearsed. He'd already gleaned that Audrey was a formidable figure in inventive sexual 'games', and could vary the scenario any way she wished.

To be peed on! Andrew's overworked cock nevertheless found new strength. He'd heard, of course, of 'water sports' but had, until initiated into the code, imagined water-skiing on Ruislip. He'd learned quickly that water sports meant that a man – or a woman – urinated on you as you lay naked, preferably in a bath. They stood above you, and emptied their bladder on to you and you sought with your lips the tang of salt and swallowed it eagerly. It had emerged from someone you adored! It had to be pure! Hard sports, he hadn't got into yet ... But, if the right person was there, he'd indulge gladly, his mouth open to receive its prize ...

Before he knew it, Andrew was forced into the bathroom and the ornate shower curtain swept aside.

'Get in, on your back!'

The porcelain was cold against his skin as he lay back. June appeared above him – it was rather dark because the bathroom had frosted windows – and she opened her legs and bent them slightly. He felt, rather than saw – except for maybe a sparkle – a pungent stream of liquid hit his eyes, making them sting. He raised his head a little, and now the gush was on his nose and mouth. He spread his lips and the strength and fire from her bladder surged down his throat.

'More!' Audrey urged thickly.

But she was done. A thin trickle, then nothing. She straightened, looking ahead at the tiled wall. He raised himself, soaking; his eyes smarting, his throat tasting lovingly of her bodily secrets; his cock thrusting. He grasped her thighs, warm thighs, and gently pulled her downwards to him. She put out a hand to steady herself as he thrust his face between her urine-smelling thighs and licked her juices like a parched man finding water in an arid desert.

Again, he lost all sense of time. The next thing he remembered was sitting naked on the cold surface of the leather couch. Opposite him, June was bent over, and Audrey, on her knees, was spreading her buttocks apart and licking her. He looked down at himself, limp between his thighs. Had he come, then? He couldn't recall. There was a half-full glass on the table in front of him and he picked it up and put it to his lips. It was vodka, neat, and he swallowed, still feeling the sting of June's urine on his tongue.

They were both naked, June bending obediently, her body at right angles, the light from the street picking out the curve of her breasts, and Audrey behind her, down low, gripping June's white thighs with fingernails that gleamed, her face pressed tightly between June's thighs. They murmured, each of them, individually, grunts of pleasure, animal grunts. He felt remote from it; as though he shouldn't be there witnessing a private ritual. He wondered if he was supposed to do anything. Having put the glass down, he began rubbing his cock and felt a spark of life.

Audrey, meanwhile, had turned June and pushed her down on to her back. She lay still, the shadows from the trees outside against the light looking as if they were thrashing her bent, wide-open legs, as Audrey crawled between them and began sucking, the sound loud in the room.

Andrew's cock rose in his hand. Without guidance, without prompting, he got up and stood over the engrappled pair, seeing only June's face turned to one side, and the gleaming back of Audrey curved as she sucked. Andrew brought his cock to full strength and began savagely to masturbate over the pair of bodies, which were beginning to writhe, twisting, groaning beneath him. The odour of sex was like incense.

Audrey raised her head. Her teeth gleamed wolfishly. 'Don't! Go in the lounge and get the box, the white box.'

'I know,' Andrew said, releasing his cock.

'Get it!'

He fled down the corridor and in the half-light felt for the box in the sports bag and pulled it out. He threw the lid aside and handled the huge dildo, the rubber cold and stiff in his hand. Not at all like his own cock which tilted upwards as he moved! God, he was close to letting go!

Back down the corridor to the bedroom. The scene had changed. June was now face down across the bed, legs wide.

Audrey stretched out a hand. 'Give it here!'

He handed over the dildo and watched as she expertly strapped the satin ribbons around her and between her legs. The black phallus stood menacingly tall. Audrey was breathing gaspingly as she bent over June and, without preamble, thrust the dildo into her. June gave a cry – but, whether of pain, ecstasy or both, Andrew had no idea. He was busy with himself.

Audrey panted as she thrust; June's fingernails clawed the bedcover. She was groaning gently to herself and muttering unintelligibly. Andrew, spell-bound, watched the scene. He wanted to come, but, again, he didn't. To prolong the swelling power was arousing in itself. He imagined, deep down in his balls, the workers pouring in creamy spunk: 'Fill her up, Harry, I reckon we're goin' to need the full measure this time!'

Now June's voice was audible. The words, jolting as Audrey worked the dildo, became louder. 'You bitch – you bitch! I'll get even with you! Cow! Wait 'til you've had enough . . . you're going to be flogged, dirty bitch!'

'Y-e-s!' Audrey breathed. 'Tell me – tell me! I want to be punished for fucking you! There! There! And – there!' She gave a huge thrust with her hips.

June clawed the bedcover, raking it with her nails. 'No!'

Slowly, ever so slowly, Audrey eased her hips away. For the first time, Andrew noticed scars on her buttocks. Faint, but unmistakably there. The dildo emerged with a 'plop' and it glistened enticingly as Audrey turned to him, holding it at the base.

'Lick it! Lick your mistress's come!'

Andrew slipped to his knees and took the slippery phallus in one hand. He opened his lips over it, tasting rubber and a tang of sexy salt. He sucked. Though it was a dummy cock, he nevertheless felt it was real in an odd way. It was, of course, still rigidly attached to Audrey and she sank back on the bed across June's buttocks to allow Andrew further egress.

'That's enough!' Audrey's words were like a whip-lash.

Andrew withdrew his mouth and licked his lips. Audrey was busily unstrapping the dildo, turning and allowing June to rise.

June gave Andrew a stare, a defiant stare. She pointed at Audrey. 'This woman has raped me! You're a witness! What – what do you think should happen to her? You saw how she ravaged me with that – that thing! Forcing it into me, no mercy! What mercy should I show her? Speak up! What are you – dumb?!'

Instinctively, Andrew said, 'She should be whipped?'

'Well done!' June said derisively. 'Get the hand-cuffs from the lounge. 'You!' She pointed at Audrey still spread across the bed. Andrew noticed stains on the dark-blue cover. 'You – get up and get ready for your punishment! You've had your pleasure; now I'm going to have mine!'

Andrew was still standing there, his cock rocketing.

'Well?' June demanded. 'What are you standing there for like a dumb, bloody idiot? Get the fucking cuffs!'

Andrew fled down the hall, his erection bouncing, found the handcuffs lying on a chair and returned swiftly to the bedroom.

Audrey was standing against a double wardrobe, legs spread, arms behind her back. June took the cuffs and manacled Audrey's wrists, pushing her arms up to the mid-section of her back. She stood, buttocks stiffened, silent. The room smelled to Andrew of sweat, and God only knew what else!

June snatched up Audrey's breeches and boots and pulled them on, zipping them fiercely. 'Bottom drawer,' she instructed Andrew, 'there!'

He slid open the drawer indicated. It was empty except for a black whip with curling knotted lashes – not unlike, he thought, one that he had bought himself! But this one had thicker lashes. He took it reverently by the grip and handed it to June. In the light, her breasts looked larger, firmer. She grasped the whip and ran her fingers through the lashes. Then she stepped back and sideways.

'Do it!' Audrey was whining. 'Do it! I deserve it!'

June pointed the whip threateningly at Andrew. 'Leave that cock of yours alone while I'm doing this! As far as you're concerned, the night's only just starting!'

Turning back, she swung the heavy lashes into Audrey's buttocks. 'Uhhh ...' It was an unreproducible sound torn from Audrey's lips. It was a shudder; a spasm. Her thighs rippled. June struck again; and again the animal grunt torn from deep within the handcuffed victim. Already Andrew could see fiery welts springing up against the pale flesh. He longed to jerk himself off, but resisted the temptation.

'Whip me! Punish me!' Audrey was moaning as June's accurate flogging fell in even stripes down to the inner curve of the twitching buttocks.

Watching, fascinated, Andrew was amazed how the moods between the pair of them could change. June the victim, then the aggressor; Audrey the aggressor, and now the victim! Where did he play his part? A feeling of fear mingled with excitement stabbed him:

he was at their mercy – unless he decided to find his clothes and leave. But leaving would be the end of it – the end of what, though? June was still whipping Audrey. God knows how many lashes she had been given! But, though she writhed, there was a grin on her face which was almost sinister. It was unreal!

Suddenly June stepped back, letting the whip lashes curl on the carpet. Apparently, Andrew thought, there had been some signal, known only to them. Audrey was moaning gently. Her behind glistened with sweat over the reddening welts.

Calmly, June said to Andrew, 'In the bathroom on the left, there's a white tube of cream on the shelf and flannel in the cupboard underneath. Fetch them!'

Andrew staggered – yes, staggered! – into the bathroom and found the tube and the flannel. His cock felt as if someone, unbeknown to him, had, at some point, poured molten metal into the slit. It was never going to shrink again! He couldn't remember the last time the thing had been a normal size!

He hurried back. Audrey lay face down on the bed. June was stroking her welted buttocks gently. She held out a hand, and Andrew gave her the tube and flannel. She squirted white cream on to the beige cloth and began wiping Audrey's bottom. 'There, there – is that better, my sweet? Just relax. My, you have had a whipping, haven't you? I wonder what cruel person did that to you? You must tell me sometime! There, there.'

Suddenly Audrey, knees drawn up, turned her body off the bed and rose to her full height. June put the ointment and flannel aside. Audrey gave a nod. Andrew looked to where the huge, moist dildo lay on the bed where it had been tossed. June dropped the whip to the floor. She slid off the knickers and breeches and, as skilfully as Audrey had done, strapped on the dildo. Andrew's heart thumped. He sensed he was about to be no mere spectator.

As if he wasn't there, they were discussing him. 'Well, he's got to be upright, otherwise –'

'I know, but the angle –'

'I can't get at him unless –'

'The ladder! We used it on –'

'Yes! What a good idea, oh, yes!' June turned to Andrew, looking him up and down. 'At the end of the hall, there's a cupboard and you'll find a ladder there, aluminium, or something. Bring it in here! Go on!'

Confused, Andrew did as he was told. The narrow door of the cupboard opened and he smelled the odour of hot-water pipes. The ladder gleamed, leaning to one side against the wall. It was taller than him, and he had difficulty, clutching it around the cold metal, in negotiating it round so that it pointed towards the bedroom. It wasn't heavy, but awkward. His mind was now a blank. His cock rubbed against one of the ladder's treads and he gasped. Then he piloted the thing carefully through the door, turned it slowly and held it upright with both hands. June, in her breeches and boots, bare from the waist up, stared.

Audrey, naked, glowing, imperious, said, 'Put it against the wall, there beyond the wardrobe. Angle it so that there's room for me to get behind it!'

He had no idea what she was talking about, but he leaned the top of the ladder against the plain piece of wall and drew the rubber-encased legs outwards until there was a four-foot gap between the ladder and the wall.

'That should be enough,' June said. 'All right, get against the ladder, facing it, and put your hands on the top tread.'

She moved to him, placed his wrists apart and snapped on the handcuffs. But that wasn't all. The next thing he knew, his ankles were being drawn apart and tied with some sort of rough material, jerked tight. What – what was going to happen now?

Audrey had gone on her knees and invaded the space between the wall and the legs of the ladder. She positioned herself, her mouth just inches away from Andrew's 'concrete' cock.

He heard June say, 'Damn! I've forgotten the KY.'

'Naughty,' Audrey said, with mock disapproval.

'I'll get it.'

Bound, Audrey's lips inches from him, Andrew wondered what KY was. Some sort of terrible implement of torture? He wouldn't be surprised!

As if reading his thoughts, Audrey said softly, 'It's cream. June's going to fuck up your behind and we need it to go in sm-o-o-o-t-h-ly. And I'm going to suck you off while she's doing it. Now, don't you think you're a lucky young man?'

Before he could answer, even if he'd been able to think of anything to say, he sensed June behind him. 'I'm just going to make it more pleasant for you. After all, it's all good fun, isn't it? Just relax.'

A hand pulled at one side of his buttocks and an icy-cold cream-covered finger sought for his anal opening. He remembered what that friend had said: 'It's like crapping – only backwards.' The finger penetrated further, exploringly.

'When did you dump last?' June asked.

The finger movement was exquisite. 'I – ah – oh, dump?'

Audrey's voice from below him. 'She means when did you crap!'

'Oh,' he said, trying to think – embarrassment was long a thing of the past! 'The day before yesterday.'

'So your arse is clean!' June's voice was harsh. 'It'd better be – if you shit on this thing, you'll lick it off!'

The finger was slowly withdrawn. Andrew's anus felt a mile wide; a truck could have been driven through it, not touching the sides! Then, he felt it: the thickness easing familiarly into him; taking its time, probing inquisitively. Then a thrust! At the same time, Audrey's lips closed over his erection. God, she could suck! As she sucked, so the entry into Andrew's behind gained strength. The twin feelings – in his behind and on his erection – were like nothing he could ever have dreamed of even in his wildest imagination. It was as if the whole core of his being was centred in those few vital inches between his bum and his cock! How long was this going on? Oddly, although he'd been bursting to come prior to this, now – although the ammunition was in the breach, so to speak – he didn't yet want to squeeze the trigger.

The room was silent apart from the sound of Audrey's sucking and the faint intakes of breath as June continued her exploration. He was totally re-laxed, now, letting them do as they wanted. How far could this thing go into him? Would it penetrate the obscure tangle of intricate intestines of which he knew nothing? Could it eventually emerge, tasting of rubber and whatever else, from his mouth? It seemed as if it was on the way, but then Audrey's tongue tickled the very tip of his knob and he could hold on no longer. Lifting his hips, he let the flood hit her tongue; felt it gushing; felt her teeth – molars? Incisors? Who cared! – biting him. Sharp pain, but good. He'd emptied himself.

For a while, time froze. He imagined being some-how an observer – himself strapped naked; June's lower half pressed against his buttocks; Audrey with his cock still far into her mouth. What an exhibition that would make if sculptured in marble and shown

– at a private viewing, of course! – at The Tate.
Worth thousands.

Audrey withdrew her mouth, leaving his cock
slackening, dangling. And, as if on cue, he felt June
ease out the dildo. Sweat stung his eyes, trickled
down his neck and gathered beneath his armpits. His
lips were like parchment. Every bone in his body
ached and, plus the soreness of his earlier punishment, his anal passage was afire. And yet ... Still
nobody said anything. A car revved up outside. If
only the driver knew!

At last – how long, seconds? Minutes? – Audrey
said thickly, 'I must wash out my mouth.' As she got
up, he heard bones crack. 'God – how long have you
been keeping that lot in there? You nearly choked
me!' She squeezed him as she crept out. 'But it was –
wonderful!'

He sensed she'd gone, and turned his head towards
June who was unstrapping the dildo. She looked at
him. 'Do you want to be untied?'

'I suppose I must,' he said. 'I'm dying to go to the
toilet –'

'Why don't you say you want to pee or piss? She
mimicked him: 'I'm dying to go to the toilet! How
refined!'

She released him. He smelled sweat. How did he
feel? He tested his legs and arms. They seemed to
move well enough. He sensed, even without feeling it,
that his behind was swollen. He stood uncertainly,
not quite sure what to do next. The script wasn't
written – or was it?

'I'm sorry.' She sounded contrite. He turned. She
sat on the edge of the bed dangling the straps of the
dildo which hung like something off a perverted
Christmas tree. It sparkled, too. 'Are you – do you
regret getting involved?'

'No!' he uttered vehemently. 'I wouldn't have missed it.' Sensing a new intimacy, he eased himself down on the bed beside her. A vein pulsed in her neck. He put a hand on her back and smoothed it up and down, the knobbly joints of her spine between his fingers. 'Is it – is it all over?'

She shook her head with what seemed like a resigned gesture. 'It's never over.'

He cleared his throat. 'What – what do you mean?'

'I don't, for Christ's sake, know what I mean!'

The toilet flushed and Audrey returned. Her pubic hair sparkled and she smelled of some kind of cologne or other. She said, 'Well, I don't know about anyone else, but I feel like some food! What's in the fridge, sweetheart? There's a bottle of white wine in my bag. Andrew, dear, would you fetch it and bring it down?' She was smiling, and she'd called him 'dear'.

He went along the corridor, his cock not quite down, and not quite up, and urinated gushingly. The urine smelled strong and it looked yellow and had bubbles around the edge. He flushed, washed his hands with soap, rubbed cold water over his face, and went, still naked, to get the bottle of wine.

He went down to the kitchen. They were there in silk-looking robes with dragon motifs. 'Can't you put something on? You look disgusting! Audrey said.

On the pale, pine-scrubbed table there was pink smoked salmon, lettuce, potato salad and soft rolls. To one side, there was a cream and chocolate gateau on a silver dish.

June replied, taking the bottle; 'He hasn't been here before! How the hell's he's supposed to know what to put on!'

Audrey, opening the wine expertly with a complicated-looking device which could well have

152

been used for some interesting forms of torture to various parts of the anatomy, said sneeringly, 'Oh, diddums! Is um fancy little boy?' Her tone sharpened. 'I've had his cock in my mouth – it's no big deal!'

June, looking at Andrew, said, 'In the spare room, there's a towelling robe, a blue one. Put that on. It's behind the door.'

He went out – scarcely able to believe he was still naked with a heavy cock weighted over his balls in front of these virtually unknown women! – and stood beside the door, listening.

'Why are you so hard on him?' asked June.

'You're a fine one to talk!' Audrey retorted. 'Take him to bed. I don't give a fuck! But, just one thing, I know you did me a big favour that time, but I think I've paid my dues. He's – well – yes, he's attractive, I'll admit that, but I thought the agreement was that neither of us would become attached, either way.'

'Attached? I don't know what you mean.' But June's voice held no conviction.

Andrew made his way upstairs, his brain buzzing. He found the robe and dragged it around him. What had started as, he imagined, a reasonably simple day, had turned into an erotic drug-induced dream. What had been in that first drink? They looked like two ordinary human beings! Friends, joined for a coffee and a cosy chat, maybe some Danish pastries . . .

'Come in,' June said, as he stood hesitantly in the doorway, aware that the robe bulged. 'Sit down.'

She indicated a seat to the right. Andrew lowered himself delicately. He was sore, without and within. Erotic. June made him a soft roll thick with smoked salmon. Lettuce, crisp and moist. Wine in a glass beside him. He drank. The others ate hungrily. Audrey's gown had slipped showing a bare shoulder; June was tightly wrapped. As she looked at him, he couldn't fathom the expression in her eyes. He was recalling the overheard conversation! 'Neither of us would become attached, either way.'

There was an old-fashioned-looking clock on the wall, round, with big Roman numerals black against a white porcelain face. The hands pointed to roughly five minutes after midnight. Midnight? Good God! His behind throbbed, but that cock of his was still on the make! It was rising, his balls tight as an unripe orange.

He heard himself say, 'I suppose I'd better think about going.'

Audrey gave a chuckle which turned into a cough. She glanced at June and said, 'Going? I'm going to whip you, my boy! That's where you're going! Upstairs into the spare room. It's cold, and there's a bare bedframe with a wire base. We're going to tie you down and thrash you with a cane and a whip, each of us, together.'

'No,' June said quietly.

'No?' Audrey was staring at her.

'No,' June repeated. 'I'll whip him. This is personal.'

'I see!' Audrey breathed. 'Well, I might as well leave you two together then!'

She got up, the robe loose, swinging away from her hips, her torso bare, the curve of the belly and the dark smudge.

'No,' June said once more. Her mouth was set.

Andrew's cock was now on full alert. He drank slowly, watching them.

June went on, 'You'll watch – and then you'll watch him fuck me! And you'll be tied.'

Audrey gave a sigh. 'As I wanted! As I wanted! Oh, God, yes – and I'm helpless?'

'Helpless,' June confirmed levelly. She looked at Andrew, her eyebrows raised, and a tingle ran up his spine. 'Do you agree? I'll flog you severely and then you can fuck me – and fuck me hard! With your cock! I've had it once with rubber – now I want it for real! Well?'

He could barely speak, but finally managed to say, 'Yes, anything.' His cock pinged. God, who cared about the time of day – or night! 'Will you wear those – those knickers while you flog me? Please?'

'We'll see,' June said and got up.

'Those knickers,' he insisted.

Now, all three were on their feet. June poured wine into each glass. Andrew noticed how steady her hand was.

'You have no rights!' Audrey barked.

'Shut up, you!' June said, then turned to Andrew. 'Take that robe off and get upstairs! The room next to where we've been.'

Andrew dropped the robe on to the back of a kitchen chair and, holding his cock steady – it seemed to have grown fatter! – he climbed the stairs and entered the room June had indicated. It was a curtainless room but with frosted windows. In the centre on an uncarpeted floor stood a bedbase with metal springs zigzagging across it. The iron rails at each end were embraced with leather straps. A freestanding, full-length mirror with imitation dull-coloured beading leaned against one wall. Opposite the bed was a double-doored wardrobe, the doors dingy and scratched. But Andrew noticed at each corner, top and bottom, were heavy brass hooks screwed into the thick, double-spliced doorframes.

He stood silently, cold, shivering, and smoothed his cock gently as he heard voices coming closer up the stairs. Audrey and June entered the room, both now naked. But June dangled a pair of long-legged knickers in one hand, while in the other she clutched the knotted whip.

June put the whip down and drew the knickers up, adjusting the elastic at the top of her kneecaps. The heavy double-gusset hung enticingly between her thighs. She turned to Audrey. 'Get yourself in position!'

Audrey stood with her back to the wardrobe and spread her arms and legs. Wrists and ankles were level with the brass hooks. Andrew, standing obediently, assumed this was something that had been done perhaps many times before.

June left the room and returned with four, short, yellow straps with buckles. She said to Andrew with a slight smile, 'You know what these are? They're execution straps. In the days of capital punishment, the executioner and his assistant would strap the victim's wrists and ankles, and he was placed on the trapdoors of the gallows, a hood over his head, the rope around his neck and then – bang! He was gone! Imagine how many doomed to die have felt these tight around them? I bought them at an auction – depraved, aren't I?' She moved to Audrey. 'Now, you're going to have them around you and you'll watch the whipping. But more . . .'

From within the waist of her knickers she produced a cream, plastic vibrator with a rounded, knurled base. Andrew had seen them in sex shops. 'Hold this!' she said to Andrew, handing it to him.

He took it gingerly. June was busily strapping Audrey spread-eagled to the front of the wardrobe, her legs wide apart. She was grunting softly.

'Give me that!' June stretched out a hand for the vibrator and Andrew handed it over. With an almost surgical precision, June thrust it between Audrey's thighs, easing it upwards. Audrey's head was back, her eyes closed, lips apart. 'In?'

Audrey nodded.

'Low power,' June said, 'it's going to take some time!'

'No, no! Please!' Audrey was twisting her head from side to side, flexing her thighs.

'Low power,' June said, and turned the base clockwise.

A buzzing broke the silence. Audrey twisted and turned.

June turned to Andrew. 'Get face down on the bed, now!'

It was awkward, but he managed it. The criss-crossed metal was sharp and cold beneath him, but somehow his cock had found an opening between the wire and thrust itself through. It was gripped tightly – as tightly as his wrists and ankles were being bound. He was stretched like elastic – like the elastic of June's knickers? – and thus his erection was pulled savagely to one side. But he could still move it vertically, and experimented gingerly. It felt as if he was having sex with the pussy of a robot.

Audrey was moaning. June took the mirror and placed it against the wall, adjusting it with, what seemed to Andrew, long practice. How many others had been on their faces, awaiting the first lash?

'Can you see?' June asked.

He could. The clever angle showed himself looking at his reflection, his naked body laid bare behind him. He could see Audrey spread-eagled on the wardrobe door, eyes open now. The whirring of the vibrator like a trapped wasp exploring a windowpane. Then June appeared in the mirror, running the lashes of the whip through her fingers. She stepped back and brought it down. It made the buzzing of the 'wasp' almost non-existent with its sound of delivered leather on flesh. Hurt? Of course! Pleasure? Indescribable!

'Flog me!' he heard himself saying. 'Punish me!'

As she whipped, as the 'wasp' buzzed, and as Audrey moaned, he gently began to move his cock within the confines of the metal springs. Suddenly, he wanted to pee! And he wanted to come! God, he'd been ready it seemed for hours, but, as June flogged him, his bottom was on fire and he had to release *something*! He let go. It wasn't spunk – it was a different itch – it was urine, hot, strong smelling, splashing to the floor beneath him.

'You dirty bastard!' June said, panting, and laid the whip hard again. 'You'll clear that up!'

A gasp from Audrey. 'Make – make him lick it! God, darling, please . . . turn this goddam thing up. I want to come!'

'Not just yet,' June said. 'I'm giving him thirty more! God, his pee stinks! It's like a bloody farmyard!'

She whipped on. Andrew, having emptied his bladder, felt no relief. The pain in his balls and his cock had, if anything, increased. He could feel it at the base, gathering, ready for a surge upwards like a released stopcock. (Good word!) He let himself accept the whip, relaxing; he glanced up and could see Audrey and June, her knicker silk twisting and shuddering as she flogged.

He could hold on no longer. It was like relieving himself but, on the other hand, not the same at all. The spunk seemed to be squeezed out of him like toothpaste: he imagined a continuous, snaky curl of come, as it dropped from his tip to join the urine below. What a combination! The strokes had ceased.

He managed to turn his head. June had dropped the whip and turned to Audrey. She turned the base of the vibrator: the single buzz of the 'wasp' became an angry hum. She turned it again, higher. Audrey gave a screech – there was no other word. The vibrator shot out of her like a bullet from a gun, to be followed by what looked to Andrew like a spurt of colourless liquid. She was thrusting her belly and hips out.

'Oh Christ – Oh my God in heaven! Jesus! Aahh.' She slumped, hanging, her head to one side.

Andrew's cock was having difficulty in subsiding. The problem was that, in moving during his whipping, he had somehow crushed the crosswires together. His cock was imprisoned and, though it was doing its best to shrink, it was still unable to withdraw.

He could see in the mirror that Audrey was being released. June steadied her as she stumbled. 'Go into the bedroom,' June said. 'I'll deal with this.'

'Thank you, darling.' Audrey shuffled out of sight.

June appeared in vision. Her knickers were down more one side than the other. The elastic of one leg was over her kneecap, the other halfway up her thigh. He stared.

'You've made a mess,' she said.

He nodded. At last, his cock had shrivelled enough to allow it to escape. His behind was swelling; he could tell.

'You should lick it up, your pee and your come,' she said.

'If you want.' Although he'd come and his cock was flaccid, he was still oddly aroused. Challenging? Make her order him to get on his knees and lick!

After a pause, she said, 'You've had enough. I think we all have. Here . . .'

She unstrapped him. His wrists and ankles were sore along with what seemed to be every other part of him. When he pulled himself upright, supporting himself on the cold edge of the bed, he looked down. His cock had angry red rings around the pale flesh.

He turned towards the mirror. His behind was scarlet: it glowed in the dim light as he did himself! He felt proud.

'Was I good?' he asked.

She was close beside him, her head level with his shoulder. He reached down and smoothed her knickered thigh, touching the rim of the tight elastic. How long had it been since that – what was her name? Hilda? – had wanked him off while he snapped her bloomer elastic?

'You were good!' She lowered the waist of her knickers and guided his hand between her thighs. The hair was soaking. She took a finger and helped him into the comforting warmth. 'Fuck me!' she whispered.

'But I've just –' he began.

'Use a second finger,' she whispered again. And she took the second finger of his right hand, pushing into the moistness to join his index finger. 'Wouldn't you like to be in there? You can do it! I'll make you hard . . .'

With that, she kneeled and took him in her mouth. He felt ashamed: it was so small, so insignificant looking. He stood meekly. Her tongue worked; her lips worked. She clasped his raw bottom with both hands and pressed him towards her. And then – my God! He was starting to grow; in her mouth! It was getting upright again and her tongue worked more furiously. Now it was upright, ready for action.

She slipped her mouth away and lay back, legs open. 'Fuck me!'

It wasn't difficult once he had positioned himself. She started him off, but his cock needed no encouragement. He slipped in, and in, and in. How far could he go?

It was like the dildo earlier on – but how much earlier? Last week? Last month? Last year?

She was whispering, her nails raking his wounded buttocks: 'Fuck me! Fuck me!'

He began to move exploratively, easing his way; he felt something – a ridge? He moved over it into the darkness.

'Yes!' she was breathing. 'Yes!'

Instinctively he began to thrust, not too hard at first, judging his speed by her clawing fingernails. 'Yes! Now! Now! Fuck me!' In, in hard – an itch; a flood from his shaft; muscles jerking . . .

'Yes! Oh, Christ! Yes!'

Her own muscular walls gripped him, squeezing hard. He'd emptied himself. He was barren like a reservoir in a heatwave. Should he move? He knew his knees were pressed against her thighs. Her belly, on his, pulsated.

She raised her head slightly in the dimness and kissed him gently on the lips. 'Roll off.'

He didn't care for the expression; it sounded too familiar. But he 'rolled off' her hip and lay on his back, his cock flopping tiredly against his left upper thigh, as if to say: 'Well, I've done my bit for today, no more.'

She scrambled to her feet. He turned and looked at the glinting pool beneath the barren bed. 'I'll clear it up,' he said and pulled himself upright.

God! He felt punished! But still he craved for humiliation. 'Make me – make me get on my knees and – lick!'

She stood above him, strong, with authority. 'I can't make you.'

'I want to grovel,' he said. 'Order me!'

'Very well! Get down and lick that mess! I want to see that floor clean, gleaming!'

He stooped, his cock flopping between his thighs. He began licking the pool. There seemed so much! On the surface of the yellow urine, white glints darted.

His come! He sucked the moisture, tasting not only the arousing salty taste within his lips, but also the scrape of his tongue across the wooden floorboards.

Her knickers dropped beside him. 'Mop up with these!'

'I'd rather wear them,' he said.

'Very well. Mop up and then put them on!'

He took them and began rubbing them across the floor. They soon became stained and bedraggled. Eventually, the floor glistened. He stood up and pulled the knickers on. They were heavy with wet but he got them up over his knees, up to his waist; they were damp and clung to his thighs like wet sails. He spread his legs. Though his cock was now down, he wanted to feel the wet silk against it, and he rubbed the sore shaft, clutching himself through the knickers. The smell of urine rose in the room. It excited him. His own pee! And his come! But this time there was no response. He remained limp and he let the knickers drop to his ankles and kicked them off.

He didn't know how long after that he left. He remembered coffee in thick mugs with a taste of brandy. He was dressed again, underpants and everything, his buttocks sore and swollen – he'd managed to glance at himself in the mirror in the bathroom – his cock smarting.

He wanted to walk. The tree-lined road cast deep shadows. There was a distant sound of sirens. He felt elated. She'd given him the soaking knickers, pressing them into his hand. Audrey, she said, was asleep. They'd be in touch through Hilda. She kissed him and squeezed his cock.

In the shadows of an unlit street, he removed his trousers and underpants, and slipped on the knickers. He watched his jerking shadow on the pavement as he masturbated . . .

6

Tales to be Told – Confessions!

The sexual psychologist was an attractive woman of around thirty-five to forty. Neat hair, a white blouse showing substantial breasts beneath what looked like a stiff brassiere. When Hanley entered the lofty-ceilinged room on the first floor of the private hospital hidden discreetly away in the Sussex countryside, and shrouded, from the passing parade, by thick pine and tall plane trees, she had stood to welcome him.

Her black skirt was tight along her hips and thighs. She wore thick-rimmed glasses. 'Welcome!' she said, advancing and holding out her hand. Her grip was strong. She motioned him to a tall-backed chair in front of the desk and sat in her own swivel, leather, chrome-armed chair behind her desk. She had a folder in front of her, open. She glanced down briefly then removed her spectacles. Immediately, Hanley felt, her whole face changed. She looked incredibly younger! His groin stirred.

An intercom buzzed beside the two pale-blue phones on the desk. She snapped a button. 'Yes?'

An inaudible screech through the box: '. . . needs . . . argh!' Crackle.

She said, 'I don't care who it is. Tell Dr Mace I'm with someone and will be for the next hour or so –'

she glanced briefly at Hanley '– and I don't wish to be disturbed! If there's a problem, refer them to the standby – what's her name? Maureen? – but don't interrupt again!'

She snapped the button up and sank back in her chair. 'It's amazing. They come to me with all their problems, most of them totally uninteresting and banal! I'm Dr Barnes, Stephanie Barnes.'

Hanley was getting an erection. He had tight underpants on, but his groin was working overtime and the result flooded into the shaft of his cock. Hurting. He said, 'I hope you don't find my problem uninteresting and – banal?'

She put her glasses on again and consulted the folder, turning a page. Hanley noticed no rings on her fingers, but she wore a masculine-looking watch with a black-and-white dial, strapped to a heavy bracelet around her wrist. She went through the ritual with the glasses again and slipped the hook of one earpiece into the corner of her mouth. 'So, you're a masochist.'

She looked away and studied the furthest wall which was covered in charts and sellotaped sheets of what looked like timetables or something. Hanley crossed his legs. Her every move seemed to give him an electrical jolt, as though, somehow, he'd been connected to the mains without his knowledge!

He could just see, over the top of the desk, her skirt around the tops of her knees. No hint of anything . . .

'I – I guess I am,' Hanley admitted, meeting her eyes.

'It's odd. I've met many men who admitted to being masochistic, but only one woman . . . and she was sixty-five, would you believe!'

His senses were alerted. Sixty-five – that was even older than Harriet, or so he imagined!

She did the glasses routine again, but studied the folder longer. Finally, she pushed the glasses down her nose and stared at Hanley over the rims. 'It seems . . . well, it seems that you belong to part of a group who indulge, shall we say, and discuss masochistic practices. And you're suddenly worried. Why?' She frowned at him, eyebrows down.

'Tell me about the woman – the sixty-five-year-old,' he asked. God, he was paying enough for her time and attention!

'What do you want to know?' The glasses were off again, dangling between two fingers.

'Well, I mean – what did she want?' He liked the growing intimacy of the conversation – before long, he'd be asking what sort of knickers she wore! And he didn't necessarily mean the old woman's, although that was a thought to keep in mind.

She stared at him. There was – or did he imagine it? – a slight smile at the corners of her lips. 'She'd been, as a nine-year-old, in a gulag in Siberia. She'd been ravished; she'd seen her mother flogged repeatedly; she'd seen her father hanged slowly in public; she became obsessed. Punishment was the only way she knew to get release. Her mother died. Under a repatriation scheme funded by UNESCO, she was sent to a convent in Somerset. There, she experienced more pain – pupils were caned for minor irregularities, if their bloomers were pulled up too tight –'

'Their bloomers?' Hanley interrupted. His shaft throbbed.

She shook her head with a gesture of irritabilty. 'Navy, elastic knickers! Classic schoolgirl underclothes! Where have you been?' She sighed and threw the glasses on to the green blotter. 'Anyway, we're here to discuss you – not anybody else. She wants what she wants, and she gets it! And not under the

National Health, either! She pays privately. We've tried to counsel her, but she takes no notice. Some of our – er – patients are like that; they don't want to be cured, if that's possible; they just want to talk.' She paused. 'Mental masturbation!'

Hanley tried to gather his thoughts. 'I, well, I was just interested. I've been the way I am since I was fifteen or so –'

'And now you're forty-five –' she peered myopically at the file '– nearly forty-six. So what's the problem? You like a whipping, yes? You like humiliation, yes? What do you want – a miracle cure?' She leaned forwards, elbows on the desk. 'Or, like the rest of them, do you just want to mentally masturbate? Go ahead! The toilet is two doors down on the right; lock yourself in and do it – and then go home! But, if you're serious, you can be cured: but it's painful and it might not work. I've known it not to –'

'What percentage?' Hanley asked, his throat layered in phlegm.

'Success? Minor! We're privately funded. If we take on a case – and they can pay – they're given every opportunity to undergo aversion therapy, but it costs. We have to bring in specialists. Each case is considered on its own merits. If we don't think you can be cured – for want of a better word – then your fee will be refunded. But, I have to warn you, even if you pay and you don't want to be, as we say, cured, we'll know and we'll take your money! Down the corridor, there is a full-scale replica of a punishment room in a prison of the early nineteen hundreds. It's cold; it has stone walls, iron bars and in the centre is a whipping post, bolted firmly to the floor. For your first test – if you agree to go ahead – you will be taken there, told to remove your clothing and you will be tied and flogged. A doctor will be present to note your, um,

166

sexual reaction to the whipping – which, I promise you, will be severe. If you show signs of arousement – and you know very well what I mean by that – the flogging will cease, and you'll be made to make yourself ejaculate before the flogging continues. If you sustain the fifty or so strokes after your – er – completion, you will be required, each day, twice a day, to masturbate in front of witnesses and then be conducted to the punishment room for further flagellation. Each day, the number of strokes will be increased until –'

'Until?' Hanley was soaking. He didn't know whether he wanted to urinate or spill his seed.

'You either pass a psychological test to convince a panel that you no longer wish to be punished – or you're sent on your way. You will, of course, have to sign a waiver agreeing to no refund whichever is the case.'

Hanley pondered. He knew, of course, which alternative he was going to take. His belly flooded with warmth. 'Do you –?'

She understood the question. 'No. The punishment is done by specially selected women.'

'But surely that defeats the object of the exercise!' Hanley countered. 'I mean, a woman flogging a man – he's bound to get –'

'But,' she reminded him gently with a conspiratorial smile, 'you'll have shot off – as I believe the saying goes!'

'Well, it's one of them,' Hanley said with a grin.

She remained straight faced. 'Of course, I have to know much more about you.' She waved a negligent hand over the file in front of her. 'This doesn't tell me anything like as much as I need to know.'

'What sort of things?' Hanley asked. His scrotum throbbed.

'For instance, do you have a fetish or fetishes? I assume you know –'

'Yes, I know all about fetishes!' Hanley tried to keep sharpness from his voice – but what did she think he was? Some kind of amateur for Christ's sake!

'And?'

'Knickers,' Hanley said.

'Well, that's not unusual . . .'

'I mean,' Hanley said, 'long ones: bloomers, directoires, pantaloons, whatever you like to call them – but they have to stretch to the knee!'

'On you?'

'And whoever's doing whatever they're doing.'

'Why? Why those? I mentioned, er, elastic schoolgirl knickers a little while ago. I noted something. Are they part of the fetish?'

'No,' Hanley said. God, he wanted to come! 'They're too short; they don't stretch down far enough.'

Her chin came up. 'And how do you know that?'

'I guessed – even if girls have to wear them, they're going to be pulled up short.' He imagined fat little thighs banded with navy-blue or bottle-green knickers!

'Supposing I told you that I know a school where the girls have to wear their navy knickers long, an inch above the knees?'

Hanley shrugged. 'I'm not a paedophile. I'm interested in the adult kind, the sort you get in old-fashioned women's underwear shops. Big ones, size twenty-eight.'

'And you have some, of course?' She was making notes.

He laughed briefly. 'A dozen or more pairs! I like them new, crisp, straight out of the wrapper. If I have

168

to wash them, they're limp, no excitement, and the elastic round the knees is never tight enough.'

'Do you wear any other items?' She was scribbling hard.

'Sometimes,' he said, 'maybe stockings, and a suspender belt; nothing up top – I'm not a breast man!'

'And how did you realise the fascination – shall we say – of these sorts of knickers?'

The word from her gave an added leap to his straining cock. Knickers! Knickers!

'My mother wore them,' he said. 'I saw a pair airing on one of those clothes-horse things. It was the way the legs dangled down to the elastic. I had to try a pair on – one afternoon when my mother was out.'

'How old were you?' Still writing busily.

'Sixteen – it was just after my birthday.'

'So you decided to give yourself a present! Go on!'

'Well, I stripped, and pulled a pair on. I got them from her dressing table. I pulled them up, and the elastic caught my kneecaps. I stood in front of her mirror, gloating at how stupid I looked –'

'Just a minute –' her pen poised '– you wanted to look stupid?'

Hanley shook his head, remembering . . . a quite summer afternoon; the curtains drawn in his mother's bedroom, intimate. He swallowed hard. 'I – I knew I was doing something wrong. A friend at school had told me he dressed in his mother's underwear when she was out. But he – he put the lot on – a brassiere, corset, stockings and knickers as well as a petticoat.'

'And?'

'Well, he masturbated.'

'Must have been difficult with a corset on!' She was rubbing the rather expensive-looking, gold-banded pen along her lower lip.

'I don't know. We didn't go into that kind of detail.' Hanley was desperately uncomfortable; hot and throbbing. Telling this stranger – attractive stranger – his intimate thoughts – along with what she had told him already about procedures at the clinic, had induced a fierce lust to be humiliated. He wished he was tied in the chair, bound by wrists and ankles. He managed to say, 'He didn't get caught; he was careful.'

'But you wanted to be caught – by your mother – wearing her knickers? And what do you imagine she would have done?' She was writing again.

'I suppose,' he said slowly, 'I would have liked her to punish me . . . with a cane – that would have been appropriate.'

'Why didn't you let her? After all, you were in her bedroom in her things; it would have been easy for you to stand there, listening for her key in the door. Stood there – and taken the consequences.'

'But, I couldn't be sure what she'd do! She'd never laid a hand on me before – how was I to know whether she'd do what I wanted! I didn't even know if she had a cane, which I doubted.' Hanley stared at her as she looked up, the glasses in her hand, but not along her ears, studying him.

'So you didn't let her catch you?'

'No, I was surprised she didn't realise, though.' Hanley surreptitiously unstuck his underpants from the tip of his cock. 'I mean, after I'd used them, I always folded them in the same way and put them back in the drawer. I never –'

'Ejaculated into them?'

'No,' he said.

She put her glasses firmly on her nose and turned a page of the folder. 'Your father died when you were two-and-a-half?'

Hanley nodded.

'So she brought you up on her own?'

'More or less.' Hanley wasn't going to mention the aunt just yet – one matter at a time!

'She never thrashed you?'

'No.'

'Never spanked you?'

'No.' Hanley hesitated. 'But from somewhere I had this – this idea of her taking my trousers and underpants down – it was important that she did it – and making me put myself across her while she spanked me with her hand.'

'It was important that she took your trousers and pants down?' The pen was busy again. 'Why?'

'I've thought about this a lot,' Hanley said carefully, 'and I think it was the intimacy of her, my mother, taking my clothes down, seeing me, you know, and putting me across her lap.'

'Spank, spank, spank!'

'Yes.' He nodded.

'And then?' She turned a page.

'Well, I'd have liked to make myself orgasm, come in front of her.' Hanley stretched. His balls were on fire.

'To add to the humiliation of being found with her things on?'

'Yes.'

'And after having her cane you?'

Hanley acknowledged with a bow of the head.

'So you sought a mother figure who would fulfil your fantasies?' She turned back a page and frowned. 'You mentioned an aunt in your original submission.' (He liked that word! Imagining himself prostrate before her as she measured her distance with a birch! Please! Flog me! Hurt me!)

Gathering his thoughts, he said, 'That was different

– it's not part of what we're talking about right now –'

'Of course it is!' Her voice had an edge. (Go on, tell me to take my trousers down and bend over the desk – six of the best!) 'It's all important, every single aspect of this. You may be of some importance to our research.' She looked up briefly with an inimical smile and then began writing again. 'If you hadn't wanted to mention the aunt, why did you do so?' Pen poised.

'I – I don't know,' he admitted. (Go on! Six isn't enough! Twelve . . . eighteen . . . as many as you like!)

'There's no point in withholding information,' she said. 'Everything is important. You won't realise it, but it is.' (Go on, another six, and make them hard!)

'I'm sorry.' Meek. Submissive. He could feel the sting of the cane! He stretched his legs, aware that his crotch bulged.

From that angle he couldn't be sure if she could see that far down, but he stayed as he was. His cock might be crooked for ever after, the way it was bent right now in protest at its unwelcome confinement . . .

She ran a finger along the page of the folder. 'You say you're a writer and you work for yourself?'

Hanley nodded. He wasn't about to give away the fact that he was a journalist! That would have put the kibosh on the whole thing!

'What do you write?'

'Oh,' he said, flexing his imaginative powers, 'politics, social things – boring really.'

'And do you make a living at it?'

'Not too bad,' he said, 'it varies. I – I wrote a novel once –'

'About your particular obsession?'

He tried a grin, very unconvincingly, he suspected. 'No! No! Far from it. It was a, well, a kind of romance, I suppose. It was published, but the royalties were nothing to speak of.' He eased himself painfully.

She stood up suddenly and glanced down at him. She saw. She knew. His crotch was practically cracking at the seams!

'Hmm.' It was a non-committal sort of 'hmm'. He could tell nothing from it. He waited for her to tell him to stand up, but she passed behind him and he turned his head to see her staring at a complicated-looking chart on a bulletin board to which were already attached a good number of yellow message slips. He admired her behind in the tight, black skirt. It was just right: not too rounded and not too thin, either. He imagined the curve of her panty elastic over the swell, but could see no visible VPL.

'I think,' she said, swivelling abruptly and facing him, 'we'll start you off with our film archives.'

She approached and put one half of her behind on the edge of the desk, facing him, arms crossed over that firm bosom. Her skirt hadn't ridden above the knees – it was too well cut – but the curve of her thighs beneath made it impossible for him to keep his eyes away.

Clearing his throat, he asked, puzzled, 'Films? But –'

'Archive film,' she broke in, 'smuggled out of Germany after the war; records of the treatment of prisoners in Ravensbruck concentration camp, which was not, as you may or may not know, a death camp. It was reserved exclusively for prisoners who had offended the State, oh, not just reactionary Germans who abhorred the Nazi Party, but guerrilla fighters, French, Dutch, Belgians, Poles, who had been caught sabotaging. It was a labour camp. Men and women worked from six a.m. to eight p.m. They worked, – God knows why! – on rock quarries, breaking up stones into powder with heavy sledgehammers. If they weren't putting enough effort into it, guards on duty would use a horsewhip to goad them on. Many were weak. They had thin, cabbage soup and bread, usually mouldy. "Ersatz" coffee, or so called, made of black beans, sour and unmilked. And corporal punishment was the order of the day!'

She paused, looking down at him from her perch. 'That excites you? The idea of a whipping?' She recrossed her legs, one bouncing on her knee. Hanley noticed her fingers gripping her arms. The knuckles were white.

He shrugged. All the time he was seeking to see what was above the enticing edge of that black skirt! 'I – I only know from my own experience.'

'Sexual!'

'Yes, sexual!'

He wasn't going to see anything under that skirt, so he might as well give up trying. He switched his eyes to her face.

She leaned forwards slightly, arms still folded. 'Well, what you're going to see isn't sexual at all! It's suffering inflicted by sadists – some of them women who were hanged after the Nuremberg Trials for crimes against humanity! Himmler, who was the Chief of the SS –'

'A chicken farmer,' Hanley said derisively, determined not to be left out.

'A chicken farmer! Did you know that this – this chicken farmer collected women's pubic hair from his victims? That he fainted at the sight of blood. But revelled in seeing the sixteen-mill films of the floggings and other forms of torture – as long as they were shown in black-and-white?'

Hanley shook his head, not meeting her eyes. Was this some kind of test? 'I didn't know that.'

She gave a contemptuous snort. 'You people, you think physical pain is fun – a turn-on! Your mock punishment rooms! Your humiliation ... knickers! But you can stop it at any time! Imagine those who can't say "that's enough!"; who have to endure the agony of being flogged by monsters whose lust is only satisfied by the intense suffering of those whom they're punishing! Do you know what being "flogged to the bone" means? It meant the victim was whipped until, literally, the backbone showed where the flesh had been thrashed away, layer by layer! And then, still hanging helpless, they were machine-gunned! You say you want to be cured of your addiction? Well, you're going to see these films in all their graphic detail and you'll be wired to a machine which will record your reactions. Your genitals, heart and breathing will be taped and the results, in order of the scenes you're going to witness, will be monitored.'

Hanley shifted again. 'But you said I'd be whipped.'

'And so you will be, no fear of that!' She slid upright, the skirt tight. 'Get up.'

He struggled to his feet not trying to hide his erection. She pressed a button on the intercom.

A harsh voice said, 'Yes?'

She said, 'I'm sending the new patient down. Show him everything.'

She flicked the key. 'Take a left out of here and go down the corridor. Two doors down you'll see a door with a thick grille. Press the button beside it and you'll be admitted. The code is Jay-haitch-one. Remember it!'

Hanley's stomach turned. He was at the same time excited and in fear. But the excitement overcame the fear. 'Will I see you again?'

'You most assuredly will! Now, off you go – and, by the way, you'll be required to strip naked.

That –' she gave a nod towards his crotch '– will be taped along wih the rest of you. We'll see if it's still in that state after the next hour-and-a-half.' She leaned towards him decisively. 'You people with your little clubs! A little masochism! A little sadism – oh! ever so gentle; everyone allowed to whine: "No, stop! Please stop!" But you're going to see the real thing: not play-acting! Not getting a hard-on with dangling whips or weird underclothes! These people you're going to see had no ideas of sexuality! They were in fear of their lives: some scared to die; others scared to live and face more torture! You – you people, I'm sure you have the Nazi insignia – the uniforms, badges and the rest!'

Hanley felt he had to interrupt and broke in tentatively. 'No, we don't go in for – for that sort of thing, honestly!' Absurdly, he felt he was pleading. Pleading!

She curled her lip. 'Don't you? What is it, then – religion? Self-flagellation? The whipping of Christ before his crucifixion? Come on!' She turned away with a swing of her hips. 'Anyway, I don't propose at this time to continue this conversation.' She jerked her head. 'Two doors down.'

Hanley hesitated. He wanted to say something, but he knew not what. Was this part of the build-up? To make him feel guilty? Cheap? Nasty? But his group had never even considered Nazi atrocities! They met because they enjoyed a certain amount of pain, humiliation, listening to stories and relieving their sexual frustrations in their own various ways.

He left the room and closed the heavy door. In the corridor, the silence was like a buzz in his ears, almost palpable. Then he noticed that the door he had just closed had a heavy lining of soundproof taping around its edges. The silence was profound, unnerv-

ing. He leaned against the pale wall of the corridor
and tried to organise his thoughts which were scattered like leaves in an autumn gale. He was still hard,
and aching. It would be something to go into this –
this – wherever he was going, have to strip and ...
He tried desperately to think of something which
might swamp the sexual feelings. At school, he
remembered, when he had an erection in class, a
friend and he used to masturbate each other. The
friend told him when he was hard at an awkward time
to 'think about something "horrible"!'

He'd said, 'I think about sucking my granny off!
That sends the old wanger down, believe me!'

But that was a long time ago, and Hanley had
never thought of 'sucking his granny off'! Still hard,
he slid along the corridor and stood opposite the
second door. Yes, it had a grille, and, yes, there was
a bell-push beside it. He hesitated; then, grasping his
cock through his left trouser pocket, he crossed the
corridor and pressed the bell. He noticed that this
door, too, was heavily taped around the edges. He
sensed, rather than saw, that he was being surveyed
through the grille. Then, with a buzz, the door
opened and he stepped into a room dimly lit from a
single anglepoise lamp to his left. It stood on a desk
upon which was a projector, a shadowy figure seated
behind it. Ahead was a white screen on a three-legged
stand. There were a row of seats – sofas, armchairs?
he couldn't tell – but he was confronted by two
figures in long, white gowns; heads covered with
white caps, surgeons' masks hiding everything but
their eyes which glittered in the dimness.

A voice on the right of him said, through the mask,
'Number?'

He couldn't tell whether the voice was male or
female. He could see only eyes and long white gowns

concealing every curve of the body. He noticed, too, that the hands were encased in plastic gloves.

With a monumental effort of memory, he remembered the code: 'Jay-haitch-one'.

'Very good.'

He was piloted to one of the chairs facing the screen. It was a wide-armed chair on one side of which was a square black box with wires running from it, three of which were coiled, snakelike on the seat of the chair with pale suction-pads attached to their tips. He also noticed two straps, like those used on aircraft, placed on each side.

A voice, he couldn't tell from which of the two figures – but again with that lack of tone to distinguish male from female – said softly, 'Would you please strip? You have to be naked for us to attach the necessary electrodes to your system.'

Hanley undressed, and a hand took each item. Jacket, shirt, shoes and socks. He drew his pants down and his erection towered in his underpants. He lowered them, too; they were soaking and he dropped them to the floor. Dammit! He was still as hard as ever! But, oddly, he felt no embarrassment. His cock, when up, was something to be proud of!

A hand – he was sure it was a feminine hand! – touched his buttocks lightly. 'Sit down.' He was guided into the chair. The straps were fastened, buckles clicked. The same voice said, 'We're going to attach three electrodes to your penis –' no hesitation! '– your chest and forehead. This will give us a reading of your reactions to what you are about to see – there.'

He turned. To the side was a flat, open laptop. The wires from him led to its base and he could see a faint, green glow.

'You can put the pad on your penis yourself, if you like,' the voice advised.

178

'No,' Hanley said, keeping the same low conversational tone. 'You do it. You're probably more expert than me – no, not probably! You certainly are!'

He felt a cool hand on his shaft and then the foreskin was drawn back and a cold, suction pad was firmly attached. It was a new sensation, something different! He relaxed, and pads were placed on his chest and forehead. He turned his head. What he could see of the green-lit, laptop screen was already displaying lines of – God knew what!

The projector began to whirr. The screen lit up. There were zigzags of lines, scratches and numbers. Then, a caption which he didn't understand in German, followed by more numbers. Finally, a scratchy piece of film, jumping and bouncing through the frame before settling down. Two German soldiers laughing into camera; a wider shot – an area of dusty-looking surface and in the middle a framelike structure; a shot of faces, bodies, dressed in striped prison clothing; the faces gaunt, the eyes hollow; a bad, blurred pan to the centre; a man, gripped by two soldiers, being dragged to the frame; hands thrust upwards and secured; legs spread and ankles strapped; a burly-looking soldier removing his jacket then rolling up his right sleeve; stretching his hand and receiving a long-lashed whip; stepping back a pace to deliver the first blow. Hanley winced; although there was no soundtrack, he could feel the pain. The whip was no cat-o'-nine-tails skilfully manufactured to accommodate those of his persuasion. Hurtful, yes, but not cruelly damaging. The fantasy!

This was a bull-whip; long and powerful, a yard or more in length. The victim arched his head and then the flogging began in earnest. Hanley, the electrode gripping the top of his cock, could scarcely bare to look. But there was a dreadful fascination in seeing the man writhing under the lash; the camera closing in, still in soft focus, but enough . . .

Hanley suddenly felt a violent pain stabbing his cock. His back became rigid. At the same time he felt his forehead banded tightly as though something had stretched across it.

A voice said, 'That's enough.'

The pain eased. He heard the clatter of a computer keyboard. Then silence; the screen flickered momentarily, and then a new angle. The cameraman had moved in. The victim hung helplessly, head down. The whipping ceased. Into frame came a figure in grey-looking dungarees and a torn shirt, with no collar. It carried a bucket and, after taking it by the handle in one hand and the base in the other, threw gouts of water at the helpless man.

The screen went black. Despite himself, Hanley felt spunk gushing into the electrode on his cock, and dribbling down the sides of the twitching shaft . . .

When Hanley had closed the door behind him, Stephanie Barnes slumped back in her chair. Her soaking, black panties, new on today, were sticking cloyingly to her pussy. And she hadn't got a spare pair with her! She got up gingerly and went to the tiny bathroom which opened off her room, pulling up her skirt and unsticking her panties, easing them down to her knees. She tore a long strip of toilet paper from the roll beside the loo and wiped herself thoroughly. Getting a fresh wad, she wiped the insides of her panties and pulled them up. Now, she felt cool and relatively dry. After washing and soaping her hands, she returned to her desk, sat down and studied Hanley's folder again.

God, she was a sadist! Yes, she'd known it for a long time and, thus, masochistic men gave her particular pleasure to interview. She loved to hear their secret lusts! Their obsessions! And she imagined dealing with them herself; having them abject before her; subject to her thirst to apply whip, cane, riding crop or birch. She had scorned Hanley regarding Nazi fantasies and religious, masochistic infatuations! But she had read books like *The Scourge of the Swastika*, by Lord Russell, and *The Day Christ Died*, by Jim Bishop, with their graphic portrayals of corporal punishment under the German whip or the Roman flagellum.

It had started, as far as she could recall, when she was sixteen and home for the holidays from convent school. Her brother Graham, two years younger, had, for some reason, offended their mother who, being a widow, had the task of disciplining. She'd heard angry words from downstairs when she was in her bedroom reading and then her mother's voice on the landing. 'Get in there! I'm going to teach you a lesson!'

Stephanie got off the bed, she was in vest and knickers, and crept to the door.

She heard her mother say, 'Take your trousers and underpants down and get across the bed!'

A drawer opened.

Graham said plaintively, 'Mama, I'm sorry – don't –'

'I told you – get undressed!'

Stephanie's heart was thudding and there was a strange pulsing between her legs. She tiptoed on to the landing.

'Go on! Take them right down!'

'Oh, Mama!'

'I'll give you "oh, Mama"! Across the bed, and lie still!'

Stephanie crept forwards scarcely daring to breathe. Mercifully, the door to her mother's room was only half-closed and she could see through the crack. Graham was across the bed, his white bottom quivering. Her mother stood to one side, brandishing a long, thin cane. She whistled it in the air and then struck.

'Oh – Oh! Mama!'

'One!'

'Mama, please! I'll be good!'

'Two!'

The cane measured its length. Stephanie felt something gripping her – a sensation of excitement! Exultation, almost! She wanted – yes – she wanted to be in her mother's place: caning her brother's bottom, hearing him cry for mercy!

'Three!'

'Mama – it hurts!'

'It's meant to! Four!'

Now, Graham's plump bottom was red with angry lines. Stephanie found herself thinking, Give him more! I want to hear him plead!

'Five!'

'MAMA!'

Instinctively, Stephanie groped for her knicker gusset. She was wet. Had she peed? Her legs shook as she watched the final stroke.

'Six! Get up and go to your room!'

Stephanie turned on her bare toes and skipped into her own room, half-closing the door. Graham came into view, holding his pants and trousers halfway up. She could see his – his 'thing'! And his bottom, angry and scored. He was sniffing hard, and disappeared from her eyeline, then she heard his door slam.

She sat on her bed, hearing her mother go downstairs. Stephanie slid a hand under her knicker waist and probed with a finger. She was soaking! She cautiously drew the finger out and put it to her nostrils. It wasn't pee! And the 'curse' had been and gone a week ago. She looked at the finger. It was slimy with a colourless moisture which glistened in the light from the far window. She tasted it. It was sort of sweet, thick on her tongue. She wiped her finger on her navy knickers, and pondered. What had brought this about? She knew things about sex from the girls at the convent, but only in the vaguest terms. What the man had; what the woman had. She'd never seen Graham's 'thing' before, dangling over two little mounds, and her senses quickened. In her mind's eye, she saw him across her mother's bed hearing the crack of the cane, his anguished cries. That's what had given her that itchy tingle between her legs, and that unfamiliar moistness!

She wished her mother had given him more! A dozen more! Two dozen! She got up restlessly, moved by feelings she had never encountered before. What did it mean? She wanted to cane her brother herself and hear him cry out? Yes! That's what she wanted! To inflict punishment, watch the weals rise on flesh and continue without mercy! She put her hand down again and instinctively began rubbing the rough knicker serge against her opening.

'Stephanie!' Her mother's voice called from downstairs.

'Yes, Mummy?' (She always said 'Mummy' not 'Mama' as Graham did.)

'I'm going to the shops. I'll be an hour and then we'll have supper.'

'Yes, Mummy.'

'And, Stephanie, leave your brother alone – he's to stay in his room!'

'Yes, Mummy.'

The front door slammed and a moment later she heard the firm click of the gate. She stopped rubbing herself, realising she was making herself sore. She put on a blouse and skirt and went to Graham's door, knocking gently. 'Graham, it's Steph.'

'Go away!' Sniffles.

'Mummy's gone out.'

'I hope she never comes back!' A sob-gulp.

'Let me come in.' Her curiosity led her on. She wanted to see his bottom, ask how it had felt when he was being caned.

'All right – if you must.'

She opened the door. He was lying on his bed on his right side, his trousers up but unbuttoned, turning in his hand one of the lead soldiers he had put in battle array on a flat square of wood beneath the window. He looked up, his eyes red, streaks of tears down his cheeks. 'What do you want?' He snorted and swallowed.

'I'm sorry,' Stephanie said quietly.

'What are you sorry about?' His lower lip came out.

'That you've been caned. Does it hurt much?' She moved a little closer and he looked up at her.

'Course it hurts! What do you think!'

Her heart thumped. 'Can I see? Your bottom?'

'No.' He turned away.

'Please?' She eased herself on to the bed. 'You know that time when you wanted to see me? And I wouldn't let you?'

'What about it?' He was fingering the soldier.

'Well, you can – if you let me see your bottom and if –'

He turned suddenly. His cheeks were flushed, his eyes glistening. 'If what?'

The sensations between her thighs were like nothing she had felt before. She was breathless. 'If you let me give you a – a pretend caning.'

'Why?' He narrowed his eyes and wiped his cheeks with the back of a hand.

'I just want to.'

'How'd you mean pretend?'

She cleared her throat. 'Well, I'll get the cane, and I'll take your trousers and pants down, and hit you very lightly, I promise. I just want to know what it feels like . . . to do it.' She had difficulty getting the words out.

He studied the lead soldier, frowning. 'And you'll show me?'

'Yes!' She nodded eagerly. 'Everything! There isn't much to see, not like you!'

He reddened again. 'You saw it just now?'

'Yes, it looked – I liked it.' She reached out a hand and touched his bare back just above his loosened trousers. 'Will you? Please?'

He nodded. 'Can I see now?'

'If you promise to let me cane you.' She got up and began lifting her skirt.

'You said only pretend!' But he watched, fascinated, as she pulled her knickers off, bundled the skirt up around her thighs and spread her legs apart.

'There! There it is!' She pushed herself towards him.

He stared.

'Now – can I get the cane?' She pushed herself a little closer.

He nodded, still staring.

'Where is it? Where does Mummy keep it?' Her voice was thick.

'In the bottom drawer of that dressing table by the window.'

'Don't move!' she said and, letting her skirt drop, she hurried out, along the landing and into her mother's room.

She tiptoed to the dressing table and gently slid the bottom drawer open. There it was, resting on a pile of silken underwear. She took it out, her hand trembling. It was long and slender and she swished it in the air, a surge of excitement flushing her as she heard the whistle in the silent room. God! Why did she feel so powerful! She slipped a hand beneath her skirt and felt; moisture was running down her thighs.

She hurried back, looking at her watch. It was all right; her mother had only been gone fifteen minutes. She closed the door to Graham's room. He hadn't moved.

She said, 'Turn over on your tummy. I'm going to take your trousers and pants down.'

He rolled over and said, 'You won't hurt me! It hurts enough as it is!'

'No,' she said, drawing his grey trousers to his knees and then his white pants.

His bottom was striped in neat lines. She gasped. 'I'll tap you lightly,' she said, 'and then give you a couple of harder ones.'

'You said –!' But he didn't move.

She laid the cane gently on him and then gave him a tap. He said nothing. This time a little harder. She was trembling from head to foot. She wanted to lash him, thrash him and hear him cry out! A little harder. He gave a grunt.

'Two harder ones!' she coaxed. 'Just two. Ready?' Without waiting for a reply, she brought the cane down sharply across his bottom.

He gave a muffled cry, his buttocks quivering. She put all her strength into the last one and it cracked as he yelled, 'You said you wouldn't –!'

She dropped the cane and sank on to the bed, smoothing him. The last stroke had left a definite welt unlike those he'd been given by his mother.

'There,' she soothed, 'all over; all over.'

She eased him on to his back, looked down and saw. When he looked up at her he was grinning shyly and instinctively she knew what to do ...

She never caned Graham again; neither, as far as she knew, did their mother. But the feeling of relish, the sexual joy of inflicting pain only increased in her self-induced fantasies.

She had an exploring mind, a restless curiosity, and one time in her late teens, when she was at medical school and had to collect some books from Foyles in the Charing Cross Road, she was surprised and amazed to see a thick volume entitled *The Whip and the Rod* amid the shelves of books dealing with all aspects of medicine. It was – she noted that the author was a clergyman! – a history of corporal punishment through the ages. Her cheeks burned at some of the graphic drawings and engravings within its pages and the various chapters with such headings as: 'The Roman Way'; 'Flogging in the Army and Navy'; 'Corporal Punishment in Prisons'; 'The Cane and the Birch in School and Police Station' ... And there were many more. She had to have it! She slid the book between the four or five others she had picked up, hoping that, when she paid, the little man at the cashdesk would tot up each purchase without comment. And that was what he did: a bored little man making out bills hour after hour, day after day until titles meant absolutely nothing to him.

She read it voraciously over and over; revelling in the stark illustrations: victims in the stocks, tied to pillory and whipping post; sailors spread-eagled on the rigging subjected to the cat-o'-nine-tails inflicted by a burly bosun. One particular drawing she dwelled on time and again: a boy, his trousers down, was being birched by a master in cap and gown. The boy's face was agonised as the thick bundle of twigs was poised across his behind ... And not the first stroke by any means as the artist had indicated vividly.

But she was a not insensitive young woman. Well aware that she was, in the eyes of the world, sexually perverted, she also realised, through further reading, that just as many, if not more, were equally 'perverted' in seeking to be punished for sexual pleasure: and that somewhere the two worlds must combine. But the various students who invited her out – and there were many – never seemed to understand her bland references to spanking or to whether corporal punishment should be brought back for certain offences such as child murder. Their reponses were equally bland and gave her no satisfaction.

She decided to take a three-year course in sexual psychology – her general medical qualifications gave her the right to select any course she chose under her grant – and she learned a good deal more about sexual aberrations than just sadism and masochism. But the idea of inflicting pain on an individual who craved the whip, cane, birch or riding crop still enthralled her totally. But they had to be willing!

Leafing idly through a tabloid newspaper left in the library, a headline caught her eye: TV PERSONALITY IN 'BONDAGE' ROMP.

She read:

'Well-known TV presenter Mark Jones has been, it is alleged, a regular visitor to an establishment in Earl's Court where leather bondage, humiliation sessions and "spanking" games are the attractions. The allegations, brought by a participant in such sexy romps, are denied by a spokesman for Jones who, in a statement said: '"These suggestions are absurd. Mark

Jones is a happily married man with two lovely children and vehemently denies these scandalous, malicious rumours brought by jealous and less fortunate individuals than himself."'

Stephanie's senses were alerted. Such an establishment must need 'professionals' to run the place! Volunteers prepared to take part in such activities to benefit wealthy clients! But how could she gain admittance to, and take part in, such 'romps'? Did the word 'spanking' conceal more serious administering of corporal punishment?

Fired up, she went to Earl's Court after lectures one evening without really knowing what she was looking for. Such a place was hardly likely to have a sign outside! But it would advertise, surely. She paused outside a newsagent's looking at cards pinned inside a glass case. Most were for bedsits to let, but one or two were more ambiguous: 'Corrective Training by Mature Professionals. Phone: . . .'; 'Discipline and Deportment Training. Strictly Males only. Phone: . . .' Stephanie's excitement mounted. Of the two, the second sounded more promising; more sophisticated, she thought. 'Strictly Male' – yes! She made a note of the number, went into a station phone box and dialled the number. It was engaged. She waited a moment and dialled again. The phone was immediately answered.

'Hello?' A woman's voice, quite cultured.

Stephanie swallowed hard. 'Oh, I saw your advertisement –'

'No, dear, men only –'

'No, no! I wonder if you ever – er – need help?'

The voice was suspicious. 'What sort of help?'

Stephanie was gripping the phone tightly. 'I'd like to see you? Explain if I may?'

Silence. Then: 'Where are you?'

'Earl's Court station,' Stephanie said, her heart thudding.

'Well, you can pay me a visit sometime –'

'Why not now?' Stephanie coaxed. 'Please?' Was she overdoing it? She didn't care.

More silence. Then: 'Very well, I can spare you a few minutes. Barkfield Gardens: turn right out of the station, second on the left. Number twenty-three. Ring the bell marked "Salon".'

In a whirl of excitement, Stephanie followed the directions. Her thoughts were scattered, dizzy. She might be taking a huge risk, but she had to know! She reached number twenty-three and paused. The house was three storeys with steps leading up to a solid-looking front door. The windows on the top floor were the only ones showing any light. Tightening her lips, Stephanie mounted the steps, peered for the bell marked 'Salon' and pressed it firmly.

A harsh voice said, 'Yes?'

Stephanie said hesitantly, 'I – I phoned a few minutes ago?'

'Top floor.'

The door lock buzzed and Stephanie let herself in. Ahead was a wide, carpeted staircase. To the right, a corridor leading to dimness. It was very quiet. Stephanie hesitated at the foot of the stairs. What was she letting herself in for? But sexual excitement drove her upwards: the allure of the unknown was too strong. She reached the top landing and paused again. Facing her was a heavy, panelled door with a spyhole. There were several keyholes. No bell, but a brass knocker with two letters intermingled. She stared . . . and the letters formed themselves into 'SM'!

Heart thumping, Stephanie tapped the knocker twice. There was a pause: somehow, she sensed she was being surveyed through the eye in the door panel. Then there was a clunk of keys and a jangle of chain. The door opened. A tall woman with short-cropped grey hair, wearing a black leather skirt, a matching black blouse and high-heeled knee-boots, surveyed her, then gave her a smile. 'Come in, dear.'

A narrow hallway was papered in dark-red which matched the thick pile of carpet. Red, bracketed lamps glowed. There was a hallstand with a number of yellow crook-handled canes sticking out of it. Ahead, a half-open doorway.

The woman closed the door and chained it. 'Come in here,' she said, brushing past Stephanie and leading the way.

Through the half-open door was a long lounge, comfortably furnished with black leather settees. There were bookcases, tall and glass fronted, neatly filled. A cocktail cabinet, open, revealed mirror-backed shelves sparkling with glasses and bottles. In vain, Stephanie looked around for any signs of what she had come for. But there were none.

'Sit down,' the woman said, 'would you like a drink?'

Stephanie sat awkwardly on one of the couches. 'Thank you. Have you a vodka and tonic?'

The woman nodded. 'Of course.' She crossed to the cocktail cabinet. Her buttocks tight in the leather. 'With ice?'

'Thank you,' Stephanie said. For a ridiculous moment she wondered if she had arrived at the wrong address!

'My name's Brenda.' She handed Stephanie a heavy, cut-glass tumbler cold to the touch, and sat opposite her, crossing her booted legs which gleamed in the light from a table lamp behind Stephanie's head.

'I'm Stephanie.' She drank, trying to keep her hand steady.

'So what can I do for you? As I said on the phone, it's men only, I'm afraid.'

Stephanie coughed. The vodka was fierce in her throat. 'No, I don't want –'

'To be whipped?' The word rang in the air like a lash.

Stephanie flushed. 'No, it's the opposite –'

'Oh,' Brenda said softly, leaning forwards, her hands clasped around her glass. 'I s-e-e. So that's it. Well, well . . .' She sat back, a little smile on her face.

Stephanie glanced up. 'I want to do it. I wondered if you needed anyone to – to help sometimes?'

Brenda drank. 'You saw the newspaper?'

Stephanie nodded.

'How did you know to pick my number?'

Stephanie shrugged. 'It was a guess . . . just a guess.'

Brenda leaned forwards again. Ths time there was no smile; her face was set, her eyes narrow. 'Just a guess, eh? Well, let me tell you – if that idiot hadn't taken off his mask until he got to the front door, none of this would have happened. But he did – and on the stairs he met someone on the way up, and he was recognised!'

'His mask?' Stephanie queried.

'He wore a mask while . . . whatever. A lot of well-known faces come here – in more ways than one!' She allowed herself a grim smile. 'But the little bastard who phoned the paper – I know who it is.'

She grimaced. 'Anyway, there's no problem. I know some of the police force here. In fact, a couple of Inspectors –' She waved a hand. 'Never mind that!' She stared at Stephanie. 'So, you'd like to join our merry little band? You may have arrived at an opportune time – one of my other girls has just left to marry one of the clients. He's a German banker, rotten with money. Anyway, that's beside the point. Have you had any experience?'

Stephanie hesitated. 'I've read a lot – and, and, I caned my brother once. I – I enjoyed it.'

'But have you ever used a whip, a crop or a birch? Really laid it on?'

Stephanie shook her head. 'No.'

'My clients expect the best. They pay good money to get what they want, and we have to provide it. However, there is no sexual contact either before, during or after what they've paid for. If they wish hand relief then they do it themselves. There is no sexual coupling!'

Stephanie nodded. 'I understand.'

'I don't think you do!' Brenda stood, took Stephanie's empty glass and went to the cocktail cabinet. She refilled both glasses and turned, holding them. 'You've had no experience, and yet you're asking me to take you on? This is a professional establishment run on professional lines! How can I possibly engage you –'

'I was only thinking of, er, part-time,' Stephanie said.

Brenda returned with the fresh drinks and sat down again. 'Part-time? Huh! When you feel the urge? Huh – again! We don't conduct our affairs in that way. We aren't an ambulance service; we don't send out 999 calls –'

As if on cue, a phone rang. Stephanie could see no evidence of a receiver, but Brenda got up unhurriedly, swung a section of one of the glass-fronted bookcases aside and revealed a red phone.

'Hello?' She grasped the receiver tightly, her back to Stephanie. 'Yes ... have you been before? No, well, our fees are variable depending on –' she turned

her head irritably '– depending on what you require.
No, you tell me! I see . . . yes, of course. We have all
the necessary equipment. Hmm . . . hmm . . . and
clothing . . .

'I think the best thing is if you come along and we
can discuss it. I'd prefer not to go into details over
the telephone . . . very well . . . I'll give you the
address.' Finally: 'Our fees start at one hundred
pounds for an hour; there is no physical contact – yes
. . . but you can tell me about it. Yes, in about
half-an-hour.'

She put the phone down and turned back. 'Well,'
she said, sitting down again and taking a drink, 'this
may be your chance – a newcomer – a guinea-pig
if you like!'

Stephanie felt herself swelling with desire. 'What
does he –?'

'He wants a whipping. One hundred strokes; a lot
of them say that! But, when it happens, they take
half-a-dozen and then plead with you to stop! But
they still pay, so that's their problem!'

Stephanie glanced around the room. 'But where?'

Brenda gave her a grim smile. 'I'll show you, but,
first, would you like to try your hand, so to speak?
It's better if you have a newcomer to start with. I'll
supervise and then we'll see.' She got up. 'Come on'.

Stephanie, her heart thudding, followed Brenda
from the room and back along the corridor. Halfway
down, to the left, Brenda stopped and gently put two
hands on the red wallpaper. Astonished, Stephanie
watched as a section of the wall swung aside. On the
other side was a metal-plated door with a peephole.
Brenda entered and fumbled for a lightswitch. A red
glow illuminated a large, square room and
Stephanie's jaw dropped. 'My playroom!' Brenda
announced. 'Let me introduce you!'

The room was mirrored from wall to wall. It seemed to Stephanie that it spread further than the wall of the stairs, and Brenda's voice, behind her, confirmed the fact. 'I bought the top flat next door, and had the dividing wall removed. A client, a wealthy client, arranged the matter. Now, let me show you.'

In the mirrors, Stephanie saw herself reflected a hundred times from every angle. And she soon saw why. In the centre of the room stood a glinting, steel piece of apparatus bolted to the lino'd floor. Various bars and stanchions reflected the light, from which hung heavy straps. As she moved tentatively forwards, she could see that the gleaming piece of equipment was, as she had been, reflected from every angle in the glinting mirrors; anyone strapped to that could see . . . She drew a deep breath, her thighs shaking.

Behind her, Brenda said, 'That piece of apparatus can be adjusted to any number of positions. Look!' She slid one of the mirrors open: behind it, hanging on rails were whips of various sizes and lengths; canes, riding crops, studded straps; a rack of thick, bunched birch twigs. She pulled open an adjoining one. Stepanie gazed at racks of clothing; uniforms; beneath, a row of riding boots. 'Now.' Yet another mirrored door was slid aside. A small, barred cell with stone floor and walls; chains hanging from the walls; a wooden bench with straw scattered on it.

'Sometimes,' Brenda was saying softly, 'we put our victims in there and chain them. They can hear, in their agony, the sounds of whipping from this room . . . Look at this.' On one side of the room was a rack pinioned to the wall. Atop it was a series of thick cables leading from a black box and beside it a red handle. The cables ended in rubber suction cups.

'After a whipping, some of my more, shall we say, devoted clients like to have a little electric shock. Oh, nothing too dangerous; these cups are attached to the tip of the penis, the anal opening and each nipple. Then, we turn on the current.'

Stephanie swallowed hard, her throat and mouth dry. She hadn't conceived of anything on this scale, but, she admitted, she'd had no idea of what to expect!

'What are you wearing – underneath?' Brenda asked.

Stephanie shrugged. 'Ordinary white panties and tights, why?'

'I've no idea what this new client wants,' Brenda said, 'but you'll have to be prepared. We have some extremely odd requests as far as clothing is concerned, but there isn't time to tell you about them now. He'll be here in a minute. Stay as you are, for the time being. We'll go back into the lounge. I'll take his money – then, do you want to do what he wants? I'll supervise as it's your first time –'

'A sort of test?' Stephanie asked, her voice weak.

'Exactly,' Brenda said firmly, 'come on.'

Hanley broke off. Harriet moved irritably, snapping her knicker elastic. 'How do you know all this?'

'She told me,' Hanley said calmly.

'Why?' Jennifer broke in.

Hanley met their eyes. 'Because,' he said evenly, 'I married her. Shall I continue?'

Jennifer eyed him scornfully. 'You never told me!'

'No point,' Hanley said easily, 'it didn't last all that long – but that's another story altogether. Now –' he met their eyes '– do you want to hear the rest?'

There were mutters of agreement . . .

* * *

Ten minutes later there was a buzz on the intercom and Brenda went to the security phone on the wall in the vestibule. 'Yes, that's right, top floor.' She pressed the entry button and returned to face Stephanie, arms folded. 'When he comes in he'll first be asked for the money: that's important – always get the money first! And no cheques unless it's a long-time, reliable regular! Nervous?'

Stephanie nodded. 'A bit – but more excited.

Brenda said, 'There's a little room beside the playroom with a spyhole. I allow some of my more privileged clients to watch now and again. I'll be in there, and, if I see you need help, I'll be right in. It's a security measure; you never know, especially with new clients.'

The doorbell rang. Brenda hurried into the hall; a murmur of conversation; the door locked and chained; and into the room came a short little man, balding, wearing glasses and a faintly shy expression. He was wearing a blue suit, and carried a holdall.

Stephanie felt a wave of disappointment run through her.

'The cash, please!' Brenda said briskly.

'Oh – yes.' The little man, with a glance at Stephanie, fumbled in his jacket and brought out a white envelope. 'It's all there,' he said, handing it to Brenda.

'It'd better be!' Brenda said sternly, opening the envelope and counting the notes. Satisfied, she replaced the money in the envelope. She pointed a finger at the holdall. 'What have you got in there? We have to be careful!'

The little man gave a weak, trembly smile. 'It's what I like to wear while – while I'm being punished for being naughty . . . I'm – I'm a naughty schoolboy, you see?' His cheeks were red; as far as Stephanie could make out there was no significant bulge in the ill-fitting blue slacks.

Sharply, Brenda said to Stephanie, her chin raised, 'Take him into the playroom and punish him. Hurry! He's only got an hour, and five minutes have already gone!'

'In here!' Stephanie said, trying to be as stern. She opened the door to the playroom and gave the little man a shove. He stared around as she closed the door. 'Now! You'd better put on what you've got in your bag – and hurry!'

He undressed, fumbling. Naked, he was a pot-bellied, skinny little fellow with knobbly white knees. Stephanie could barely see his cock, a shrivelled little piece of nothing dangling between his legs. She felt a surge of anger. His thin, white buttocks showed no signs of punishment.

'Hurry up!'

She didn't really want to whip a little runt like this! Cowering little prick! She watched as he put on a shirt, short, grey trousers to his knees and old-fashioned grey socks with coloured tops. He looked at her meekly.

'I'm a naughty boy – I need punishment from my headmistress.'

'What have you done?' Stephanie asked curtly. She felt a surge of sexual power.

'I was caught smoking behind the bicycle sheds.'

'Very well.' Stephanie stood above him. 'You've broken the rules – now you must accept your punishment.' The words came easily to her, she was surprised to find. 'You'll be birched!'

'Birched?' He looked up fearfully. 'Birched?'

'You've never been birched?' Calmly, Stephanie crossed the room and took up one of the bundles of twigs, whistling them in the air. A rough handle was made of black industrial tape woven round and round. 'Have you ever been whipped?' She turned, holding the birch threateningly.

He cowered. 'I've been spanked . . . but some time ago.'

'You said you wanted a hundred strokes – that's what you've paid for, and that's what you're going to get!' Stephanie moved forwards. 'Take your trousers down!'

'Can you?'

'Bend over!' Stephanie ordered, and the pitiful little figure bent, hands on knees. Gingerly, Stephanie pulled down the short, grey trousers. The thin, white thighs trembled. He was nothing! A miserable specimen! She told him so, and then brought the birch across his bony posterior. He yelped like a whipped dog.

'Shut up!' Stephanie commanded. 'Do you want to be strapped?'

'No.' He shook his head, still bent. 'It's hard; it hurts!'

'That's what it's meant to do,' Stephanie told him, preparing for another slash; drawing the birch back in readiness. 'You asked for a hundred and you're going to get a hundred! Value for money is our motto!' She laid the birch across the already reddening welts of the first blow.

'No! I'm sorry! I'll – I'll never do it again, Miss! Please let me off! My mum'll see!'

'You'll have four more!' Stephanie said. But the sexual thrill had gone. This creepy little nothing! He wasn't worth it; he couldn't take what he'd paid for!

She whipped him savagely four more times, the force of the blows sending him staggering, a ridiculous figure with his scrawny legs and his hands over his smarting buttocks in an absurd attempt to protect himself.

He turned to her, his eyes pleading. His shrivelled cock dangled, a long piece of ragged foreskin hanging stupidly.

'No – no more!'

'There's no money back!' Stephanie told him. Although she hadn't been told by Brenda, she instinctively knew this would be the form. 'We're not allowed to touch you – you know that.'

He nodded, wearily removing the shirt, shorts and socks. 'I know.' He lifted his flaccid, minute cock from beneath. It flopped tiredly, what there was of it. 'Look at it! I thought a good – thrashing would give it some life . . . it used to.' He shook his head and began to dress in his own clothes. 'I just thought . . .' He looked wistfully at Stephanie, still holding the birch. 'I'll think of you at night in bed, wishing . . .'

He finished dressing quickly, and gave a deep sigh, as he gathered his belongings together. 'Thank you,' he mumbled and made for the door, a pathetic, forlorn little man with aspirations beyond his frail abilities, Stephanie thought.

Brenda entered with a smile. 'Disappointed?'

Stephanie replaced the birch. 'I'd have liked –'

'To give a real flogging?' Brenda came close, put an arm round Stephanie's shoulders and then ran a hand down the curve of her back to the top of her buttock mound. 'And so you shall,' she whispered, 'and so you shall.'

'Les?' Jennifer asked.

There was a pause for drinks all round. Simon did the honours, his cock large in his underpants. Nobody took much notice of each other. They stared ruminatively into their glasses.

Hanley mocked them. 'Cat got your tongues? And you know what sort of cat I'm talking about!' To

200

Jennifer: 'Yes, in answer to your question – AC–DC, the ideal combination!'

'Very convenient!' Jennifer responded, her lip curled derisively.

'Look who's talking!' Harriet unexpectedly broke in. She stood, glass in hand, her outsize knickers drooping over the elastic at her knees. 'You've had it both ways, my girl! I know that well enough, so don't criticise others – you wouldn't be here if it were otherwise!' She raised her chin, exposing loose folds of flesh, and Hanley was reminded of the actress Dame Edith Evans with her immortal line in Oscar Wilde's *The Importance of Being Earnest* – 'A HANDBAG?'

He'd been down on Harriet one time, with Jennifer whipping his buttocks, as he spread the older woman's fleshy, white thighs apart, seeking with his tongue the slit; dry and odd-tasting to begin with, and then a flood of moisture salty and strong as he buried his face and hungrily licked the soaking lips as Jennifer flogged. An older woman!

For a long moment, there was silence in the room. Nobody stirred. Hanley felt all the eyes penetratingly on him.

It was Jennifer who broke the silence. 'Gross! Fucking gross! That's the most unbelievable, stinking, dirty, filthy –'

'I get the message,' Hanley said. He leaned forwards. 'I thought when we got this friendly little group together there were no holds barred – about what we wanted, about what we told each other and what, within certain parameters, we were willing to enjoy. Thought we were uninhibited – you, you and you have told us things you'd never dare mention to another human being. It's a kind of release – just as whipping, or being whipped – is release of another kind.'

Again silence. Again Jennifer the first to break it. 'There are limits.' Her voice was low.

'Are there?' Hanley queried. 'Have we ever set guidelines? You say there are limits – who set them? You? All of us?'

Harriet broke in unexpectedly. 'He's right. There are no limits. There can't be. We're here because we're all perverted; we have tastes which only the minority have. But *we* have them! And we should be able to confess to each other all our thoughts, all our sexual fantasies – otherwise there is no point meeting as we do.' She turned abruptly to Jennifer. 'Who are you to set limits? Huh!'

Again, silence. Hanley suggested, 'Who wants to hear the rest of the clinic story? There's still a fair way to go; we can indulge anyone's desires at the moment.' Silence. 'Very well, I'll go on. Just as a reminder, it's me telling the tale as Stephanie told it to me . . .'

Hanley gave Jennifer a glance. 'Brenda wasn't a "les" – not as far as Stephanie was concerned –'

'Or as much as she told you!' Jennifer broke in with a broad grin. Hanley ignored the interruption . . .

That was Stephanie's introduction to the professional game, and her disappointment obviously showed as Brenda said encouragingly, giving her a drink, 'They're not all like that, I promise! I have regulars, but I thought I'd see how you dealt with a newcomer.'

Taking a drink, Stephanie asked, 'Did – did I do all right?'

'You were very patient,' Brenda said with a slight smile. 'The little runt! I can't stand so-called men who arrive here boasting about how much they they can take, and then snivelling, whining after the first few strokes!'

Stephanie said excitedly, 'I'd have liked to have tied him up, and flogged him until –'

'Yes, dear, but don't let your imagination run away with you. You have to be symphetic even if you don't feel like it. A number are little men – like yours tonight – who are failures; they know they're failures: life has passed them by. They have ugly wives who no longer have any sexual attraction. So, in their frustration, they visit prostitutes – and, by the way, we aren't prostitutes; we don't sell our bodies. We provide an expert service for what's required. I like to think we are experts in our art. I pride myself that we are as expert in what we do as electricians, computer know-alls, or doctors. Never forget that! Now –' She opened a black-bound appointment book and flicked a page. 'Yes, in two days' time, one of my favourites. He's a professional soldier, a lieutenant in the Household Cavalry. After guard duty at Buckingham Palace, he always visits me for a flogging – and I mean, a flogging! And in his case, and his case only, I make an exception: while he is still strapped, I masturbate him. He has a huge cock. Perhaps you'd like to be part of this? He always stays for two hours; it might be instructive for you, my dear.'

Stephanie swallowed hard. 'How often do you whip him?'

'Roughly twice a month,' Brenda said, 'after the tour of duty at Buck House, as they call it. Would you like to be here? He'll arrive at two. I suggest you – have you riding breeches and knee-high boots?'

'No.' Stephanie shook her head.

'I suggest you acquire some. Black breeches and black boots. The breeches, or jodhpurs, must fit extremely tightly around the crotch and down the thighs, and the boots must be with exceptionally high heels. You will also require a white blouse with a high collar and long sleeves. Also, black elbow-length leather gloves. I can give you the name of a quality store in New Bond Street where you can obtain all these items – they're not cheap but, if you are to continue here, you'll need them plus other items which I'll tell you about later. Have you the money? The items I've listed will be upwards of two hundred pounds.' She raised her eyebrows questioningly.

'I have the money,' Stephanie said quickly. Her heart was fluttering strangely. 'May – may I sit down for a moment?' She was damp between her thighs.

Brenda was all concern. 'Of course, my dear. I'll get you another drink.' She hurried to the cocktail cabinet. 'It must be a shock to you, all this, so suddenly, I realise that.' She handed Stephanie the glass and sat down beside her. 'Drink that, you'll feel better.'

It was vodka again, and fiery.

Brenda moved so that their thighs were touching. She whispered, 'When you feel better, I want you to give me twelve strokes with a cane on my bare bottom. Will you do that?'

Stephanie's senses swam. She felt stronger and took another gulp of vodka. 'Yes,' she said, her voice sounding strangely different. 'I'd like to very much.'

Their shoulders touched. Brenda said, 'And lay them on hard!'

'I will,' Stephanie promised. Her voice seemed to have a strange echo in her ears. She thought of the handsome, young officer whom she'd see in two days, and her groin swelled and her belly heaved with excitement. With a none-too-steady hand she put the glass down.

'I'm ready,' she said firmly.

Hanley paused as Jennifer said with a familiar lip-curl. 'Lesbo? Oh, no!'

Harriet broke in. 'I agree – why would this woman want twelve cuts with the cane. From what we've heard, she's supposed to be the dominatrix.'

'Exactly,' Hanley confirmed.

'Exactly – what?' Jennifer said again.

Hanley sighed. 'She wanted to know what it felt like to experience a whipping, caning or flogging – whichever you like to call it – so that she would know from the infliction of pain on herself, so that she would realise how her clients felt,'

'You mean to say – sorry to break in –' it was Peter, apolgetic as usual 'that this woman had never had it before? She sounds, from what you've been describing, that she'd been in the trade for some –'

'Exactly!' Jennifer's voice was like a whip-crack. 'For once, he's made a good point.' She gave Peter an evil grin and gently swung the thin-lashed whip she was toying with. 'This woman would have known anyway what punishment was like! They all do! And the only reason she wanted this – this Stephanie to whip her was because she's a dyke!'

Hanley said, with some irritation, 'Does it matter, for Christ's sake? Really?'

He stared at Jennifer bluntly – but don't go too far, he told himself – you probably need her more than she needs you. His eyes were on the dangling whip.

With her extraordinary change of mood, which had always fascinated and surprised him, she gave him a genuine smile. 'All right, lover, don't get uptight: not yet, anyway.'

Simon, who'd been fondling himself and saying nothing, suddenly piped up, 'Where – where's all this going? I mean, we're sitting here listening –'

'Well, isn't that what we always do –' Jennifer turned to him lazily like a relaxed, elegant cat, stretching her long, black-stockinged legs '– before we, shall we say, get the show on the road? What do you want, little boy? A smacking just to whet your appetite, apart from anything else?'

Hanley suggested, 'Shall we postpone the rest of the story until another time? Personally, I'd like a whipping –' he was bone-hard '– and I imagine the rest of you would like to indulge in one way or another.'

Jennifer scrambled lithely to her feet, the black whip firmly in her grasp. 'Get up there to the post,' she ordered, 'and get those pants off!'

'There were many others,' Hanley said when the group met a week or so later. He was referring to Brenda's clients and his wife – briefly – in her participation. You have to know the background,' he explained patiently, 'to understand how she became head of this aversion-therapy clinic –'

'Which is what you started to tell us about in the first place!' Harriet snapped.

For once, she was fully dressed in a black, high-collared blouse and a long black thigh-hugging skirt beneath the hem of which peeped glistening black ankle boots. Simon, whose fetish was silk, elasticted underwear, had no doubt in his mind that long knickers nestled tightly an inch or so above her kneecaps.

Hanley, still smarting deliciously from the flogging Jennifer had administered the week previously when everything had become a little uptight, and each in their various ways had released their frustrations, said, 'I'll just tell you one more event before I get back to the clinic.'

Simon asked, 'About the lieutenant in the Household Cavalry?' His voice quavered.

Hanley gave him a knowing grin. 'I wondered if

you'd choose that one!' He looked around. 'All agreed?'

Jennifer said dreamily, 'They wear tight, white moleskin breeches, and thigh-length boots with silver spurs, breastplates and plumed helmets; they all have to be over six feet tall even to be considered. And, when they're finally selected, they're each horsewhipped by the Queen on their naked bums and, if they make a sound, they're put in the Tower of London, chained and flogged daily for the rest of their lives!'

'Were it only true!' Simon breathed.

'How'd you know it isn't!' Jennifer sneered at him. 'Anyway, they wouldn't take you, you skinny little fucker!'

Unusually boldly, Simon said, 'They might like this!' He pulled the waist of his pants down and his erection towered upwards.

'Put it away,' Hanley said quickly. 'Wait 'til you hear the story.' Despite himself, he felt a surge of longing at the sight . . .

It was a week later, after a session involving the joint flogging of two gay young men who clutched each other as the punishment was inflicted by Brenda on one side and Stephanie joyfully wielding the whip on the other, when Brenda told Stephanie that the lieutenant would be paying a visit in two days' time.

Meanwhile, Stephanie had visited the shop in New Bond Street where the mere mention of Brenda's name had brought a scurry of devoted activity. She emerged with slim-fitting jodhpurs, boots and elbow-length black gloves. At home, she dressed up and stood before the mirror in her bedroom. Her heart missed a beat: God, she looked sexy! All she lacked was a whip or a riding crop in her hand menacingly poised.

The lieutenant was due at two in the afternoon. 'He's always punctual,' Brenda said.

'He – he won't be in uniform?' Stephanie suggested hopefully. She had a vision of this handsomely garbed young man strapped to the whipping frame, and she pulling on those thick breeches, folding them over his boots to allow his buttocks freedom for the whip. In her fantasy, he wouldn't be wearing underpants . . .

'No,' Brenda said and smiled understandingly. 'He could hardly arrive in full dress on his horse! He's in civvies, but he soon strips, and he's ready for the whipping post. That's what I like about him – he's eager for it! Thirsty for it!'

'Can I –?' Stephanie asked, her heart thudding.

'We'll have a drink when he arrives, and I'll introduce you. I'll flog him at first and then you can take over. He also likes the birch; he had it at boarding school and you can give him some lashes.'

Stephanie frowned. 'But what about the marks – the welts – when he undresses in front of the others?'

Brenda laughed. 'Oh, they joke about it! He's not the only one, by any means; most of them, you see, are ex-public school; they've been caned, slippered, birched; and, if that goes on for very long, certain types will begin to enjoy it – to come, ejaculate.'

'Does – does he?' Stephanie ventured.

'Quite often. But if he's on the brink – so to speak – then I usually finish him off.'

'Can I?'

Brenda smiled. 'We'll see. Let's not work everything out in advance. Sometimes the unexpected can be much more interesting!'

The two women eyed the ormolu clock on the marble mantelpiece in the lounge. Stephanie was in her jodhpurs and boots. She felt strong, dominating,

208

wearing no knickers beneath the thick material. Surprisingly, Brenda was dressed 'normally' in skirt, blouse, grey stockings and stiletto-heeled court shoes.

In answer to Stephanie's query, Brenda said wryly, 'He likes things done his way!' And left it at that.

The clock chimed mellowly; the doorbell rang harshly. Brenda hurried to the front door and pressed the release without even querying who was there.

Footsteps bounded up as Brenda opened the door. There were mumbled greetings and then in came a tall, slim young man with wavy, curly blondish hair, a lean face with dark eyes and a wide mouth already smiling. His tweed jacket was perfectly cut as were his beige corduroy slacks. With his checked shirt he wore a neat striped tie which looked as if it might mean something.

Brenda said, 'This is Stephanie. Stephanie – Rupert!'

His grasp was strong. 'Hello, you're new!' He turned to Brenda. 'Where did this luscious creature emerge from?'

Brenda smiled. 'She's a volunteer, and a very avid one.'

'So I see.'

He had an engaging grin, Stephanie thought, watching him shed his jacket and fold it carefully before putting it down on the back of the couch.

'God, it was hot on parade this morning! I had two troopers in my section faint. I'll be for it on Monday!' He accepted a drink from Brenda.

Stephanie took her own glass. 'But it's not your fault if men faint because of the heat!'

Rupert drank deeply. 'Oh, but it is! I have to make sure they eat a decent breakfast before parade. Oh, they'll get a good telling off, and so will I – but I won't get flogged spread-eagled to a gun-carriage as they used to do in the field, so I'm expecting to be severely taken to task by you this afternoon!' He glanced at Stephanie. 'Both of you.'

She glanced down and saw the swell tightening his groin.

'How long today?' Brenda asked practically.

'Oh, I think two hours,' Rupert said matter of factly. He reached for his jacket and brought out a cheque book and a silver ballpoint, looking up at Brenda. 'Cheque OK? It's Coutts & Co. – you've had them before.'

'Fine,' Brenda said.

Rupert wrote the cheque with a flourish, tore it off and handed it over.

Brenda frowned. 'But this is more –'

'Well,' Rupert said mischeviously, 'you've got an extra hand to think about.' He stood up, the bulge in his trousers more prominent. 'I think I want somebody to take my trousers and underwear down and slap me hard while I bend over. Then we'll go in there and you can punish me as you see fit for my failure to do my duties on parade this morning.'

'I will,' Brenda said and, without any more ado, unzipped Rupert's trousers and drew them down firmly.

Stephanie stared. He was wearing white boxer shorts with little buttons down the front looking as if they might burst at any minute with the thrust of his cock. Brenda slid the underpants down and Stephanie hungrily eyed his erection, the foreskin already tightly stretched.

He said with a grin, 'It's been doing overtime thinking about this afternoon. Now, who's going to spank me?'

He pushed the pants to his ankles and bent meekly, supporting himself on one arm of the couch. His thighs and legs were well muscled, silky black hair gleaming.

Brenda nodded to Stephanie. 'Spank him! He's a naughty boy!'

Heart thumping, Stephanie tightened her black gloves and moved into position. Now, she could see that his buttocks were wealed and scarred, right down as far as the backs of his knees. She imagined the lash falling, and momentarily contrasted this with that pathetic little man of a few days before. She slapped across the centre of the twin mounds. Rupert grunted. She slapped again, putting the whole weight of her upper and lower arm into the effort. He grunted again with what sounded like animal pleasure, and offered himself more obviously to the gloved punishment. His cock bobbed enticingly as she struck again and again, feeling an almost unsupportable surge of naked, sexual power.

'Harder!' He was muttering in a voice unlike his own. 'Mummy! I deserve it. I've been naughty! Strip me! Whip me! Punish me!'

Stephanie glanced at Brenda who stood, arms akimbo. She nodded. 'Ten more – then he'll be over this particular episode. He doesn't always want this . . .' She was talking, Stephanie realised, as if the bent, submissive body of Rupert wasn't there at all.

As she slapped on, her hand stinging almost as much as she imagined Rupert's behind was, she sensed a disappointment. She wanted to flog – or see this handsome young man flogged – naked, enduring his punishment not like a mummy's boy, but like the strong, masochistic victim he purported to be. She gave the final slap and Rupert straightened slowly, his cock rigid.

'All right – in there! The fun's over! Strip!' Brenda said sharply.

Naked, Rupert was a magnificent specimen, Stephanie thought. Broad-chested, hairless except for the thick pubic outcrop like a forest of undergrowth from which a single, giant tree thrust itself proudly, he moved enticingly, his reddened buttocks moving sensuously, into the mirrored room. Obediently, he positioned himself against the two vertical bars of the whipping apparatus, spreading his legs.

'Fasten his ankles,' Brenda said, as she strapped the willing wrists.

Stephanie bent and gathered the leather restraints, buckling them tightly. She rose, acutely aware that the crotch of her jodhpurs was sticking to the insides of her thighs. She realised she was little short of orgasm. Mesmerised, she watched Brenda select a heavy whip from the rack and position herself to one side of the helpless Rupert. And, without preamble, she lashed. The sound was violent in the silence and Stephanie felt her cheeks flooding. Brenda flogged again, grunting with the effort. Rupert made not a sound as the punishment continued and as thick, new weals spread across the tautened buttocks.

After thirty lashes, Brenda handed the whip to Stephanie. Breathlessly, wiping a hand across her damp forehead, she said, 'Take over.'

'Riding crop!' Rupert said peremptorily.

Brenda took a thick, plaited crop from the rack which tapered to a tassled end. Stephanie took it in place of the whip, measured her distance and struck the centre of the quivering buttocks. The result was startling. Whereas Brenda's whip had raised a light flush on the flesh, the first stroke of Stephanie's caused a scarlet weal. Possessed of a fury, a sexual obsession which she could scarcely have imagined, she whipped the obsequious bottom, watching the flesh visibly swell before her burning eyes.

She was in a flogging frenzy, flagellating the bound body of her willing victim.

A faraway voice said, 'That's enough.'

Brenda stepped forwards and took the crop while Stephanie stared pantingly at her handywork, at the results of her first real flogging.

'That girl knows how to lay it on!' Rupert said faintly.

'Yes,' Brenda said. 'She's a quick learner. Do you want to –?'

'Bring me on . . . I'll tell you when to stop.'

Brenda, lifting her skirt delicately, kneeled in front of Rupert, took his cock in her left hand and guided it between her lips, gradually taking in the whole of the rigid shaft. She worked her jaws gently and Rupert moaned.

After a moment he gasped, 'Stop!'

Brenda immediately withdrew. The cock glistened in the light, hard as ever.

Rupert was shaking, sweat running down the elegant curve of his back. 'Let her . . . finish . . .'

'Hand relief,' Brenda said, 'that's what he wants, but slowly. Have you ever masturbated a man before –'

'It doesn't matter!' Rupert interrupted hoarsely. 'Let her!'

Stephanie moved to Rupert's right side. Suddenly, she recalled that moment with Graham after his caning, when he'd turned to her with that shy grin and she'd . . .

His cock, when she enfolded it, gripping it between the fold of thumb and index finger, was slippery like an eel. She watched the tightened skin move silkily within its muscular strength, the foreskin drawn way back exposing the pink-red knob.

'A little quicker,' Rupert whispered. 'That's it . . . slower now . . . now quicker.' Within her hand the cock seemed to grow even more stiffly and she clasped it with the rest of her curled fingers. 'Squeeze my balls!'

With the other hand, Stephanie cupped the tight mounds, feeling, as she did so, Rupert's body become even tenser.

'Squeeze hard – and do it up and down! More, more! Squeeze!'

Stephanie did as she was bid, both hands beginning to ache. Between her legs moisture dripped. She was conscious of nothing but Rupert's strained torso, his flat belly and that great throbbing piece of manhood in her hand. Brenda and the rest of the room might have been a million miles away . . .

'Now! Let go!'

Stephanie released her grip. Thick spunk spurted in an arch, strong-smelling, and splattered to the floor. Again and again the muscular activity drove more outwards until there was a final, thin dribble.

Brenda said, 'Leave him.'

'But –' Stephanie began.

'That's the way he likes it,' Brenda said sharply.

She glanced down at Stephanie's jodhpurs and smiled enigmatically. Stephanie followed her glance. There was a spreading patch on the reinforced crotch, dark against the light-coloured material . . .

'He likes it to be watched going down,' Brenda said. 'Stand in front of him.'

Rupert's face was drawn but he gave them both a tired smile. 'Look,' he said, 'look down and tell me how stupid the thing looks!'

His cock, the foreskin loose, was now beginning to sag gently; it dwindled further until it hung over the testicular mounds which themselves had shrunk and now dangled.

'God!' Brenda spat. 'What an object! You're not a man! What do you think?'

Stephanie swallowed hard. 'It doesn't look much.'

'Fiercer!' Rupert hissed.

'It looks ridiculous!' Stephanie summoned all her imaginative powers. 'The stupid bit of – nothing! It's pathetic! I've seen boys with bigger ones than that!'

'Small boys!' Brenda added. 'You're worthless! I've half a mind to flog you again!'

Rupert said, 'I need to pee.'

'I'll get a jug,' Brenda said, and left the room.

Rupert met Stephanie's gaze. 'Thank you.'

Suddenly, she wanted to cry, to put her arms round him; soothe his pain.

Brenda returned with a silver jug, took Rupert's slack cock and inserted it. The metallic sound of strong-streaming urine against the metal was loud and enticing in the room . . .

'Oh, water sports!' Simon unexpectedly piped up with some glee. His pale face was flushed.

'Shut up!' Jennifer gave him a sideways look. 'I'll give you water sports!' She eyed Hanley. 'Where the hell is this story going? I thought we were supposed to be hearing about your redemption – Paul seeing the light on the road to Damascus!'

'I never mentioned redemption!' Hanley said with feeling. 'Why, in hell, would I want to do that? I'm giving you background about Stephanie and the clinic –'

Harriet interrupted. 'Of course. You're absolutely right; background is all important: knowing about the past can sometimes explain the present. I know that from Jeremy –'

'Oh, God!' Jennifer sighed. 'Jeremy – always fucking Jeremy!'

Harriet bristled. 'My girl! If you'd ever had a relationship like –'

'Yeah, yeah!' Jennifer glanced at Simon. 'Fancy a whipping?'

'Oh, yes –!' Simon began.

Hanley held up a hand. 'I'm going to finish this story before anything else. After that . . . well, it's up to you what you do. It's important that I get back on to the main track. What I found out about Stephanie –'

'Your wife!' Jennifer sniggered with a look around at the others.

'My ex-wife!' Hanley corrected. 'What she told me is part of the story of how she came to be at the aversion-therapy clinic, all right?' He flicked a page of his notebook and studied it. 'Yes, here it is. She was reading a book one day, and found this passage from an article by a Professor Bronowski who, I believe, was something of a television pundit at one time. I quote: "The wish to hurt, the momentary intoxication with pain, is the loophole through which the pervert climbs into the minds of ordinary men".'

'Or women!' Jennifer added.

'Or women,' Hanley conceded, with a brief nod. 'Shall I continue?'

Nobody responded and Hanley drew a deep breath . . .

At Brenda's 'salon' there were more encounters with the weak and the willing. The bizarre, the pitiful, the dressers-up, the meek, the boastful; those who wanted their genitals flogged; or the soles of their feet as with the 'bastinado' in the Far East. This caused some difficulty because the soles of the feet had to be raised in a position to be caned which meant the victim, masturbating, had his head well below his ankles as they were secured vertically to an iron bar.

Stephanie, though, became tired of the repetitious acts she was required to perform: the soft strokes on quivering, wrinkled behinds; the entreaties: 'Whip me!' eventually resulting in pathetic pleas to stop. She wasn't getting what she wanted: that intoxicating feeling of inflicting real pain and observing the result! There'd been others like Rupert, the Guards officer, but nobody as rapacious for punishment, humiliation and the joy of being hurt both mentally and physically.

Still with her daytime job, Stephanie was joined one lunchtime in the canteen by a vague friend, Joyce, whom she suspected, but had never been able to prove, was gay. Joyce had a copy of the BMA job lists in her thick-fingered hand – she also had a disturbing growth of hair on her upper lip which Stephanie found disturbingly disgusting – and shook her head unhappily. 'Here's a job I'd go for.' She turned the list to Stephanie and pointed to an item ringed with a red chinagraph.

Stephanie read, 'A private clinic in Sussex requires an additional counsellor to its staff which deals primarily with patients seeking aversion therapy. No particular qualifications are required but the applicant – who must be female – would have to have understanding of the various abnormal symptoms which it is the object of the clinic to try and help patients come to terms with. Please apply in writing, with references, to . . .'

'Might be fun?' Joyce suggested.

Stephanie shrugged and handed the list back. 'Sounds a bit odd.'

Later, having remembered the address, she wrote a response. She was, she said, qualified to deal with 'unusual' cases and, while not mentioning her brother by name, implied that her experience might equip her for the post in question. She gave her age, her marital status, together with a hospital reference and one from Brenda, which, without going into details, gave assured confidence in Stephanie's ability to handle any kind of sexual problem.

She heard back within three days, was invited for an interview and, after something of a grilling about her knowledge of sexual aberrations – in particular, of sadomasochism – was offered the post. The woman principal who interviewed her, tall, getting on in years and whose blue-clothed body looked rigidly corseted, had a gleam in her eyes which Stephanie found exciting in a way she couldn't quite analyse.

'She'd been there for two years when I met her,' Hanley said.

'So, at last, we're getting to the point!'

Hanley didn't have to check on whose voice that was!

'Why did you go?' It was Harriet following up with a supplementary. 'I mean – why? Surely you didn't wish to be – what's the word – cured? You've been a masochist since your teens, according to your own story.'

Hanley hesitated, for once lost for words. His real intention in booking into the clinic was, of course, to enlarge his research. But he could scarcely admit that without giving the whole game away. Playing for time, conscious of curious eyes, he said levelly, 'Good question, Harriet, and let me just say that genuinely at one stage I thought it might be an idea to, well, change my habits.'

It wasn't a convincing answer, he knew well enough, but, without a pause, went on, 'You want to hear the rest of the story? Remember, I'd had my first taste of anti-aversion therapy with that black-and-white film of a Nazi flogging and I'd come –'

'And almost electrocuted yourself!'

Hanley ignored Jennifer's caustic aside. 'Now to the next stage . . . You have to remember that I only heard her side of the story afterwards, so now I'm only going to give you my story of what happened next . . .'

The figures in the dim room removed the electrodes and motioned for Hanley to stand. His cock drooped, but he could still feel the exciting tingle of the electric shock. On the far side of the room, a door opened letting in a shaft of grey light.

'Through there,' a voice said. All the voices, he'd noted, had a muffled sound.

Aware of, but not embarrassed by, his nakedness, Hanley made his way between the shadows and through the door which clanged decisively behind him. He was in a windowless room with bare walls and empty except for a solid-looking wardrobe on the far wall. But there were chains dangling fron the walls; thick chains with handcuffed ends and his heart began an unsteady beat.

There were no signs of torture instruments nor means of bondage; but beside one set of chains there hung leads, with serrated-edged metal clips, running up to a box high on the wall with a red handle. The red-and-black wires looked to Hanley nothing more evocative than the 'jump leads' used to start a car with a flat battery.

He waited. The silence was profound. Apart from his nakedness, he felt in other ways exposed to an unknown which both aroused him and gave him twitches of apprehension. He had only ejaculated a few minutes before in the other room, but he felt his scrotum tightening and his flaccid cock beginning to rise.

He leaned against the wall nearest him, the cold dampness cooling on his skin. Then suddenly, the wardrobe opposite slid smoothly aside revealing a narrow opening and through this into the murky light stepped a figure clad from head to foot in glistening black latex rubber which clung to the body like a second skin. The face was masked with narrow slits showing a hint of glinting eyes. To Hanley, it could have been a slim man or a wonderfully shaped young woman. No telltale bulge in the crotch area gave any clue.

'Face the wall.' The voice was clearly distorted by some audio device and sounded metallic. Hanley did as he was told. 'Raise your arms above your head and spread your legs apart.'

Hanley complied. Swiftly the leads were gathered and a clip was attached to the head of his cock. He grunted at the biting pressure. Then others were attached to each nipple. A hand rose slimly above him and pulled down the red handle from the box on the wall.

A buzzing sound. Hanley's body stiffened – an incredible sensation totally unlike that he'd experienced in the other room while watching the public whipping. This was like an itch, a masturbatory itch, in his cock, but like no other he'd felt before during the final stages of masturbation. Allied to the tingle of his nipples, the buzz gave him an extraordinarily feeling of helplessness even though he wasn't bound. The very fact that no restraints confined him made him paradoxically feel more unable to move.

The current wasn't too strong, and went in waves as if some remote control monitored the increase and decrease of power. At full erection now, the clasp cut into his cock as the foreskin stretched. A glance over his shoulder showed him the silent, motionless figure in black watching him with arms folded. Then it turned, went to the wardrobe, opened it and took out a cat-o'-nine-tails with knotted lashes which hung almost to the cold stone floor. Hanley braced himself for the flogging to come. But, instead, the lashes tickled his back and buttocks teasingly; up and down; shoulder blades to ankles; tantalisingly foretelling what might be to follow.

Then, from somewhere above his head, a sound, unmistakably the sound of a whip or cane falling on bare flesh. Grunts, then cries and finally screams as the castigation continued. A woman's voice rising high in desperation. 'Please, no more! No more!'

Hanley recognised the voice immediately: it was that of the woman who had interviewed him earlier and who now, he saw with fascination, was beginning to peel the latex from her body; and, when she pulled the mask over her head, he was sure. She stood before him naked and then, spreading her legs, began flagellating herself with the cat-o'-nine-tails. Strongly, mercilessly, back, buttocks and thighs. She flogged herself, not looking at him, but at the ground, as though she were performing some private religious penance.

Music cascaded from the unseen speakers thundering with increasing intensity to a physical climax. Hanley recognised it immediately. It was the erotic 'Thus Spake Zarathustra' by Richard Strauss which formed the basic theme of *2001: A Space Odyssey*, Stanley Kubrick's groundbreaking film. It was overwhelming – but more so because, in the privacy of his flat, Hanley had frequently masturbated and thrashed himself to its towering uplifting, orgasmic climax.

She flung the whip carelessly to the floor and Hanley stared at it hungrily. She eased one door of the wardrobe back and Hanley heard the sound of liquid spilling into glasses. She turned, a glass in each hand. 'Vodka all right?'

Hanley, overcome by her beauty, even more so by the vivid purple, red welts on her thighs, nodded. 'Thank you, vodka's fine.' He started to turn and move towards her, but she shook her head.

'Stay where you are.'

She brought him his drink and he took it, drinking deeply.

She asked, 'Surprised?'

'Surprised?' Hanley met her level gaze. 'Surprised at what?'

'That it was me?' She drank slowly, watching him.

'I hoped,' he said. 'Is that enough? Are you going to –'

'Whip you? No, not just now. I want you to stay exactly where you are now and face the wall. Finish your drink and hand me the glass.'

Hanley did so, passing the tumbler over his shoulder. 'What's next?'

'You'll see.'

'When?'

She moved to his side and he smelled sweat; not rancid male BO, but fragrant, musky, woman's body emission. 'You're here to be cured.' Her voice was almost a whisper. 'And whether that's what you want or not –' he noted the emphasis '– you'll do as instructed.'

'Yours to command,' Hanley said, attempting irony.

'Yes.' No irony.

Facing the wall obediently, Hanley heard a rustle of clothing and then a sliding sound. When he tentatively looked over his shoulder, the wardrobe was back in its place, and he was alone. The cell-like room seemed suddenly to have grown colder. Hanley shivered. Up to now erotic warmth had kept him from feeling any kind of temperature but gradually his naked body was being gripped by biting icy fingers stabbing his flesh. He looked up. Was the ceiling of the room lower than it had been? He squinted. The ceiling was tiled with paste-covered squares and they appeared to be lowering. No! He glanced at the walls – no! They, too, couldn't be advancing four-square towards him. This wasn't possible. He ran his tongue along his lips and tasted . . . So, she'd put something in his drink! Fair enough! He could take all this. (Besides which, it would make good copy for the new book!)

Like the majority of sexual masochists, he relished the erotic mystery of suffering helplessness – sometimes to be unaware of what might happen next; to be blindfolded, naked; hearing whispers around him; a hand driving him to his knees as he crouched awaiting the first lash. Sometimes there was no lash. Sometimes, a hand would smooth gently between his legs and masturbate him, no sound; no indication if a male or female hand was stimulating him to a climax.

This was different, though, and clearly meant to be. He was not tied; he was obeying orders to face the wall. Still, the room seemed to diminish both vertically and horizontally. It was now a faceless cube encroaching from all sides. He'd been drugged. She'd poured the glasses from behind the wardrobe door: what had she dropped into his glass – some kind of hallucinatory drug? And for what reason? How the hell was he supposed to know!

'You're here; you're under no pressure; you can walk out, collect your clothes and go!' But he knew he wasn't about to. His genitals swelled as the room continued to embrace him sinisterly in its menacing constriction . . .

* * *

'But why?' Inevitably, it was Jennifer.

'Why what?' Hanley asked. He was hard. Should he demand a whipping from Jennifer before he continued? He could tell she was in the mood by the way she was drawing the thin-lashed, knotted thongs through her slim fingers. 'D'you want to hear the rest as it happened or –?'

'I certainly do,' Harriet broke in harshly. 'Let him tell his tale the way it happened. After all, none of us has a train to catch, do we?' She raised her fine eyebrows, the heavy folds of her knickers drooping to the elastic legs poised on her kneecaps. 'Besides which, I have a problem to sort out with young Simon here.' She glanced at the boy with a knowing smile.

'A problem –?' Jennifer interjected with a smirk. 'It doesn't look like a small problem, at any rate!'

Indeed, Simon's cock was towering, wet and throbbing. He sat relaxed, lazily smiling at the group as he stroked himself suggestively. The power was there, and he knew it. He might be skinny, but . . .

Peter edged nervously into the debate. 'It sounds like, um, well, that drug called . . . I've forgotten –'

'You're useless!' Jennifer scorned. She looked at Hanley. 'Why? All that bogus metaphysical crap! Walls coming at you; the ceiling coming down! Why?'

'I'll tell you,' Hanley grunted, 'if you'll give me a minute.' He was aroused and wanted the lash.

He stood, as did Jennifer, and bent across his chair. The others watched as Jennifer gave him twelve, stripelike strokes across his behind. He felt better. The joy of being whipped in front of an audience always was an added spice to the punishment.

After pulling his briefs back over his stinging buttocks, he sank into his chair. Jennifer's face was flushed with sadistic lust as she sprawled on to the leather couch, gently tickling herself with the whip she had just been using.

Hanley drew a deep breath, feeling his rigid cock through his underwear. 'What happened in that room was, of course, induced by a drug of some kind – don't ask me what.'

'But why?' Harriet demanded. 'The question's been asked before, I know – and if necessary I'm prepared to take the consequences for being boring and that must never be allowed to happen in this elite little group –'

'Twenty-five strokes of the cane!' Simon put in.

'Not nearly enough!' Harriet responded with a jerk of her head.

Hanley, a vision of Harriet tied and being thrashed momentarily impairing his thought processes, said patiently, 'The disorientation was clearly meant to confuse me. But I was never told that until afterwards. As I've said, the walls and ceiling closed in on me and I closed my eyes . . .'

How long it had been, he had no idea. He'd fallen into a deep sleep and had dreamed he was being flogged. The pain was cutting into him and eventually the dream turned into reality as his eyes opened and he realised he was stretched face down on a hard surface, his hands and ankles bound. Lashes were falling on his buttocks and the backs of his thighs. The pain was both excruciating and arousing. Was he still dreaming? He managed to turn his head and his eyes were immediately temporarily blinded by a white light. He could see nothing except two black shapes, and, as they moved within the lighted umbra, so he felt the sting on his flesh. He was still in that half-blurred state between sleep and wakefulness and thus abandoned his body to the whipping, luxuriating in the pain, soothing as a hot bath. He was floating on a cloud of agony.

'Don't let it stop!' he pleaded mentally. 'Please. Don't let it stop!'

It did eventually, and silently the floggers left; the light was extinguished, and he was alone again, still bound. Dawn must have been coming up because he noticed through a small, double-paned opening in the ceiling a filter of light which grew stronger. Gradually, as his eyes became accustomed, he realised he was stretched naked on a bed, his wrists and ankles tied to the iron bars at the foot and the head. As far as he could see, the room was otherwise empty.

Silence reigned. He was hard from the whipping and rubbed himself wiith increasing intensity against the rough, blanketlike material beneath him until he ejaculated and lay exhausted in the cold puddle of his own spunk.

Suddenly, from somewhere above and around, as in the punishment room – what was it? Days, hours ago? – there came the sound of whip against flesh; loud, stark in the semi-darkness.

A female voice said, 'Don't – not to her! Flog me to death if you like! But not her!'

Then, once more, the giant crescendo chords of 'Thus Spake Zarathurstra' flooded the room as the whipping sounds diminished and then faded away completely.

Hanley was neither hungry nor thirsty, but he badly wanted to urinate. After a flogging it had always been the same. With the thrilling idea of a young boy wetting the bed, Hanley eased himself a little and allowed urine to pour from him, the splattering loud on the floor beneath. He eased every drop of urine out, and then relaxed, comfortable in his bondage. The acrid stench of urine assailed his

nostrils and he wondered what the punishment eventually might be inflicted on him – and by whom?

What he knew was this: that, whatever measures
the clinic took to 'cure' him of his masochistic
inclinations, they would not succeed. But he was
relishing the prospect of them using every means,
both mental and physical, to try and persuade him
otherwise!

Stephanie was well aware, of course, that she had a
devoted punishment-craver on her hands. Was there
no way she could arrange for him to be flogged
without his gaining erotic arousement from the
experience? As a sadist, she wanted the thrill of
flogging a victim who was terrified at the prospect. It
was all very well to use a whip on someone's bare
flesh who begged for it; something else to lash the
buttocks of a victim unable to tolerate the pain and
making no mistake about expressing the fact loudly
with moans after each biting lash.

That was what she wanted to hear, and her pussy
swelled and pulsated at the prospect. Old women
were no good to her! The one she'd mentioned to
Hanley, who gloated when the prospect of a whipping
came about, was merely a naked body bending to the
cut of the whip, cane or riding crop, strapped
willingly to a flogging frame and begging for more.

Her thoughts – as she sat in her office, her skirt up
and knickers to her knees so that she could feel the
sensuous slippery feel of the leather chair on her bare
buttocks, and as she stimulated herself, legs as far
apart as her knicker elastic would allow – returned to
her young brother whom she'd caned and then
masturbated. He'd turned to her shyly revealing his
erect, pink cock (not large, but stiff) and she'd caught
it in her grasp and rubbed the taut shaft until he'd

227

raised his slim torso and thin white spunk had spattered from his stretched foreskin.

Yes! She wanted a boy she could birch! That image of the schoolmaster flogging a bare-bottomed pupil swam into her mind as she brought herself to orgasm with relief tempered at the same time with frustration.

Her brother had been an exception – after all, he was only just fifteen! – but, as she fingered herself, withdrawing her hand now and again to relish the odour and bitter-sweet taste of her orgasmic juices, she knew she wanted a tall, fresh-faced nineteen-year-old, innocent of the taste of the whip; unwilling, yet, as she knew, even thrashed men sometimes achieved an erection: to see his cock rise as she flogged his bottom and even as he suffered was still paradoxically aroused. She'd whip him until he came! But afterwards? Money would have to exchange hands, and a good deal, as well. He would have to have no knowledge of where he'd been brought – that wouldn't be difficult – and taken to some anonymous spot and dumped with money in his pocket and most importantly vivid marks across his buttocks. Who knew, he might find a taste for the birch, whip or cane and seek more! She might even be doing him a favour, whoever he might turn out to be.

She'd birch him, she decided, dreamily post-orgasm. She'd make him take his trousers and underpants down – they'd be dark-blue – not strip him naked, but strap him to the frame in another room. She'd use fresh birches (she could always get a good supply) and thrash him, revelling in his screams and moans as the welts rose on his flesh. Maybe, if his cock was hard, she'd kneel in front of him and reduce the agony of his wounds by taking him in her mouth. But initially he had to be unwilling, dragged, roped, trembling . . .

She stood a little dizzily, pulled up her knickers and adjusted her skirt. She washed her hands and tidied her hair. In the mirror of the small bathroom she stared at herself. Her eyes were very deep.

Hanley had been unstrapped and was lying naked on his bed savouring the bruising pain of his recent whipping when Stephanie entered unannounced. Hanley noted immediately the creases across her skirt between her thighs and his cock began to respond. She stood looking down at him.

'You won't be cured, and you don't want to be. I'll refund your fee personally if you'll do me a favour.'

Hanley struggled up from the bed a little, aware that his cock was on an upwards slant. Was she going to flog him senselesss? He wouldn't have put it past her!

She moved to the small window, her back to him. 'I want a boy, about nineteen –' her voice was soft '– I want to birch him. He'll be well paid, and we'll have to make sure he has no idea of where this is. Most important of all, he's got to be told in advance what's going to happen and I'll need your help to get him strapped to the flogging frame. I want to thrash him until he comes – or as close to it as possible.' She swung round. 'Can you help?'

Hanley studied her. It was difficult to imagine what was going on in the mind of this tall, stern woman whose attractiveness only added to her erotic impulses. His cock was upright, proud. He said, 'Sit down, and touch me.'

She perched on the edge of the bed, drew her skirt up above her knees, then cupped his balls in her left palm and stroked him with her right thumb and forefinger. 'I want it,' she said, not looking at him.

Hanley drew a deep breath. The image forming in his mind – of a slim youth bound and birched –

possessed him joltingly. 'It won't be easy. I know places where the kids hang out who've come from the sticks to find jobs ... but I don't know what sort you're looking for, do I?'

She was caressing him gently, a faraway look in her eyes. 'He has to be tall, slim, good-looking, shortish hair. I don't care about his clothes – he won't have them on for long, anyway, if I have anything to do with it.'

Hanley said, 'Yes, whip him, but not to excess. Control your impulses. I'm yours to be flogged any time – but remember, a nineteen-year-old may never have been spanked, let alone whipped!'

'I know.' She nodded. 'I know how far I can go.'

'But what will I tell him?' Hanley asked. The hand on his cock was becoming more demanding by the second. 'That you want to birch him?' He felt a muscular twitch deep down.

'Say you're from a charity organisation – you can think something up – you care for homeless young men. He'll be only too keen if you offer food and a comfortable bed for the night –'

'As well as a bloody good flogging?' Hanley broke in, adding, 'Move your hand up a little ... ah, yes, better.'

'Will you?'

'Yes,' Hanley said, 'I will – as long as I can watch.'

Her hand wrenched him and he spilled spunk over her fingers and wrist.

She said, as she licked his spunk, 'I know how far I can go. When I come, I'll know to stop. But I've got to hear him scream, moan, begging me, pleading with me to stop. If I whip his behind raw, it won't do any lasting damage. The buttocks are there to be flogged, and that's what he's going to get.'

Hanley said, 'You might turn him into a convert; masochists are born, not made. It's in them from

230

birth, only they don't know the pain and pleasure principle until, if they're lucky, a whip cane or riding crop is laid across them. Your victim might discover that fact and beg for more. Won't that have defeated your aim if you're really after the ultimate thrill?'

She gave a nod which could have meant anything and muttered, 'I've thought of that.' Then she added, 'It's best if you look around after dark. The seafront where these homeless kids sleep; at night he won't know where you're taking him and you'll drop him off somewhere in the dark as well after I've finished with him.'

'And you'll pay him?' Hanley asked.

She slapped his flaccid cock and stood. 'Yes, I'll pay him – and you, too.'

Hanley knew the sort of youngster he'd be looking for as he made his way that evening in Stephanie's Mercedes to Brighton seafront some twenty miles away. He was afire with the idea of seeing Stephanie birching a protesting young man, but who, at the same time, was being aroused. It was a fine, starlit evening with a breeze coming off the sea as he parked, left the car and sauntered along the front. He needed to find a youngster, apparently homeless, sitting in one of the beachfront shelters – tall with slimness suggesting his naked body strapped for the birch. And he wouldn't know what was in store! Until that moment when . . . He was getting a hard-on, and the pressure stretched the skin of his whipped buttocks. Luckily, he was wearing a trenchcoat which concealed the telltale uprising within his underpants and trousers.

He strolled watching the inhabitants ot the shelters. Mostly they consisted of elderly couples staring glumly out to sea. What did they have, he thought!

Never been flogged, humiliated or wanked off! Probably some of the old women with their long skirts would be wearing knee-length pink interlock bloomers but to their dull, half-assed husbands that would mean nothing!

He was about to return towards the centre of town, promising himself a drink in the bar of the Grand Hotel before he resumed his quest, when he noticed a lone figure in one of the shelters. From the back, he looked slim; a decent haircut, anorak collar pulled up. Hanley circled him and glanced at him as he passed on the seaward side. He took in enough – the young man was pale and his tight jeans were mounded around his crotch. Beside him was a cheap-looking rucksack. He didn't look up as Hanley went slowly by, but the impression was of a slim face with long lashes and a wide, sensitive mouth. As he wandered round again, taking his time, he imagined this figure naked, bound, being flogged with Stephanie's birch. Too much!

He drew a deep breath and stood before the young man, his speech already rehearsed several times. 'Hello, are you all right?'

The eyes which looked had long lashes and the pupils glinted in the light from the streetlamps.

'Who are you?' The voice had no discernible accent, wasn't aggressive. Rather, it had a plaintive ring to it.

'Well,' Hanley said, 'I'm part of a group who do charity work and try to help youngsters who may be down on their luck. You look as if you don't have anywhere to go tonight and our place is only a few miles away. A good meal, a warm bed and some money to see you on your way.' (He didn't add, 'and at least one good flogging'!) He went on, feeling slightly two-faced, 'You're a good-looking young man and there're a lot of nasty people around. I'm sure you know what I'm talking about.'

At this point Harriet, who had been gently masturbating Simon as his hand crept beneath the elastic of her Dks up the inside of her thigh, interrupted: 'You were taking a big chance – gently, dear – weren't you? Did you feel you needed to satisfy this – this woman's lust –'

Jennifer broke in. 'You're a fine one to talk about lust! The kiss of the whip! We've seen you take it enough times!' She looked across at Hanley who was mixing drinks and placing the glasses neatly on a silver tray. 'Well, slave? Do your job and sharp about it!'

The drinks were handed out; Simon ejaculated on to the pink silk of Harriet's knickers. Peter had taken his pants down and was trying desperately to get some stiffness into his floppy cock; Jennifer watched Hanley as he resumed his seat, the erection beneath his underwear only too apparent.

'Harriet,' Hanley said, taking a drink, 'in answer to your question about the young man, he was only going to be whipped by a woman with professional expertise. As I've already mentioned, she told me that she knew how far she could go flagellating his bottom.' He looked round at the group. 'We've all been whipped and have whipped as well; we're special people, not good people by any means, but our pleasures are derived from inflicting and receiving corporal punishment and whatever other pleasures we can obtain from the benefits of it. Do you want to hear the rest?'

Peter suddenly got up, ripped off his underpants and went to the table, picking up a short whip with knotted lashes. Turning to them, his cock hanging loose, he began flagellating himself, legs wide apart.

'Flagellation,' he was moaning as he flogged himself, 'flagellation. Flog yourself, you bastard! Punish that stupid bit of nothing hanging down!' He grasped what there was of his cock and thrust it outwards, thrashing the limp shaft as he did so. 'There! There! There!' Gasping now as he lashed himself. But still his cock didn't rise and eventually he sank to his knees as the others stared.

Hanley said, 'Listen to the rest of the story and keep the whip handy, Peter. I swear that before very long that cock of yours will be as stiff as a poker. Stay where you are, on your knees!'

'I'll get the fucking thing hard!' Jennifer scrambled to her feet and stood over Peter, sliding her black, lace-edged panties down and thrusting herself towards his face.

'Wait!' Hanley said sharply. 'He'll get his cock up – even *he* will – when he hears the rest of the story. But stay as you are, love, the sight of your delicious, knickerless bum will inspire us all!'

'What's your name?' Hanley had asked as he sat down beside the slim figure.

'Jonathan. Is – is this on the level?'

'Of course,' Hanley replied. He pretended to fumble in his pocket. 'Sorry, I thought I had a card with me. Look, my car's parked a little way up the road. I promise you you'll come to no harm.' (You'll come all right, Hanley said to himself, but as to harm, well . . . Again excitement rose as he pictured the scene.)

Jonathan said, 'All right. I'm hungry. Some mates have let me down.'

'Let's go, then,' Hanley said, his heart beating faster. He picked up the rucksack. 'What's in here?'

Jonathan said, 'Some clothes, underwear, odds and ends.'

As they walked to the car, Hanley, eyeing Jonathan's long, slim legs in his jeans, wondered what sort of underwear? Tight briefs? Boxer shorts? Well, he'd soon know and at the prospect his scrotum began to tighten.

In the car he said, 'It's not far. Where're you from?'

'Leicester. I came down here 'cos my mates said they could get me a job.'

'And they've let you down.' Hanley turned on to a side road and flicked the main beam. 'I suppose you're broke?'

'Flat,' Jonathan said. 'I spent my last fifty pence on a chocolate bar.'

'Never mind,' Hanley said, 'you'll have some food, a good rest and some cash to be going on with. Here we are.'

He swung the Mercedes into the tree-lined drive and ahead the white-stoned house rose like a ghost in the moonlight. He cut the engine, got out and opened the door for Jonathan who reached for his rucksack and stood surveying the house.

'Are you sure this is OK?'

'Of course,' Hanley said.

The front door had opened and Stephanie stood in the light. She was all in black – black polo-neck, wide black whipcord jodhpurs and knee-length high-heeled boots. Christ, Hanley thought, as they approached, why doesn't she have a fucking whip or a birch in her hand to complete the picture!

He said, 'This is Jonathan. He's from Leicester. His mates have let him down and he's hungry, tired and broke!'

'Well, Jonathan, welcome.' Stephanie put a hand on his shoulder and guided him into the hall.

God, Hanley thought, as he followed and shut the door, before very long that hand is going to be holding a birch, and –

The accoustically sealed door to the 'clinic' was shut, Hanley noted with relief. It wouldn't have been good if Jonathan had been greeted by the sound of a lash cutting into bare flesh. He knew that three floggings were booked for that night. Stephanie led the way into the reception room which was cosy and homely. There were long settees – perhaps significantly of gleaming black leather – and side tables. An electric fire glowed in the fireplace with fake flames curling up the back surround.

'Sit down, darling,' Stephanie said. 'Would you like a drink? Beer or something stronger?'

'Beer please,' Jonathan said, sitting down. (You won't be sitting as easily as that very soon! Hanley thought and again his balls tightened and his cock gave a throb or two.)

Stephanie took a can from a corner cabinet and pulled the ring. She handed it to him with a smile. 'I know you lads don't like glasses; you prefer to drink it straight. Now, I'm arranging for some food – a fry-up, as they say. Does that sound good?'

Jonathan nodded. 'Thank you.'

Hanley noticed he was eyeing Stephanie's breeches and boots as she stood commandingly in front of him.

'Good,' she said, 'it won't be long. By the way, what's in the rucksack?'

'Just some clothes,' Jonathan said, gulping beer, 'underwear and stuff.'

'Dirty, I suppose,' Stephanie said with a tight smile. 'We'll sort it out later. I'll see to your food.'

She motioned at Hanley and he followed her into the hall. She whispered, 'The room's ready. The birching block's in place and there're two birches soaking in salt water.' Her face was flushed.

Hanley asked, 'When?'

'After he's eaten. I'm going to tell him straight out what he's in for. In detail. I want to see his reaction. I'll have handcuffs ready and we can get him down to the birching room between us. He'll have to be stripped, of course, and bound to the birching block. You haven't seen one, so far – it's a long bench with straps to restrain his shoulders, waist and thighs. Of course, his bottom will be bare.' She put out a hand and touched Hanley's swollen cock through his trousers. 'It's going to be fun, you'll see!'

He watched her as she went down the hall, the jodhpurs swinging sensuously, the gleaming boots clicking on the patterned marble floor.

Hanley was in an agony of frustration as he watched Jonathan devour his food. He had another beer. Stephanie appeared quite calm, although he guessed that, beneath the breeches and whatever colour knickers she was wearing, the sexual pressure was mounting.

Finally, he finished and sat back. 'Thank you. You're very kind, really.'

Stephanie leaned forwards. 'Jonathan, you've been picked out because you're going to be flogged! I'm going to flog your bottom. It will hurt agonisingly, but it will do you no damage. Afterwards, you'll be given money. There's no use protesting or attempting to get out. You're going to be whipped so accept it and take your clothes off – everything. Now!'

His face had gone pale, his mouth half-open. 'You won't – you can't –' His voice was thick.

'Oh, but we can and are about to,' Stephanie said evenly.

'But – why? I haven't done anything! Why do this to me? I don't want to be whipped! I'm scared. What're you going to do –' His voice faltered.

237

Stephanie stood up. 'What we're going to do is this: you'll be taken to a special room and, after you've been stripped, you'll be strapped down and I shall flog you until your bottom is raw. You can scream, beg and plead – the louder the better, the rooms are sound-proofed – but you will not be released until I'm satisfied with the state of your bottom. You will be treated medically and, as I said, you'll be well rewarded. Now, are you going to strip yourself, or do we have to do it for you? It doesn't matter either way because in the end you're going to be whipped, whipped and whipped!'

He started to get up, but Stephanie was too quick for him. Like a magician she produced from some-where a pair of handcuffs and threw him face down on the couch, pulling his arms behind his back before snapping the metal over his wrists.

'No – no please. I'll do anything . . . please don't whip me! Please!'

Between them, they got his trainers and socks off. Then his jeans came down revealing a pair of dirty-looking white boxer shorts. His shirt was more difficult because of his cuffed wrists, so Stephanie simply ripped it off as far as it would go.

'We'll get the rest off when he's tied,' she said.

Her face was aflame. She rolled him on to his back. His cock was flaccid, surrounded by a thick bush of hair.

He stared up at her, his face contorted. 'Please . . . please don't –'

Hanley was now fully erect, filled with sadistic desire. He'd never had such feelings before, always getting turned on by the thought – and the adminis-tering – of leather on his unprotesting flesh. But now he had a thirst to see this young man flogged!

Between them they got him to his feet. His knees were giving way and now he was crying, tears running down his cheeks. 'No! I don't want to be whipped! I'll do anything –!'

'All you'll do,' Stephanie said, as they dragged him to the door, down the hall and into an unmarked room on the right, 'is let yourself be bound and flogged!'

The room was small and windowless. In the centre on the hard, stone floor stood a long bench, heavy straps dangling ready. Hanley saw a bucket in one corner out of which stuck the taped handles of two thick birches.

They forced him face down on to the bench. Suddenly, he seemed to have given up the struggle and was limp as they tightened the straps. Without warning, he urinated, a dark stream which poured through the bench and on to the floor.

'Right,' Stephanie said, 'that'll be an extra hundred strokes.'

She took one of the birches from the bucket and swished it in the air, droplets of salt water flying off.

Jonathan lay perfectly still, except for his white, unblemished buttocks which were quivering violently. Stephanie took up her position above and to one side of her victim. Hanley tore open his trousers and pulled out his erect cock. At the same moment, the first crack of the birch landed squarely across Jonathan's buttocks. He gave a loud cry and his body jerked spasmodically.

Then the deadly accurate, rhythmic birching began in earnest.

He was strangely silent as the thrashing continued, deadly: the coloured welts rising as she flogged the already swelling buttocks.

'Damn you!' She was breathing heavily as she thrashed the birch. 'Damn you – scream, beg! I've given you fifty. There's one-fifty to go. Beg, plead!'

She continued to birch the bottom, now almost grotesquely swollen and deep red.

Hanley was close to ejaculating, and Stephanie noticed. 'No,' she said, pausing with the birch in mid-air, 'no, don't – it's going in his mouth after I've finished, and while it's in there you're going to have your bottom in shreds! You haven't seen my best whip yet – I've been saving it. So stop wanking off while I get on with what I'm doing!'

Hanley released his cock, but drew his trousers and pants down as he watched. A few minutes later, Stephanie reached out a hand. 'Give me the other birch; this one's had it.'

She threw it down, the twigs broken and torn. He brought the second birch from the bucket and handed it over. She shook the droplets off, as she'd done with the first, drew a deep breath and resumed flogging Jonathan's tortured bottom.

At last, he turned his head and gave a loud moan. 'I'm going to – I'm going to –'

'He's going to shit!' Stephanie said.

Sure enough, loose faeces bubbled out of Jonathan's back passage and ran down his legs, joining the trickling stream of sweat. The stench rose in the room, combined with urine and sexual activity. Stephanie flogged the mess with extra vigour.

'Don't – don't you faint,' she was saying as she laid the birch on, 'because if – if you do, we'll wait until you revive. I'm not flogging a body that's not feeling anything!'

What could Jonathan say? Hanley thought as he resisted the impulse to touch his cock. He was tied up in a place he didn't know, naked and helpless and being mercilessly flogged! Wouldn't he be aroused eventually? The pressure on the straps had forced Jonathan's lower half into the bench, so he could not tell whether Jonathan had an erection. He, himself, would have done! Hell, he'd have come twice by now with the punishment Stephanie was administering with undiminished fervour. She had unbuttoned her jodhpurs and lowered them, sliding a hand inside her black panties.

Jonathan's buttocks continued to produce a sluggish, crawling dribble of excreta as each stroke landed. It was almost, Hanley thought, that each stinging stroke of the birch induced another motion within the flogged youngster's bowels. He urinated again, but only a trickle.

Stephanie had obviously been counting. 'That's two hundred,' she said as she flung the birch down and stepped back.

Jonathan's buttocks and thighs at the backs of his legs were like a crimson sheet. Sweat dripped; welts rose. His bottom was twice the size of normal; a huge mound of flesh on which no paleness of untortured skin was visible.

Stephanie turned to Hanley. 'Strip off, and keep that cock stiff! You haven't come, have you?'

Hanley shook his head and removed his clothing.

Stephanie kneeled beside Jonathan's head. 'All right, you're going to suck my friend's cock and I'll whip him at the same time. Your punishment is over – as long as you keep your mouth open and let him enter. If you refuse, I promise you I'll turn you over and I'll thrash your cock and balls until there's nothing left. Believe me, I'll do it!'

All it seemed possible for Jonathan to do, as Hanley watched keenly, was give a weak nod. Stephanie got hold of his hair and jerked his head upright.

She motioned to Hanley. 'That second drawer; the top whip.'

Hanley, his cock throbbing like a spring, went to the drawer. The whip was heavy as he grasped the leather-bound handle, thick as a broomstick. Nine lashes hung heavily, each knotted, and with small slivers of metal and bone tied at lengths to the leather, plaited tails. He brought the whip to Stephanie and handed it over. She gave him a grim smile as she ran her fingers through the lashes. 'You'll get your pleasure, I'll get mine!'

Still holding Jonathan's hair so that his face was tilted upwards, Stephanie gestured to Hanley. 'All right, get it in!'

He moved in front of Jonathan, took the shaft of his cock in his right hand and thrust the exposed knob to Jonathan's mouth. The thin lips opened and Hanley felt his erection slide into a warm, moist interior. There was a bite of teeth, temporarily, on the shaft of his cock, but he slid in further, at the same time feeling the fire of Stephanie's whip biting into his buttocks. He thrust; she flogged; he pushed into Jonathan's mouth as far as he could and then felt the flicker of tongue on his tip. He ejaculated instantly as the whip continued to lash him, jerking his hips and thighs into Jonathan's throat.

He said, 'All right, I've come.'

His buttocks were afire; in her sexual excitement, Stephanie had lashed his upper thighs, fairly sensitive skin. He slowly withdrew his still half-hard cock from Jonathan's mouth, and Stephanie let the boy's hair go; he slumped back on the birching block, spunk dribbling from the corners of his mouth.

Hanley found himself saying, even though he had just come, 'I want more flogging – but I've got to have knickers on. And I want him to thrash me – no, not just thrash: whip my skin apart. But I have to have knickers! You know that!' His cock was rising again. 'Well?'

Then she got up. 'He'll stay hard. Get hold of your cock and push it out towards me.'

She picked up the whip, as Hanley did as he was told, and she brought the curling lashes down on the rigid, vein-enhanced, eager recipient of the genital flogging about to lift him to unknown heights of masochistic delight . . .

The group was silent as Hanley concluded his story. Nobody moved; nobody felt for themselves. It seemed to have gone beyond the bounds of even their excessive perverse sexual longings.

Hanley awoke in his own bed. His cock was huge and throbbing, straining at the leash like a dog trying to sniff for familiar scents. Hanley grasped himself, and then let go. He wanted to suffer; allow the rising tide of spunk to thrust upwards as he lay there, naked, spread-eagled on the damp sheets, allowing nature to take its course as and when it decided.

And wasn't this the core of the 'problem'? Nature had decided his sexual tastes, and those of his clan: Harriet, Jennifer, Simon and the rest. The whip, cane, birch, riding crop had governed their lives.

But it would never be satisfying to the ultimate degree: there were always more borders to cross; but he was tired. He got up, his cock stiff and unyielding, and stood naked in front of his mirror – as he'd done long ago in his mother's bedroom after she'd given him a stinging thrashing. He'd wanted more over the years, but had been too shy to ask.

He took the loaded handgun from a bedside drawer, checked that the chamber had five rounds, and held the barrel to his temple with his left hand. Masturbating with his right, he imagined his mother stripping him naked and flogging him mercilessly, her skirt halfway up her thighs, and grunting with the effort.

He could see her in the mirror, and, as he felt the fiery spunk surging up the shaft of his cock, he squeezed the trigger of the handgun.

NEXUS BACKLIST

This information is correct at time of printing. For up-to-date information, please visit our website at www.nexus-books.co.uk

All books are priced at £6.99 unless another price is given.

- - - - - - ✂ -

Please send me the books I have ticked above.

Name   ....

Address ....

....

....

.... Post code ....

Send to: **Virgin Books Cash Sales, Thames Wharf Studios, Rainville Road, London W6 9HA**

US customers: for prices and details of how to order books for delivery by mail, call 1-800-343-4499.

Please enclose a cheque or postal order, made payable to **Nexus Books Ltd**, to the value of the books you have ordered plus postage and packing costs as follows:
    UK and BFPO – £1.00 for the first book, 50p for each subsequent book.
    Overseas (including Republic of Ireland) – £2.00 for the first book, £1.00 for each subsequent book.

If you would prefer to pay by VISA, ACCESS/MASTERCARD, AMEX, DINERS CLUB or SWITCH, please write your card number and expiry date here:

....

Please allow up to 28 days for delivery.

Signature ....

Our privacy policy

We will not disclose information you supply us to any other parties. We will not disclose any information which identifies you personally to any person without your express consent.

From time to time we may send out information about Nexus books and special offers. Please tick here if you do *not* wish to receive Nexus information.   ☐

- - - - - - ✂ -